POLMENA COVE

POLMENA COVE

Mary Lide

St. Martin's Press
New York

Library of Congress Cataloging-in-Publication Data

Lide, Mary.
Polmena Cove / Mary Lide.
p.   cm.
ISBN 0-312-11877-5
I. Title.
PR6062.I32P65   1992
823'.914—dc20   94-34236   CIP

First published in Great Britain by HarperCollins Publishers

First U.S. Edition: January 1995
10 9 8 7 6 5 4 3 2 1

To all my children,
to remember their Cornish inheritance.
With love.

INTRODUCTION

St Marvell is a small fishing village on the north coast of Cornwall. Once famous for its pilchards, still well known for its Music Festival, in some ways it is typical of its kind. With its cobbled streets converging on a harbour, its winding lanes, its overhanging cottages built into cliffs, it is the sort of place that looks its picturesque best in summer, a place where nothing much ever seems to happen, a little world set apart, slumbering in tranquillity. Like everywhere else it has its private life, its past, its dangerous secrets.

Here the sea is king. In calm weather it is benevolent. Fishermen fish, children paddle, gulls dip and cry. Waves curl lazily in lines of foam. Underneath, there are reefs and currents, rocks and surf. And the great Atlantic swells which in storm turn waves to breakers, feet high. In storm the sea becomes truly majestical, cruel. As the graveyard of St Marvell Church testifies.

The church stands at the top of the hill, half hidden by yew trees. Small and grey, resembling the cottages it keeps watch over, its lichen-covered tower leans slightly to the east, tilted, like the trees, by the prevailing west wind. Around its base cluster gravestones marking the resting place of fishermen, drowned at sea. More slate slabs line the walls, these for men whom the sea has never returned, not even for burial. Beside them, fresh flowers are laid every week, a ritual of ongoing mourning and remembrance.

Among these many memorials one stands out from the rest, a stained-glass window, erected at the turn of the present century. Called sometimes the Polleven window, from the family whose wealth paid for it, it is also known locally as Ben Trevarisk's folly, Ben Trevarisk being the name of the fisherman whose rescue is here commemorated, along with the death of his would-be brother-in-law, who was drowned in rescuing him.

The design of the window is typically Victorian. Huge violet crested waves beat down on crimson boats, stylized to resemble those of Galilee; sailors cling to spars in a sea of robin-egg blue. Gold lips frame the wind's open mouth; a gold halo surrounds the drowned man's head; the Gothic text is scrolled in gold, lines of it, a saga of it, capped with verses from the Bible.

The story it tells of storm at sea, of fishing perils, of self-sacrifice, is familiar to all seagoing communities, in fact many families in St Marvell have known the same; some there might even resent this gaudy display of grief and thanksgiving. Yet none would claim the grief or thanksgiving less, the bravery less, because depicted in such bright ornamental profusion; a few might even argue that a storm of such gigantic proportions required a memorial of equally impressive size.

However, in the midst of all this extravagance, certain details have been omitted. Some, such as the vastness of the pilchard shoal, again the largest of the century, perhaps explain Ben Trevarisk's stubborn refusal to abandon it despite all warnings. More important, the rescue was actually achieved by two men, although only one is mentioned, the one who drowned. That the second man was son of the rich landowner who paid for the window and that he survived to marry Ben Trevarisk's sister (by whom he had already had a child) reveals another side of the story, a hidden side. Love, betrayal and bitterness, the window makes no mention of these, nor the interwoven lives of two men from very different backgrounds, joined to a simple fisher girl whom fate made their nemesis. And if afterwards it was with the money from that rich marriage that Ben Trevarisk celebrated his return to life and made atonement to a man who had lost everything, the secret story still remains – although in truth it all happened twenty years before and really was no secret, just waiting to be drawn from its hiding place.

CHAPTER 1

'Just look at the sun on the water, Em. Doesn't it make you want to ring out? I feel like St Enodoc's church bell.'

Lily Polleven, daughter of Julian Polleven, the son whose family had built the window, had been singing as she walked along, her voice rising larklike in splendid shining tones. Now she stopped, spun round on her toes, her dark skirts flaring. Her plait of honey-coloured hair thumped against her pale blue blouse, her hat dangled carelessly by its ribbons. When Em Trevarisk didn't answer, Lily eyed her cousin. But Em continued to lean on the gate, gazing silently down the slope of the field to where the rough grass was dotted with primroses. The lack of response was so unlike Em it made Lily nervous.

The girls had just come from St Marvell, where Em's real father, Ben Trevarisk, the rescued fisherman, still lived in pious reformation with his wife, Charity, and where Lily had happily left Em to domestic errands. Em likes responsibility, Lily thought, she likes bustling round with delivery lists, she likes making visits and listening to news – all the things that Lily's mother usually took care of and Em oversaw in her Aunt Jenny's absence.

Em's sense of duty always made Lily squirm. 'I'm off,' she'd cried, escaping to the far more interesting surroundings of the harbour and fish and boats. But it was only after the village had been left behind and the ritual visit made to the recent war memorial, where Em's oldest brother was listed among the dead, that Lily had sensed the extent of Em's change of mood. She's not full of local news, Lily thought, I don't mean gossip, but stories of people and events that everyone confides in her. She's not mentioned her parents or her other brothers, although I know she's been with them. She hasn't even talked of the Music Festival, and usually she'd be full of that.

Lily wanted to make Em tell her what was the matter; by not speaking, Em shut Lily out and that was something Lily hated. Although very alike in looks, with the same fair hair, same green-grey eyes, Lily knew of course that Emma Trevarisk was quite different from herself, was quieter and more reserved. Em would not have sung in public nor danced in a public lane. But usually she would not have minded Lily's doing so; in her own way Em was not without her own sense of the absurd, not immune to her cousin's fun.

Lily spun on her toes again. Her eyes shone like the sea which expanded in a glistening arch below the fields. She stretched her arms as if willing a wind to waft her off the ground like one of the real larks still singing overhead. 'Mind your skirts,' Em should have said in the dry tone that hid affection, treating Lily like a gambolling lamb or a colt with too long legs. 'There's a bramble thorn.' Or a nail, or a piece of barbed wire, or any other danger which her careful glance had spied. Instead Emma Trevarisk could not be stirred from her silent contemplation. In a day which was meant in truth to lift the heart, Lily thought, blackthorn budding along the hedge, violets pale-scented, grass upspringing – all signs of an early Cornish spring – it was as if her cousin, who loved the countryside with a passion, didn't even notice it.

Lily looked at Em again. Suddenly she seems older than she is, Lily thought, noting how Em's wide forehead was slightly knotted in a habitual frown as if she contemplated the woes of the world. Anxiety coupled with annoyance caused Lily's voice to rise a notch.

'And scarcely a ripple, the ocean's a pond,' she cried. 'Doesn't it make you glad to be alive?'

It was only then that Emma spoke. 'He's not glad,' she said. 'He's a dead man back from the dead.'

Lily's exuberance immediately vanished. In this spring of 1920 it might be a joy to be alive, but there were thousands, no, millions of young men who were not. Scarcely a family in the village hadn't known some loss, Em's brother among them. But Lily knew Em was not talking of her brother. Young Ben Trevarisk had died early in the war, had been regretted, mourned over; that sharp grief had passed. This 'he' referred to Will Pendray: the whole village had been full of it – a soldier who had survived the war only to return home an invalid, mentally deranged, they called it.

'I went to see Will,' Emma was continuing. The words poured out. 'While you were on the quay. They said not to, but I did. Remember how strong he was, why, he used to be a wrestler. Remember how, years before the war, when you were twelve, we went to watch him at St Winnow's Fair.'

Tears were running down her cheeks now but she paid no attention. 'Remember how he caught his opponent round the waist and lifted him up in the air before throwing him to the ground. And when everyone clapped, he smiled as if he were glad they were pleased. That was what he used to be like, Lily, full of life. Reliable as rock. Why, they said at the mine if there was someone to be trusted, trust Will. Today he sat hunched in a chair like an old man and wouldn't even look at me.'

She scrubbed at her cheeks. 'His mother says he spends all day like that, afraid to move,' she said. 'And at nights, if he sleeps, he tosses and turns, or moans so loud he wakes her up, as if he still dreams of being in France.'

Then she did turn her soft sad gaze on Lily. 'They say he wishes he were dead,' she said, 'cries it out, as if he feels guilt at coming back.'

Lily put out a hand to touch her cousin's, vexed that in any way she should have given offence or been insensitive. She too leaned on the gate as Em continued to speak of

3

Will Pendray, every word unconsciously perhaps revealing Emma's liking for a man who might once have been regarded as her 'intended'. Or future intended, Lily thought, for it was over three years since the army had taken Will, and she herself only remembered him vaguely. But Em, older than her by some five years, had not forgotten. Em had been over twenty when Will had left, old enough to have written to him, to have dreamed of him, to have waited for him to come home. Now, as Em spoke, a picture emerged of a tall young miner who had smiled a lot, only to be reduced to a husk of a man, all pith torn out.

'They say he's afraid of everything,' Em was saying, 'afraid of going with his mates, afraid of returning to the mine, afraid even of stepping out of doors. What's to become of him, Lily, if he won't work? His mother, poor old soul, is beside herself. And there's his Paw's boat, the "Seagull", rotting in the harbour and no one to use it if he won't.'

And what's to become of me, she might have said, I can't marry a man who's rotting away from grief.

The thought that Em might have married, or even considered marrying, was something that Lily herself had never really faced before. She knew that letters to Will had been written and replies had come; within her own family at least, where Emma lived as an adopted daughter, it was a close-kept secret, to be joked and teased about with affectionate restraint (for nothing was official, Em was young and Will Pendray, away at war, and after the war still in hospital, could not be expected to support a wife). We've always spoken kindly of him, Lily now thought, he's always been liked. If any outsider, had they known, had suggested that Em, related to the Polleven family, should aim higher than a miner, well, they'd have got short shrift. But that was while Will Pendray was away; now he's back, it's different. Em belongs to me, she thought, suddenly rebellious, more like a sister than a cousin. There's never been a time at Nanscawn Farm without Em; Em can't marry and leave just like that. She can't leave until I do first.

4

Yet uncomfortably, Emma's words touched a nerve. I'm almost twenty now, Lily thought. What has it been like for Em all these years? To be parted from someone you love, to be constantly afraid for him, to hide all you feel and never show it, and then when he does return to be unable to visit or talk to him because he doesn't remember you – how does Em bear it? I couldn't. And now perhaps to have to put dreams aside for good because of what the war's done to him. It isn't fair. Overcome with her own selfishness, Lily wanted to throw her arms around her cousin and rock Emma as once, years ago, Emma used to rock her when she fell and cut herself. 'There, there, my handsome,' she wanted to imitate the soft Cornish voices she loved, 'don't 'ee fret. Things'll turn all right in the end.'

Suddenly the five years that separated her from Em seemed a gulf that hid all kind of dangers she didn't want to learn about. If that's what loving means, she thought, I'll keep well clear of it. I'll not be caught in that same trap, not if I can help it.

After a while Em straightened up, shook herself as if shaking off a burden. 'Best be moving on,' she said. 'There's still a chill in the evenings.' She smiled at Lily, the generous smile which transformed her face and made her beautiful. 'Shouldn't be bothering you with my worries,' the look said, 'shouldn't grumble. William's home at last, that's what counts.' And drawing Lily's arm through hers, resolutely Emma Trevarisk began to walk ahead as if to leave this new sorrow behind.

The sun was still warm and the evening cold a couple of hours off when they came to a turning in the road. One way led inland towards Nanscawn Farm where they lived, the other, a footpath, opened on to the cliffs. Here Lily hesitated. 'Let's not go home just yet,' she wanted to say, 'what about another mile or so more, to the point and back.'

As if guessing her wishes, Emma smiled consent. By common agreement both girls continued along the left-hand track which steepened here into a climb, became rougher, rapidly mounting up to an unprotected headland without trees, where the few gorse bushes were flattened by the prevailing western winds and the grass was pitted with rabbit holes. Always on their left, the jagged cliff was broken into deep chasms, forcing them into detours away from its edge. Peering over, they could see sea pinks clumped in crevices, their round flowers bobbing, and, below these, the bodies of nesting gulls in white feather clumps. Below again, straight below, where the sun cast shadows down sheer defiles, a jumble of rocks began. Even on a calm day like this there was a line of foam fretting at their base and the sound of the sea came up in a subdued throbbing.

At the top they paused to admire the view, mile after mile of cliff and promontory, extending in both directions into a purple haze. Then Lily tugged at Em's arm and pointed. A short distance eastward a dark green line sloped in a V, a narrow vein of twisted vegetation between two high cliffs. Against the green now a thin coil of smoke showed. 'Someone's down in Cove,' Lily said.

This was their private name for Polmena Cove, an isolated bay carved out between two headlands like a crescent moon. It was reached by means of the narrow valley which formed the V, cut out from the rock face by a swift-flowing stream. Cove was an unusual place, partly because of the valley's rich undergrowth of bush and tree, in marked contrast to the desolation of the rest of the region; partly because it could be easily reached, amid a stretch of headland otherwise inaccessible. But, most unusual of all, the tidal beach it led to was sandy and flat, a rarity in this jagged tumble of rocks and cliffs.

Lily and Em looked at each other in surprise. They knew Cove well, had spent much of their childhood at play on the beach at low tide. As few other people ever bothered to go there, they considered it almost as their own and in their family it held many memories. Most important of all, at the foot of the valley, under the cliffs, was a 'cabin' or hut, long boarded up and empty. It too was special, the place where

Lily's mother, as a young girl, had stayed with the fishing family who had once lived there.

The reasons for Jenny Trevarisk's staying in the cabin were many, not unknown to the cousins although that had happened so long ago they scarcely ever thought of it. But they helped explain their feeling for Polmena Cove. That Lily had actually been born there in the little hut, had lived there with her mother as a baby, enhanced the feeling of belonging. And certainly Lily loved Cove with a passion; summer or winter it was her favourite place. She loved the peace of it and its simple beauty. Most of all she loved its sense of secrecy, hidden from the world and forgotten, a place where she could go and claim it as her own. The thought now that someone might have broken into her birthplace was more than she could bear. 'Come on,' she cried. And, not waiting for Em to answer, without another word she hitched up her skirts and began the climb down towards the entrance to the valley.

If you didn't know where the valley was, she thought, as she forced her way through the gorse and bramble which masked the entrance, you'd miss it altogether. Only the sound of water, deep down and hollow, running in a tunnel under roots and stems, tells where it is. So whoever's come, it must be someone local, no outsider could have found it.

The impertinence of this invasion drove her on, although the thickets tore at her clothes and hair and Em was left struggling behind. But when she came to the cleft in the cliffs where the descent to the sea actually began, she faced another unwelcome surprise.

A barrier had been placed across to bar the path, a pile of old planks of wood. 'Driftwood,' Lily panted, as she tried to pull it aside. 'Someone must have brought it up from the beach. Dragged, more like. Whoever would dare?'

Unable to move the heavy pieces, she scrambled over in a flurry of petticoats and hurried down the track. At this time of year, when each tree and bush was just breaking into leaf, an arch had formed overhead, through which the light shone dim green-grey. For Lily it was as if she were moving under water. She wanted to stop and admire the delicate traceries of the twigs, coated now with a downy covering, their buds sticky with sap, or turn aside to part the underbrush where bluebells were already pushing through last year's debris. As Em panted to keep up with her, 'Look,' she wanted to say, pointing to the ferns which hung from lichened branches, 'Listen,' as birds fluttered in protest and the stream tumbled and fretted under its layer of stones, 'Feel,' as the day's heat lay trapped there in its velvet glove.

The track was barely visible, a faint traced line through the bracken, like a badger path. Usually by summer the brambles and the nettles grew so thickly they had to be hacked away but, 'Someone's already pruned them,' Lily said, 'just enough to hide the path.' And when they came out at last on to the beach, burst out into the sun as swimmers surfacing from the depths, 'Look,' Lily cried again. 'What do you make of that?'

In front of them stretched the little cove, its sandy beach half covered by the outgoing tide. It was empty, nothing but the tracks of sanderlings which scurried along the edge, dipping and pecking like bobbing wooden birds. Against the shingle bar where the stream emerged and where in season irises and marsh buttercups vied for space, another pile of wood had been newly stacked: fishing boxes, broken crates, timbered logs, all the flotsam of the winter storms trimmed and arranged for firewood.

'And look at Wheal Marty.' Lily pointed dramatically to the other side of the cove where the cliffs rose equally steeply. Halfway up this eastern cliff was a kind of dark patch cut against the shoots of new bracken like a square-cut hole. It was the entrance to an old mine, known as Wheal Marty, so old no one remembered when it had last been worked. It had always seemed inaccessible from the beach but now they could see how a faint line had been hacked through the undergrowth, winding its way up the cliff towards the opening; and how the rocks around the entrance had been dug away, for the colour was different, no longer black but rust-coloured, tinged with orange and ochre as if someone had taken a brush and daubed paint on them.

'And there's the fire.'

On the other side of the stream, crossed by a large coping stone, a well-defined path ran against the edge of the beach, here mainly shingle, towards a kind of ledge. Sheltered by an overhang, out of reach of wind and tide, the ledge held a small building, more like a hut, its wooden walls and sod roof, reinforced by stone, blending into the cliff above. Today its door stood wide open, and from its granite chimney came a curl of smoke.

'What cheek.'

Hands on hips, Lily bristled, and clamped her lips. Once more not waiting for Em, she started off towards the hut, crossed the bridge and scrambled up on the ledge in righteous indignation. She came to the door, paused for a moment, went inside. When Em reached the ledge she reappeared, holding something in her hand.

'I thought as much,' she said triumphantly, 'someone's had the nerve to settle in. Cleared the rubbish out and parked himself just as if the hut belonged to him.'

She pulled at Em's arm to make her come to the door. And when reluctantly Em did, showed her the dirt floor, neatly raked, the open hearth where a banked fire burned, the plain deal chair and table, set with plate and mugs. 'Nothing else,' she said, 'except a pile of tins; he's stocked up food for himself all right.'

The two girls looked about them curiously. Then Em shivered. 'Come away, Lily,' she said. 'It's like, well, like walking on a grave.'

'More like the cottage of the three bears,' Lily said. She waved the object she'd picked up, a man's cap, khaki, with holes showing where insignia had been ripped off. 'Except not a single bear. An ex-soldier by the looks of it. And there's his greatcoat by the fire.'

'Come away, Lily,' Emma repeated, her voice sharp. 'We shouldn't be here.'

'But I've never been inside before,' Lily said. 'You know we always wanted to but it was too well locked and the windows were boarded up. Does it look like you remembered it when mother lived here?'

Emma shook her head, again reluctant. 'I was too young,' she said at last. 'I don't remember much.'

'But you must have been inside before,' Lily persisted. 'You must have seen it then. It can't have changed. That fireplace'll have been used for centuries. And there're the stairs.'

Before Em could stop her she darted up a steep flight of wooden stairs, narrow and vertical, like a ladder. Her feet went tapping along the beams, there was a rustle of straw, a grating sound. When she spoke her voice sounded muffled. 'And a little window right beneath the roof so from the outside you'd not notice it. All covered with spider webs but the glass still intact.'

After a while she slid back down, her face and hands streaked with dirt. 'No bed or furniture,' she said, her eyes shining with excitement. 'But a partition to make two tiny rooms. The roof's got great holes in it and so has the floor. And the cob walls are green with damp. But give them a coat of paint, mend the floors and resod the roof, you'd be snug and cosy up there. Perhaps that's what some of the wood'll be used for.'

Em had gone from the ledge and was already climbing across the stream towards the beach. 'Wait,' Lily cried. 'Don't you want to find out who the trespasser is?'

Em turned round. 'No,' she said, in her quiet way determined, her voice not quite even. 'We're the trespassers. And whatever poor soul has found refuge there, leave well alone.'

For a moment Lily looked abashed. Then her natural exuberance took hold. 'But it's mine!' she cried. 'Mother always used to say it was her home. If it belongs to anyone, it belongs to me.'

There was another long silence then, full of the past, full of things done, not done; said, not said. 'Listen,' Em said at last. 'You know that's not true. If you were born here it was by chance, because your mother had nowhere else to go. Your father was still in Africa, a prisoner of the Boers, and everyone believed he was dead. For all their importance his people thought they were too grand to help, and my people wouldn't, even although my father is your mother's only brother. The Martin family owned the hut. Beth Martin and her brother, Jeb. When Beth married and Jeb was drowned saving my father's life, the hut was shut up. The cottage never "belonged" to your mother; she just stayed in it until your father came back for her.'

It was a long speech for Emma, but she still hadn't finished. 'So if someone now is making use of it,' she said, 'it's none of our affair. And I can't help thinking perhaps he's an ex-soldier, perhaps he wants to hide away a bit and get used to peace after all that war.'

She added, 'That was what your mother did, thinking your father was dead and having to look after you on her own.'

Once more Em's sensible reply quieted Lily. More subdued, she followed her cousin back down the beach and let the older girl lead the way across the flats where the waves curled and hissed in long sweeps of foam. The sand was still damp from the outgoing tide, and behind them their footprints left slight hollows for water to fill, the only set of human prints among the birds' claw marks. Except for the orange-red stains around the mine, the stacked wood, the coil of smoke, nothing else had changed from the way it always was.

When they had come right out on the sands, they turned to stare back at the hut. It nestled under the cliffs like an animal warren. As if remembering something, Em said, 'Your mother always claimed it was the view that brought her back to life. After you were born Beth Martin drew the curtains and said, "The winter's gone, it's spring again." And your mother felt the spring come in the room and lift her out of bed.'

Lily was kneeling, pretending to be looking for cowrie shells.

11

She turned over the broken shards and the wet strips of seaweed, letting the damp sand trickle through her fingers. Her voice came out muffled. 'What was my mother like in those days, Em? Surely you remember that?'

Em's worried frown lightened. 'Just as now,' she said simply. 'Pretty as a picture.' After a while she added, 'The first time your mother came to our cottage in St Marvell we were all eating fish stew. She stood in the doorway and asked for Ben Trevarisk. That would have been her father, your grandfather and mine, the first Ben, but as my father and my oldest brother were called Ben too, we all stared at her. Well, until then we never even knew our father had a sister. After grandfather's death she'd been brought up far away from us, on Bodmin Moor. I'd never seen anyone her like before. Until I found out she was my aunt I thought she was a queen.'

She said, 'And after you were born in Beth Martin's cottage up there, she'd sit with me sometimes on this beach, and show me all the shells she'd found, and teach me their names and tell me how to cook them, all the things she said she'd learned off Beth Martin and Beth Martin's brother, Jeb. And after Uncle Julian returned safely from Africa, and Jeb Martin was drowned, she and Uncle Julian went to live at Nanscawn Farm, taking you and me with them.'

All this Lily knew of course. All that happened years ago, Lily wanted to say; every Sunday I can read about it in the plaque beneath the stained-glass window. In fact it's always been a bond between us both, that just as my father was given back life so was yours. But I'm talking of the, well, call it the Martins' hut, what it was like in those days, was it as bare and simple as it is now? I'm curious, she wanted to say, and since mother and father are away you're the only one left to ask. What was it really like? How was it for my mother to be living there?

She continued to let the sand trickle through her fingers. Other questions, not completely formed as yet, wound themselves in and out of her thoughts. And what was it like for me to have been born a fisher child? My father was an officer, a member of the Cornish aristocracy, with a title to inherit when his own father dies; what did he think when he came back and found mother and me living as we did?

These were ideas that had not occurred to her before. Vaguely she wondered why. She sensed somehow she should have thought of them. But that is what I'm like, she thought, drifting along, never touching on one subject long, never bothering to probe as Em does.

Her lack of interest had never bothered her before. She had the sudden perception that perhaps henceforth it would. She didn't know if she liked or disliked the idea, or what it would mean to her.

But Em didn't, or wouldn't, help her. Em didn't, or wouldn't, remember anything else. 'Ask Aunt Jenny,' was all Em would say. 'She and your father can tell you when they return. But I'll repeat, Aunt Jenny and Uncle Julian would say the same as I've done, leave well enough alone.'

Em put her arm around Lily. 'Until they come back, let Cove keep its secrets. Myself, I rather like the idea of someone's making use of Beth Martin's cottage again.'

With that Lily had to be content, but all the unanswered questions pricked at her, like thorns. As she and Em started back up the path, she dawdled, constantly turning to look round, hoping perhaps to see if the new occupier of the hut had returned. Whoever he was, and wherever he had gone, there was no sign of him – only the coil of smoke from the banked fire behind them, the cleared track they trod, the planks of wood crisscrossed to bar the entrance to the path.

CHAPTER 2

Nanscawn, the Polleven farm, lay back from the sea, on a road that ran between Rock and Delabole. The farmhouse itself stood within the shelter of a stand of trees so that it could not be seen until the girls came along the farm track. On either side low hedges topped with may and beech opened to pasture grass, beyond which the sloping land gave way to fields of grain just showing through the dark ribs of ploughed earth. In front of the house the track widened into a more formal drive with room for horses and carriages, and in recent times for a motor car (which Lily's father, at present abroad, had taken with him). Behind the house, however, the drive reverted to a familiar farmyard with cobbled stones and watering trough, and a kennel for a couple of dogs, which now came leaping out in greeting. 'Bother,' Lily said, wiping the muddy pawprints from her skirt, already much dishevelled from her scrambles in hut and on beach. 'It's a good job no one's home to see my clothes. There isn't time to change.'

Em watched her as she ran up to the steps into the kitchen, her new hat swinging by its broken ribbon, its silk roses already crushed against the straw. Half exasperatedly, she thought, Lily's like a flower too, a bud opening to the sun. Not yet full blown, not yet flattened by experience, but light-hearted, a butterfly, full now of her own concerns, bubbling with curiosity about the cove, dying to find out more about the old hut and its previous occupants. My own predicament will be put aside and forgotten. Not intentionally, of course, not meanly, but simply as being of less consequence. Such curiosity about the past is natural, Em thought, trying to be fair. But surely the present's equally important; more so, since it deals with real living people and their real difficulties.

Once again Em shook herself. No room for thoughts like that, she told herself, that way lies bitterness. William's out of hospital, not cured perhaps, but that's in God's hands, God will provide. Rather concentrate on what is known and good.

She contemplated the farm which had been her home now for many years. The original house was old although its façade was Victorian of the previous century. Made of Luxyllian granite, its pink stones shone in patches under a covering of ivy. It was not its air of prosperity that pleased her, although it had that, nor the contrast with the cottage at St Marvell where the rest of the Trevarisks still lived, all crowded together like pilchards in a tin, the fisherman's house with its rank smell of fish and its slatternly disorder in which her mother, Charity, thrived and which she herself always tried unobtrusively to tidy when she went there. No, it was the sense of belonging, of being wanted and loved for herself, that she felt here at Nanscawn and had lacked in her own home, a lack of affection her aunt, Lily's mother, had immediately recognized and responded to.

Thinking of Aunt Jenny made Emma's face light up again. 'You were my first child,' Aunt Jenny had always said. Well, she and Uncle Julian were not Em's real parents perhaps, but in all other ways they had acted as parents to her since childhood. And that, despite troubles of their own which might have daunted anyone.

'We had a stormy start,' Em heard Aunt Jenny say, her voice still keeping its soft Cornish burr. 'Storms and their aftermath run through our lives. But after storm comes calm. Praise be, that's how it is for us.'

And she would smile at her tall husband and he would smile

back and take her hand. That's what married life should be like, Emma thought; that's what Will would have understood if Will were his real self. A line of poetry her aunt had once taught her came into her head and repeated itself as she followed Lily up the steps. 'Out of loss comes golden gain.' So it had been for Jenny and Julian Polleven, so perhaps it would be for her. But for her cousin Lily, and Lily's brother, all was golden from the start, without loss or pain.

Lily was in the scullery, washing her hands. She came into the kitchen, drying them on an old piece of towel and trying to comb her hair straight. The kitchen, older than the rest of the house, was of ancient origin, built within the ruins of a former abbey church. In odd corners there were still traces of Norman stone and arch, some tucked in sideways or upside down as if later builders hadn't known what to do with them. It was a room that seemed to have grown rather than been built; the girls always felt at home in it as if, given a chance, any number of previous inhabitants would appear to make them welcome. This sense of warmth and well-being was enhanced by the copper jugs and pots which gleamed from the shelves of an old pine dresser, and by the bundle of farm kittens, asleep in a purring huddle on the sloping slate floor.

Left on their own as they now were, they would have preferred to eat their tea at the refectory table, would have preferred to sample Hetty's saffron cake and currant buns rather than a more formal meal. 'Master Michael Robert's asked for 'ee in the dining room.' Hetty, the housekeeper, rattled tins, not quite daring to make a face. 'Hurry, my lovers, don't dawdle.' She flapped her apron as if shooing hens. 'He'm some teasy these days.'

Michael Robert was Lily's younger brother by a scant year. He was leaning against the mantelpiece, poking with his boot at the fire. The table was set for three but he had already served himself from the covered dishes on the sideboard. A glass of wine stood half empty at his place and he now moved to gulp it down as the girls seated themselves. 'I'm starved,' he said with the angry scowl that these days had earned him the reputation of being 'teasy'. 'What's kept you so long?

'Up to no good somewhere, I'll be bound,' he added when they didn't reply. 'I spotted you, scuttling along the lane, guilt written over you, like cats in cream.'

That he wasn't really interested where they'd been, or what they'd done, was apparent in his tone. Working himself into a paddy, Lily thought, watching how he poured himself another glass of wine. She and Em exchanged glances. Michael wouldn't want to hear their news, although once he would have done; he wouldn't be interested in Will's return, nor the stranger in Polmena Cove.

Michael, as the girls more simply called him, was not like them in looks at all, although until recently he had been very like his real sister in spirit, full of boyish enthusiasm and boundless energy. Come to think of it, he did not really resemble anyone; again, until recently he had seemed what he was, a typical round-faced, blue-eyed, tousle-haired farmer's lad, fond of horses and dogs, fond of the countryside. Farming was what he had always wanted to do and, having recently left school, he had at first embarked on it with his usual vigour. 'A throwback,' his father had teased. 'Like the old Pollevens. We were good yeomen farmers once, before we grew too big for our boots and forgot what farmwork was.' And in those days Michael had laughed and taken his father's teasing in his stride.

Now Michael's boyish looks had been supplanted by a resentful air which gave him a sulky look, a sulkiness which increased when again the girls did not immediately reply. 'You're always having secrets,' he burst out. 'Not that they're worth much. But if you've been to St Marvell as you said, you should have returned hours ago. You knew I was going out.'

He added petulantly, 'And since Lily was invited too, it would have been courteous not to be late. There's a dance tonight, at the Club. But she can't go looking like that, as if she's been dragged backwards through a hedge.'

Beneath the petulance he sounded almost relieved, as if, thought Lily, he doesn't want me to come. She noted how, as if to hide that thought, he took another hasty drink and pretended to attack his food, although he was really toying with it. He's nervous, she thought, and then, I wonder why.

Drink loosened his tongue. He began to shout. 'For God's sake, can't you keep yourself neat? A chap's friends'd be ashamed of you like that.'

Lily was hurt. Although she and her brother had never been close, they had always been good friends. Now, since their parents were away, he seemed to take perverse pleasure in being disagreeable. In his father's absence the new, disgruntled Michael Robert liked to swagger, ordering his sister and cousin about, seemingly never satisfied with anything. Their father hadn't meant Michael to behave like that when he left him in charge.

'Your mother and I have agreed,' their father had said. They were all sitting in the living room, Julian with his leg propped up. 'Your chance, old son, to run the farm.'

As Michael had flushed with pleasure, 'You'll be in command, with Em and Lily to look after you.'

He had smiled at them, then grimaced as he tried to stand up. 'Time your mother and I took a break,' he said.

Behind his back Lily and Em had glanced at Jenny Polleven. Although she continued calmly with her needlework, her wide forehead, so much like Em's, was suddenly knotted in a frown. Mother's worried about father, Lily had thought, and doesn't want him to know. She's pinned her hopes on this new cure he talks about, this spa place he's heard of, but she isn't sure. She's just willing it to work; she's just praying that it will.

Lily herself knew that ever since her father had been young, a soldier in Africa, his leg had troubled him, an old war wound. Over the past year or so it had grown worse. Mother wants everything to go smoothly while they're away, she thought, so father won't be bothered. And so it should, she thought now, there's nothing to go wrong if Michael didn't act the fool. Father'd never approve of all this talk of Club and dancing, he'd never allow Michael to drink so much.

She decided to humour her brother, genuinely conscience-stricken by her forgetfulness. 'There's time to get ready,' she began, 'but it doesn't sound my kind of thing . . .'

'Your kind of thing.' Her brother's anger was rekindled, having found something to focus on. 'And what's that? Trudging over ploughed fields, scrambling through ditches, like a fisher brat. Act like a lady for once. Why don't you admit you forgot? You'd forget your head if it weren't screwed on.'

His voice held a note of sneer now which also was new. It made Lily flush. 'Come on, Michael,' she began, 'that's not fair.'

'Call me by my real name.' Her brother's voice was sharp. 'Michael Robert Polleven.'

He stressed the middle name. 'Robert Polleven. For my grandfather, Sir Robert Polleven of Polleven Manor. A gentleman, in case you've forgotten that too.'

'And you're beginning to sound like him.' Lily became defiant. She put down her knife and fork and crossed her arms. 'Sir Robert this, Sir Robert that, until you'd think the world revolved around him like the sun. Father doesn't bother with all that stuff. And if your friends are that stupid, I just won't come.

'And you shouldn't be drinking so much,' she added virtuously as her brother tipped the bottle empty. 'I'm sure father didn't say you could. Nor that you could stay out to dawn like you did last night and the night before. He left you in charge, but the men do all the work.'

Michael pushed the bottle aside with an even angrier gesture. 'Bugger that,' he said, his voice indistinct. 'I can come and go in my own house as I please. And drink what I like. And you've no reason to talk, spending hours with that drunken old fisherman you call uncle.'

Again Lily flushed. 'That's mean,' she cried. 'Uncle Ben's

your uncle too. And he doesn't touch anything stronger than tea.'

'By the pot.' Michael Polleven's voice was slurring. He reached under the table, produced a second open bottle which he proceeded to wave at them defiantly before he poured it, partly missing the glass so that the red wine ran over the polished wood. 'At least I know how to carry my liquor,' the new Michael Robert boasted. 'At least we keep a good cellar in this godforsaken hole.'

Again the girls exchanged worried looks. Michael Polleven had loved Nanscawn, had hated every moment away from it and his horses and dogs, had counted the days until he left school and could remain at home for good. That had been a year ago; what had happened in a year that could have changed him so?

'Nothing to boast of in Uncle Ben's tea-swilling.' Concentrating with difficulty, Michael returned to the charge. 'Ask her.'

He gestured unevenly towards Emma, who had remained silent during this exchange. 'Ask her what Uncle Ben was like before he found God and abstinence, before he almost drowned himself. And drowned Jeb Martin instead.'

He stuttered over the last word. 'She'll tell you that without the Pollevens he'd be dead. And she'd be nothing.'

Another drink. 'And so would mother, if father hadn't married her.'

That was too much. 'Don't you dare speak like that!' Lily cried. 'If father heard, he'd be furious. I wish he'd come back.' While Em, rising from the table with her plate of food untouched, said, 'Leave him alone, Lily. It's the drink. He'll be sorry when he thinks over what he's said.'

'I said she knows all about the effects of liquor.' Michael's voice had slurred, the 's' sounds came out like 'z's. 'How often did she make allowances for her father when she lived in Ben Trevarisk's house? How often did she make mother suffer in her stead before your "Uncle Ben" turned them out to starve?'

He pointed an accusing finger. 'But Cousin Emma was wise. Cousin Emma feathered her own nest first,' he said, with the same belligerent sneer. 'Knew which side her bread was buttered on, by God she did. Sucked up to mother to make sure she'd be taken care of, out of the fish oil stink into cosy living at Nanscawn Farm.'

'That's not true.' Again Lily rose to the defence. 'Em wasn't much more than a baby when she came to Nanscawn. Her father didn't turn her out, mother brought her, ages before you were born. If anyone belongs here she does.'

Em had gone very white. Only her eyes held their colour as she stood looking at her cousin. 'I was wrong,' she said at last. ''Tisn't just the drink. The drink gives him the courage to say what's in his mind. But why tonight?' She said to Michael, 'What makes it so important to say all this tonight?'

He didn't answer, sat there with a truculent sneer until the girls had gone. That'd set the fox in the barnyard, was all he could think; that'll show them up, sneaking back with their silly secrets. When the immediate effect of the wine had worn off, he took himself up to his room to duck his head in water from the ewer. Then, dressed in evening clothes, left over from his father's day and slightly shabby, he went down the back stairs to avoid another confrontation with the girls. Taking his bicycle from the shed, he mounted and pedalled quickly down the lane.

The fresh air made him feel better. He let it whistle through his hair, bent his shoulders, forced his legs to go round and round. A sliver of moon was visible over the hedge, a nightjar churned; he rode on oblivious to them and the fields on either side. Once he wouldn't have been. Now as deep in thought as Emma, he couldn't be bothered with any of that as with guilty truculence he defended his position.

'The courage to say what's in his mind,' Em'd said. Well, he admitted to himself, there was something to that; but then Em had a knack of guessing at truth, one of the things he hated about her. It wasn't that he really hated Em, of course, in fact she had once been something of a favourite. He had been as fond of her as he was of his mother. It was only, why did she have to be right about everything, that got under a fellow's skin.

It was true that the resentment had always been there, the resentment that Em came before him in every way, even in his mother's choosing her, adopting Em to be first, showing preference. And he, the son and heir, had perforce to be content with being second, second to his cousin, second to his sister, two older females who ruled the house and took precedence over him. But that was only part of it. Again he pedalled furiously, his trouser cuffs tucked into his socks out of the mud, his face beaded with sweat as he worked up speed.

Had his father not been off in some godforsaken spot nursing some old injury obtained in the Dark Ages, he would have taken the car, with or without permission, not had to cycle down dirty lanes like a poor farm labourer. It wasn't right, he thought, his round face contracting, he was as good as the next man, a landowner's heir. Polleven was as old a Cornish name as there was. Those bastards at the Club, for all their confounded sneers, weren't heir to half as much. Polleven Manor was on the cards one day, and the title too. But not yet, there was the problem. Grandfather Robert was old, but he wasn't about to kick the bucket for a good few years. And if rumour were true, his grandfather's fortunes weren't all they were said to have been. For the time being, his father was left to pick up the slack, would have to provide something for his only son, should already have made some provision for him, not let things slide. And a son moreover who wasn't illegitimate, even if his mother were a fisherwoman.

In those two words, 'illegitimate' and 'fisherwoman', lay all his resentment. He wasn't sure which was worse. Not that these details of his parents' story were new: his mother and father had never made a secret of their past nor the difference in their status. Their misfortune to be parted by war, the dislike and prejudice of both their families, were facts he had known about since he could first remember. But they didn't have to live with the consequences. Lily might wish for her parents; for the first time in his life Michael was glad his father was away, else he might have had it out with him.

'Why did you and mother ever meet?' he wanted to cry, goaded into saying it. 'Why did you look so far beneath you? Or if you did, why did you have to marry, and if married, couldn't you have gone somewhere else to live? Not stay here at Nanscawn, within sight and sound of it; not flaunt it, bring it into the house, by adopting Emma Trevarisk.'

Once more he put his head down, stood up on the pedals, gritted his teeth as the open wind caught him, cycled faster. As the crow flies his destination wasn't far, back along the road his sister and cousin had followed, then veering eastwards to the coast. It was imperative that he get to the Club tonight more than any other time. 'Why tonight?' Em had asked him. He let his feet flap on either side as he coasted now down the last hill. If he ever had the chance he'd tell her why, the same reason why it was important that he reach there early: to see and be seen, to show that it didn't matter either, nothing mattered, and he was as good as the next man, even if he knocked someone down to prove it.

The Club, as it was known, was a new building close to the sea. As he had done last night, and the night before, and for many previous other nights with growing frequency, Michael would leave his bike where it couldn't be found, buried in the rhododendron bushes which grew in front of the hedge. The hedge had been built to hide the coastline and shelter the site, to make it seem more urban and presumably civilized. With Cornish perversity the bushes were already springing up with unexpected vigour, would soon reach tree height. Like many things Cornish they wouldn't fit into an accepted mould, burst out of traditional confines. Although they covered the rawness of the surroundings and softened the brick-and-wood façade, there was something about their rich jungle cover that gave them a slightly tropical feel, as if all kinds of wild things lurked within their growth.

And so Michael himself felt as if he too were some wild savage, peering out of darkness into a civilized world. Straightening his clothes and dusting himself down, he strolled with pretended nonchalance up the drive, pausing to look at the motor cars which were parked on either side, their polished sides gleaming in the faint gaslight. All the cars in Cornwall gathered in the one place, he thought, contrasting their glittering perfection with his father's battered Lagonda, its mud-splattered side dented where a rock had hit.

Just before he reached the doors he paused again. Already it was dark. From the open windows the sound of music ebbed and flowed like a tide. There was the usual hum of voices, the clink of glasses, the babble of laughter from the owners of the cars. He knew all about them now. They motored down at weekends from places in or around London to take up temporary residence in the equally new villas that had begun to sprout across the cliffs behind Rock and Trebetherick. Or they left these cars here for 'country use' and travelled down on the Waterloo to Padstow line, dressed in tweed plus fours like country squires, with their gear, their golf clubs and fishing rods and guns, spilling from the guard's van, to settle in for the Cornish 'season', throwing their weight about, subduing the 'locals', lording it over the natives. Among whom he was counted, despite his Polleven rank and name!

That the Club had been called an architectural monstrosity, built for these new villa invaders and pandering to their taste, that real Cornish people, as if outsiders themselves, could only come as guests, didn't matter to Michael. Monstrosity or not, it drew him like a magnet. Or rather, its members did.

They were all related, the 'Clubbers', as they called themselves, were intermarried or were neighbours or worked together in the business world of the city. They had names like Bunny, or Ginger, even Boy, for God's sake, Boy for a man fifty years old. During the day, they went fishing or playing golf on the Club's new course, carved out of the sand dunes, while their evenings were spent drinking whisky and smoking cigars in the Club's bars. Or dancing with the girls they brought down with them.

Thinking of the girls made Michael even more hesitant. The girls were true tinsel, they dazzled. With their short bobbed hair, their fashionable short skirts, they made Lily look a frump. Their shrill voices, gossiping about playwrights and musicians, and painters – about people, never their work – were as foreign to him as if they spoke a foreign language. Yet at the same time drew him, like a wasp to treacle. After all these nights of standing on the edge, an obvious onlooker, a hound puppy with too large feet, he was just beginning to pick out the faces behind the painted lips and mocking laughter, beginning to feel at ease with them. Making progress finally he'd thought, until last night that is.

Among the young ladies there was one he especially admired from afar, Iris, Iris Duvane, cousin to his friend, Farell. Again he rocked back and forth on his heels, his face tight with worry. 'Iris's quite keen,' he heard Farell say again as he had said last night, making Michael's heart thump with delight. They had been playing billiards, well, he wasn't much good at it, and Farell had been drinking and had to keep one eye shut when he took aim. The room was thick with cigar smoke. Next door the flimsy wooden partitions muffled but didn't drown the drone of older men's voices, serious talk theirs, of money and business ventures, of the world's economy after the war which had gained them most of their wealth. On the veranda beyond a girl squealed, other girls laughed, young laughter, and young men his age chuckled indulgently. Everyone was enjoying himself, no doubt of that, had to enjoy himself, this was Pleasure Palace; Farell's mocking nickname stuck.

Farell had closed one eye, measured along the cue, made a dab and missed the shot. 'Your turn, old man,' he said. He leaned against the panelling, drink in hand, twirling the glass so that the light caught at its amber contents. Farell himself wasn't an exact stranger, was someone whom Michael himself had known from school days. Meeting by chance, graciously Farell had allowed acquaintanceship to be renewed. In school it hadn't seemed to matter when Farell had jibed Michael about being from a 'backwater'. 'A Cornish galoot, lost in the Cornish mists', could be made to sound exciting, dashing, reminiscent of pirates, swashbuckling pirateers, Drake and Hawkins and Raleigh and all Michael's youthful heroes – Farell had nothing in his background to rival that.

Now Farell was a city man, in train to enter his father's business. In the Club, Michael was permitted to mingle with others like him, embryo lawyers and stockbrokers with their briefs and papers and their own portfolios, with homes of their own in those important up-country places – and with sufficient cash to rent out Cornish villas and strut around in their mock country clothes.

Michael hated their attitude, he hated them. Yet at the same time he envied and wanted to become one of them. In their eyes he remained what they had dubbed him, what he had become, a country yokel up to his knees in muck, a stay-at-home farmer without a spark of imagination or charm.

Although conventionally dressed by day, at night perversely Farell affected the latest style of country clothes, loud checked knickerbockers and paisley pullovers. His hair was sleeked, parted in the middle, black, accentuating the pallor of his skin. He boasted of his dislike of the out-of-doors. 'While the pater bangs away at golf balls, I sleep,' he'd said. 'Pater always fancied being a country squire.' He'd sniggered. 'Can't see him on a horse out hunting, a red-sacked ton of wheat.'

Michael had leaned over the table, pretending to concentrate. Farell's next words froze him dead. 'I say, Polleven,' Farell had said, in the carefully modulated up-country voice which hid so much malice and which Michael remembered from their school days, 'I say, Polleven, I hear someone's squatting on your land.'

That had been news to be shrugged off in calculated

indifference. 'Another army drifter,' Farell had continued, with a nod towards the bar where a group of slightly older men clustered, the ones who had been in the war. Even Farell was in awe of them – they didn't say much, didn't have to, just kept to themselves, what they had experienced setting them apart from everyone, making the rest seem like silly children crying for the moon. Their very presence always made Michael uneasy, as if they weren't all outside glitter, as if they at least had something of worth to them.

'A war-worn old lag,' Farell had gone on, although he said this last softly so as not to be overheard, 'an out-of-work drifter, pretending to be a hero.' He squinted at his glass. 'Squatting in a hut, I hear, down at Polmena Cove.'

And in reply to Michael's own non-committal mutter, deliberately loudly now, 'I say, isn't that the hut where your mother lived as a fisherwoman? Before your sister was born and your father had to marry her?'

The words had stung. Like fire they scorched. To know a thing, to have it part of you like some living legend, is different from having it spat out in public for the world to snigger at. The ball had ricocheted off the table and rolled across the floor, lucky the green baize hadn't ripped. 'Steady on,' Farell had said with his little laugh. 'No need to break the place up. But a pity, old man, don't you know, a pity. Iris's been quite keen.'

So that was why tonight was so important – to show he didn't care, to show Farell his words had left no mark – and to prove to Farell's cousin, Iris Duvane, that she was a nothing to him. And why, despite his hectoring, or perhaps because of it, he was relieved that Lily hadn't come. But even having to think like this left a sour taste. He shouldn't have had to think at all.

'I shouldn't have to be ashamed,' he told himself, as he screwed up his courage, 'not of mother, sister, cousin, the whole crew. I shouldn't have to be ashamed for feeling shame.'

He shook off these unwelcome thoughts, took a deep

breath, looked around him as if taking stock, like a man about to jump into the deep end of a swimming pool. Then he swaggered up to the doors and pushed them open, to face those friends he was so afraid of.

Left in the house, the girls heard the front door slam and breathed a sigh of relief. They had sought refuge in the former nursery which gradually they had taken over as their own sitting room. It was on the third floor under the eaves, and there they crouched before the hearth, trying to light pieces of damp wood with an equally damp match.

'At last,' Lily said. She sat back on her heels and blew wisps of hair out of her eyes, her hands too black to touch anything. 'What a pain.'

But it was not of damp wood she spoke and Emma knew what she meant. Michael these days too often was a 'pain'. Not in the way of a younger brother who interfered and teased, and never before so offensive, so determined to wound. Yet at the same time unhappy, depressed, as if, Em said now, he were two people in one skin and never certain which one was which.

'But I don't understand him,' Lily broke out. The thought surprised her and she repeated it. 'I don't understand him, and I always used to. When we were younger I always knew if he was in trouble, don't you remember, Em, when he broke his arm hunting, and I said he had, before they brought him back. He has never wanted anything else except to live here with us. But now he doesn't like us any more. Except you know him as well as I do, I'd apologize. He'd no call to lie like that.'

Emma was quiet. It could have been the heat that made her cheeks turn red, for she was holding sheets of newspaper across the fire to make a draught. Or the smell of scorching which made her eyes water. After a while she said, 'When I was a little girl they say that my father seldom went out fishing in his boat. Most of the time he sat at home, letting it rot, just like Will Pendray does. And they say it was drink that did that to him, destroyed him, soured him and my mother until I think they loathed each other.'

She took a breath. 'And so Michael didn't lie about my father's drunkenness,' she said, 'nor about his behaviour to your mother. There was some old story from their past which left him bitter against her. And Michael didn't lie either, that when the storm came, against all sense, although the whole village begged him not to, my father insisted in staying out to prove himself as good a sailor as the first Ben Trevarisk had been.'

She didn't add, 'And it's true that all these things are reasons why your mother wanted to have me with her, out of harm's way.' But it was clear that she thought this by the way her eyes darkened with old unhappiness. Nor did she contradict when Lily cried out, 'That doesn't give Michael the right to use them, as if they were sticks to break our bones.'

'It's all in the past,' was what Em insisted, 'no reason to dwell on the past. But no reason either to be ashamed of it, let it be. And if I were you,' and now she did hesitate, not liking to interfere, 'I'd not mention Cove to your brother or say anything about it, let it be too.'

In Polmena Cove the light from an oil lamp lit up the wooden walls, the floor, the ledge outside the door. Louder now with the incoming tide, the sea surged on the beach, a swishing of sand as the ripples spread, a sucking withdrawal. The wind had risen, and with it the Atlantic swell; grit rattled against the shutters, and the dry grass soughed. The new occupant of the hut sat in stockinged feet in front of the fire, muddy boots stuffed with paper set to dry. After years in the trenches he knew how to care for boots; for years before that boots and their care had been his work. On the table were spilled the rocks he had just brought down from the mine; he had sorted them roughly into piles by colour and shape, would presently take his book and study them. In his hand he held his cap, twisting it as Lily had done. He had retrieved it from where she had thrown it; by the lamplight had found traces of sand, knew that in his absence someone had entered his home. Like Michael Polleven he brooded, his face in shadow. Beside him, against the wall, a gun barrel gleamed.

CHAPTER 3

If Em really believed that Lily would 'let things be', she underestimated Lily's curiosity. Lily might not be given to brooding but she was not likely to follow Em's advice. Nor would she wait for her parents' return. She soon devised a plan to visit Polmena Cove again, without telling Em what she was about, and certainly not telling Michael. She ignored her brother, something she'd never done before, calling an uneasy truce which for the time being suited her as well as him.

Nor did Lily feel comfortable about going down the valley to Cove. For some reason the thought of the path which had been so painstakingly blocked – and from which there was no escape if someone were watching it – was unpleasant. She decided therefore to go by boat, convincing herself that the distance from St Marvell by sea was in fact shorter than by land, given the direction of the prevailing wind and the windings of the cliff path. She waited for the next fine day, when the Atlantic was once more glassy smooth, convincing herself too that the trip was one she had often made with her parents in the past and ignoring the fact that she had never managed a boat alone, and what was more, had never brought it back again. Nor had she ever lied before, although she told herself she was not really lying, as she caught the local bus and came into St Marvell Square, as she'd told Em, to shop. And having entered one shop as proof of that, she immediately went down to the quay.

St Marvell's harbour was called The Cut because of its narrowness. It was where all the little village streets converged and the world of fishermen and fish concentrated round a cobbled pier. And where sooner or later everyone passed by to chat and gossip. That what Lily had in mind would at once become common knowledge, eventually to be spread abroad even back to Nanscawn Farm, bothered her not a scrap – or only in so far as how at this moment it might hinder her. 'What do 'ee want to do that fer?' someone might ask, ''tain't fitty fer a maid.' But if she pretended an hour's fishing was all she had in mind, again not exactly a lie, she liked to fish; if she asked one of the local fishermen, with luck he might let her borrow a small skiff, or, better still, offer to take her out himself. And, once on board a boat, she had no doubt about her ability to coax any oarsman into compliance with her wishes.

'Just a little further,' she'd plead, 'just round the next cliff. Just a moment on the beach.' Then she could scan the ledge where the hut stood, search for signs of life. If no one was in sight, she'd take the opportunity to duck inside, poke in cupboards and drawers, search through the scattered clothes, empty pockets, find what she was looking for. What exactly she hoped to find, what she would do with the information when she had it, were things she hadn't yet thought through, had not really considered.

The tide was halfway out but The Cut was still under water. On one side of the harbour wall were the wharfs where the daily catch was unloaded. She avoided them. Within a large stone building, known as the 'cannery', the fish was processed by the fisher girls. Her own mother had never worked there, had been employed in the fisheries at the rival port of Zennor, but the job was similar: hard, and long and evil-smelling. It was part of her mother's past that even she preferred to ignore.

On the other side the boats were moored, side by side,

their sails furled. She was too late to see them come in after a night's trawling but some of the crews were still at work. Those who knew her by sight waved or smiled as she went by, greeted her by name and asked after her father's health, then went back to coiling nets or swabbing decks or mending sails. They didn't stop to chat and she knew better than to interrupt. She knew there weren't many fish about and the fishermen were worried; the catch had been poor after a series of poor seasons. She couldn't help noticing how even in the past year the number of boats had declined. Called Padstow luggers, they were judged too slow and cumbersome these days to compete with modern motorized trawlers. At this rate, she thought, soon there'll be none left!

Ducking under mooring ropes, skirting the place where her uncle kept his boat, she hugged the shadow of the wall, still hoping to enlist the help of her special friends. She was about to withdraw in frustrated defeat when she spied a figure seated on a bench at the pier's end.

The hunched look, arms crossed, head bowed, gaze fixed on the ground, gave her a clue to the man's identity. Quickly she crossed in front of him and leaned down to touch his arm. As he flinched away, 'Hullo, Will,' she said loudly, too loudly, a bright tone to encourage convalescents.

The look he gave her made her falter and her voice lose its artificial note. 'Poor soul,' she wanted to say. 'Poor dear soul.' The laughing young man Em had described was gone. Instead she was looking at what might have been a skull, its bones cleanly drawn as if the flesh had receded. Only the eyes were alive; they shone dark and tortured, as if opening into hell.

'Lily Polleven.' The man spoke haltingly, dragging the name up from some deep recess. 'Miss Lily, Emma's little cousin.'

At least he remembers me, Lily thought. And he remembers Em. And he's come outside, surely that means he's getting better. But he looks . . . she had no words to describe his looks except they gave her the sensation of being scrutinized by someone who wasn't of this world, and who certainly wasn't sure what it was he was scrutinizing.

Not knowing what else to say and embarrassed by that unwavering stare, she added in her usual bright way, 'I'm here to go fishing, if anyone will take me.'

It was only when he repeated the words to himself that she realized how provocative they were.

To her astonishment and dismay Will Pendray put his hand on the back of the seat and pushed himself upright. 'I'll take 'ee,' he said, 'fishing's something I ought to know about. I used to . . .' His voice trailed off. Without waiting for her response he turned and walked back towards the harbour steps, moving unsteadily as if he were being jerked on strings, as if even his legs wouldn't obey him. But with a strange air of command as if he expected her to follow him.

Lily knew she shouldn't accept, even if the offer were meant. Why, he didn't look as if he had the strength to stand upright let alone manage boat and oars. Yet she didn't like to refuse. If I go along with him now, she thought, pityingly, when we reach the boat I'll change my mind without letting him guess the reason. Yet when he had made his way to where his father's dinghy was tied up (by instinct she supposed, for he kept his gaze fixed on the paving stones), when he had slowly and laboriously loosened the painter and held the 'Seagull' trim, again she found she hadn't the heart to contradict him, although his hand trembled on the gunwale, the veins standing out like those of an old man. Reluctantly she stepped on board, uncertain what to do next and angry with herself that she had so foolishly encouraged him.

She noted at once that the little skiff was dry and clean as if someone had recently repaired it. Instead of making her feel better it added to her uncertainty. She was sure that Will himself was incapable of such forethought. Nor did the fact that after all she had obtained what she wanted, albeit in this unexpected fashion, diminish her alarm. Yet once again, although she knew she should somehow think of a way to thank Will and get out, she let herself be seated in the stern and waited while he struggled to fit the rowlocks. She told herself that perhaps it would do him good, might even give him confidence – but she knew that what she was encouraging was wrong and dangerous.

She clung to the side, pretending to smile, until it was too late to move, until he had pushed off, unshipped the oars and settled down to the stroke. And for a few moments perhaps it was safe as under the startled gaze of his mates Will rowed Lily Polleven out of St Marvell harbour in professional fashion. When the first surprised shouts broke out, they had reached the nearest headland (although by then the solemn splashing of the blades half deadened the commotion).

Once round the point Lily felt better. In actual fact this was where she should have felt most uneasy. Round the point was where the wind was always worse and today was no exception, the calm waters inside the harbour roughened here into ripples that danced darkly off the rocks. And round the point, out of sight of the village and its inhabitants, she and Will Pendray were truly on their own and must manage as best they could. Yet for a while Will continued to row without difficulty, again perhaps by instinct, for he said nothing and his shoulders bent and pulled as if the weight of the dinghy and her weight within were nothing. As indeed they well might have been to a former miner and Cornish wrestler. It was only when she told him where she wanted to go that he hesitated.

'Polmena Cove,' he repeated her. 'That's a far piece off.' He leaned on his oars, letting the boat drift. 'That's a distance.'

For the first time since he had climbed on board he raised his head as if looking round. 'And them cliffs, like tunnels,' he said, 'closing hard.

'Can't abide tunnels,' he said, 'like trenches, dark and cold and wet. Can't abide being under them, might be trapped.'

Lily watched him, watched the cliffs, watched the swing of the boat. There was no danger yet but they mustn't drift. There were currents here and reefs under the surface where the white foam spun. It wouldn't do to get too close to them.

35

'I'll come sit beside you,' she said, 'look, I'll help.' With infinite care she slid next to him and put her hand out. And a third time by instinct he made no further comment, allowed her to take an oar and row with him.

It was difficult, for he was tiring and she had to pull hard to keep the boat in line. But gradually, as the water began to chuckle under the stern again and she saw the rocks slip past, she let herself relax. The sun was hot and dried the salt in white patches on her skirts; when the wind died, in places the sea was so clear she could look over the side down to sandy bottoms where great black patches of weed floated like underwater forests. To cheer him up and to keep herself cheerful, she began to sing, old fishing shanties, familiar songs and ballads that he would know, keeping time with the music as she rowed. It was only when they rounded the cliff enclosing Cove that danger returned, full and threatening.

She had known the tide would be out, had taken that into consideration. It was essential to her plan. No one could object to a boat coming in on the tidal flats. And even if he did, surely she could as quickly get away again before he could come out to her. And if she could land without being seen, she could leave the boat, have Will wait by it while she explored the hut, and yet have time to push off before the tide turned. What she had not counted on was the surf. Or the rifle shot.

That it was a rifle even she recognized, although it was perhaps not aimed at them, for it seemed to crack spontaneously, echoing and re-echoing so many times that instead of one shot it might have been a volley. It set the seagulls clamouring. They rose in flocks, swirling like white snowflakes, their screams of indignation at being disturbed ricocheting off the rocks.

'What's that?' Will Pendray let go his oar and cowered, then, as if seeing for the first time the white foam that surged across the beach in front of them, tried to stand up. ''Tis bubbling,' he said, his voice coming in short gasps. ''Tis frothing like phlegm. Got to get out of it.'

Coming in to land through surf was not difficult for an

experienced oarsman, as presumably Will must once have been. Lily would not have ventured on her own perhaps, but she could tell him how to do it. You aim the boat towards the centre of the beach, she'd say, where the risk of current's slight; you wait for the right wave, not too high, not too fast, and ride it in before the next one breaks. The trick when you land is to jump out fast and pull the boat up the sand before another wave catches it. But to shift balance by standing up, to drop your oar so the boat goes broadwise to the waves, that's asking for trouble.

'Sit down,' she gasped. She backfeathered with all her might, trying to turn the prow. 'Don't move.'

Will sagged back on the seat, his hands lax. Already his oar had swung loose and now, as a wave partially hit the boat, it floated clear away. Momentarily freed of the drag the boat righted itself, then once more began to swing parallel to the waves as Lily struggled to keep it on an even keel. It was not the threat of capsize which frightened her – they were close to shore, the water was probably shallow and, if they themselves went with the waves, eventually they would be washed in. But William might not be able to swim and in his present state might not even try. And if a current got hold of him or the backwash sucked him out, she was not sure she could hold on to him, let alone support his weight. And even if they both came safe to shore, she could not right the boat, certainly not drag it, waterlogged, up the beach by herself. The loss of a boat was a serious thing. And then how to get William home across the cliffs, or herself for that matter . . . all these difficulties flashed through her mind in quick succession as she bent her back, pulling and backwatering with her single oar in a desperate attempt to prevent the inevitable from happening.

If the waves had not kept coming with maddening regularity, if the beach had been closer and had not suddenly looked so dark and inhospitable as the sun went in, if she had been twice the height and had had twice the strength, she might have had a chance. As it was, her struggle only exhausted her. When the boat heeled over so that the first wave broke on top of it, she could only grasp the side with all her might and shout to Will to hang on to her.

The 'Seagull' was stoutly built, it survived the first blow. But there was no way it could survive a second. It listed sluggishly, wallowing now, half filled with water. Her own oar gone, she put her arms around William trying to protect him so that when the next wave came, both could go with it.

'Hold on,' a voice said. 'You'm in some mess.'

It seemed to come from the depths of the ocean, so close and unexpected that Lily cried out in fear as she hadn't before. And even Will seemed to come alert, making vague splashing efforts with his hands as if trying to bail. A man's dark head bobbed up, the water deeper than she had thought, for he was swimming and certainly out of his depth when the waves swept over him. Two hands appeared over the prow, grasping for the painter. One mighty heave, another, he had the prow pointed shorewards again. Then, using the waves themselves, sometimes letting the boat cream along of its own volition, surfing with it in a smother of foam, he began to tow them towards the beach, his hands steady on the piece of rope. Wet and shivering, Lily sat with her arms still about William, holding on to him for comfort, too cold and wet to wonder where this help had sprung from.

It was only when at last they had come into the shallows where the boat ground with a crunch that she took in their rescuer – a young man of middling height, slight, almost thin, his dark hair matted with sand, his clothes dripping, for like them he was fully clothed. But it was his eyes that marked him, very bright in a sun-darkened face, bright with rage and with some other emotion she could not name.

'Out,' the man said. He was panting with effort and as he moved she saw how difficult it was for him to walk. Where his trouser leg was pulled up, a hideously vivid scar stretched down from his knee, a scar recently healed. He saw the look and scowled. 'Don't just sit there like a bump on a log,' he snapped. 'You can still lose this boat.'

He limped round the side, leaning on the edge for support, assessing the possibilities. And assessing Will too, for when he spoke to him his voice was soft. 'Come on, old son,' he said, 'nothing to it. Just swing yourself up.' And as Will allowed himself now first to be coaxed into an upright position, and then gradually eased over the gunwale, 'What the hell do you mean bringing him out in this?' he accused Lily.

He didn't wait for her answer, didn't expect one, got Will on his feet, supported him in to where the surf was no more than a ripple. 'Stay there,' he said, 'I'll be back.'

Then once more to Lily, 'What are you waiting for, to be carried? Heave.'

He paid no attention as Lily scrambled out in ungainly fashion. He ignored her as she too stood in the swirling water, her skirts fanning in a circle about her knees. He began to pull at the rope, taking most of the weight across his shoulders, but obviously expecting her to pull as well. And so she did, although she was already beginning to shiver, knuckles blue with cold, palms so blistered that the salt stung. And bit by bit, using the impetus of each fresh wave for leverage, together she and the man managed to drag the boat clear of the water, free from immediate capsize, by which time Will had sufficiently recovered to help them pull it up the beach.

Satisfied, the man left them, limped off to where he had left a couple of large buckets. He kept one himself, handed one to Lily. As she bailed over one side, he took the other, all the while carrying on a running commentary for Will Pendray's benefit.

'Getting the water out,' he said, 'or enough so she'll be lighter to move up to the cliffs. Out of the tide, above high-water mark. She'll be safe then until we can find another pair of oars and row her back.'

He shot a look at Lily. 'Wherever that's at,' he said. 'Silly fool, out to sea in a cockleshell.'

Lily paused, hands on hips, her hair blowing. She was aching all over now, no longer cold, for the work had warmed her. 'I know this coast,' she said. 'If I'd had both oars, I could have brought her in. If I could have got past him to the stern, I'd have sculled with the remaining oar . . .'

'If.' The tone was cool. 'If wishes were horses, beggars would ride. I heard you, singing like some blasted mermaid, watched you turning round and round in circles. Long enough for me to get down on the beach myself and bring my water buckets with me. What did you think you were doing, paddling in a kitchen sink?'

'It would have been easy.' Lily was insistent. 'If you hadn't fired at us, and frightened Will. He's been ill, you know,' she cried in righteous indignation. 'You scared him into fits.'

He raised his eyebrows, his mock resignation making her anger grow. 'It's illegal to own a gun like that,' she said coldly, 'you might have killed us. It's your fault.'

Without replying the man bent, scooped, poured. When at last he straightened up his face no longer showed emotion, was blanked off, reserved. 'Family retainer, I suppose,' he said, mimicking Lily's way of speaking, 'ordered him to come, made him do it. Frightened, is it, why, he's frightened of his own shadow.'

He straightened up, 'No excuses,' as she began to argue. 'Haven't you heard of shell shock?'

Lily was silenced. It was a term seldom used in Cornwall as yet, but her father had used it. And perhaps it meant something to Will. For he now came forward in his hesitant fashion and, gripping the side of the boat, said, ''Twasn't a shell, 'twas the waiting. Don't hurry, they told us, walk, not run. And so I told the men; I was their sergeant, it was up to me, wasn't it? Walk, not run. And that was the last words they ever heard, mowed down in rows because they trusted me.'

He was crying too, great tears, and shaking. And the unknown man was holding him and saying, ''Tis all right, 'tis over,' gentle as a woman. And then the two men were pulling the boat once more, easier now it was lighter, sliding it up over the wet sand, both of them taking the strain together so that it glided and crunched with each heave like cutting through a crust of bread. And when they had brought it high enough up under the cliffs beside the stream, and tied the rope around a rock they used as a bollard, 'Come and dry off then,' the unknown man said. He made a grimace to include Lily. 'Though I suppose you know the way already since you've been inside my hut before.'

He looked again at Lily, a quick look. And as she opened her mouth to protest, 'And don't tell me the opposite. I know when someone's been in my house.'

Lily pressed her lips tight and followed him as he led William up to the ledge, his hand companionably around the other's shoulders, although that may have made for easier walking for himself. On land it was painfully apparent how lame he was. Like my father, Lily thought, but that didn't make her like him any better. And just as Will obeyed, meekly acquiescent, so she made herself as meek, although it took almost as great an effort. For it had darted into her mind with the speed of light that now, in spite of all these difficulties, she had in fact obtained what she wanted, no, more than that, was on the very brink of finding out all about this stranger who had been so rude to her.

The hut door was closed today and a new padlock barred it. He dug into his pocket, waved a key mockingly, stood aside to let his guests enter. 'Drip away,' he told Lily, in the same mocking fashion. 'Sorry there's no woman's gear but you're welcome to a blanket and towel. You'll find them upstairs.' And as she hesitated, 'I wasn't exactly expecting company, was on the way to fetch water from further upstream where it's not so salty. But as I think you know what happened when I left the door open, I make sure now to keep my property locked whenever I'm away.'

He gave a mirthless grin. 'I presume you know where upstairs is, you left enough sand there when you came snooping before.'

He ignored her then, busied himself with helping Will, seating him before the hearth on the packing cases and helping him off with his wet jacket. Left to her own devices,

Lily went up the narrow steps where scattered tools and boards suggested repairs were in progress. She used the towel to change under, wiping her hair dry and wringing out her skirts. When he shouted up to her, she threw down her clothes in a bundle and, wrapped in an army blanket, whose coarse hair tickled, sat down on the window ledge where her mother had once sat. With her elbow she rubbed a clean spot and gazed out at the beach and sea.

Suddenly the enormity of what had happened swept over her. We might have been drowned, Will and I both, she thought, and it would have been because of me. If that man hadn't come out to save us, risked his own life perhaps, we might have been washed under. The thoughts galled like the blisters on her hand. Yet as she sat there, torn between remorse and irritation, gradually a sense of peace prevailed after the excitement and flurry of the past half-hour. She had the strangest feeling of having sat like this many times, like some half-forgotten dream she caught a glimpse of memory and when she put out a tentative finger to touch the rough-hewn timber, she felt it warm and solid as if the past were embedded there. When presently the man reappeared, dressed in dry clothes, a cup of tea in his hand, she started as if she had almost forgotten his presence.

'We're decent down below,' he said, gruffly, 'your friend's asleep. Better for him to rest. Come and join us and get warm if you'd care to.'

He waited until she had come down the steps, for the trailing blanket hampered her and she found she was moving stiffly as if sitting in a cramped position had settled in her bones. After she had seated herself before the fire on a second upturned crate, he looked at her thoughtfully over the tin mug. 'Sorry about the reception,' he said, but without much conviction. 'I don't fancy people prying. So I take the gun to warn them off and keep the door locked. But I got good at shooting in the war; I know what I'm aiming at. And if I'd known who Will was, I'd never have fired at all.'

It wasn't much of an apology, and Lily, who found she was

expecting him to say, 'If I'd known who YOU were,' resented it. Any thought of thanking him went out of her head. 'I've a right to be here,' she said, 'we own this cove.'

'No, you don't.' The answer came out as bluntly. 'I'm Richard Chote and it's mine. And if you aren't the one who came before, I beg your pardon. If you are, then you're lucky I didn't catch you rummaging through my things.'

He added, 'In any case 'tis you who needs to do some explaining, trespassing on my land.'

He was leaning against the beamed mantel shelf where clothes were dimly steaming. She could see how thin he was, dressed only in a shirt and trousers, his ribs almost showing like a half-starved horse. Beside him, wrapped in the army greatcoat she had spotted before, Will lay huddled, eyes shut. For a large man he too looked small and defenceless. The words her father once had used came into her head, 'The ragtag ends of an army.' She had the uncomfortable feeling that she had blundered into some secret coterie of men and soldiers where she was not wanted and should never have intruded.

It was not pity now, stronger than that, a feeling that reflected what Emma had tried to express, a wanting to withdraw and leave alone, as one might regret having disturbed some animal in its lair. And as she was at heart an honest person and unused to subterfuge, perhaps these feelings were reflected on her face. The man's stiff shoulders relaxed; he sighed.

'There,' he said more calmly, 'who am I to speak. You'll have to forgive me, Miss, I'm not fit these days either for human company.'

He nodded at Will. 'Seen that happen many times,' he said. ''Tis the effect of the trenches. 'Tisn't cowardice although there are those who will call it that. But they're the ones who weren't out in it. Lots weren't,' he said. 'So that's why I've come here to be alone and get away from society I don't like.'

He looked up, his eyes bright. 'But you still haven't

answered me,' he said, 'or told why you came before and why a second time.'

Lily opened her mouth to protest. 'I did,' she was going to say. An unexpected noise outside made her jump up instead.

CHAPTER 4

The door burst open. Framed in it stood Em. Forgetting her own appearance, Lily gazed at her cousin. She had never seen Em look so dishevelled, hatless, her hair loosened from its neat bun, her face mud-streaked, her skirt ripped. 'You're safe. Thank the Lord,' Em was crying. 'I saw the boat.'

She clasped Lily to her, alternating hugs with shakes. After a while when her voice had steadied, she said as if excusing herself, 'Someone spotted you with Will. Thought we ought to know. Telephoned the farm and, imagining the state we were in, came up on a motor bike.'

Again she caught hold of Lily. 'Brought me to the turn, then I ran.' She tried a smile. 'Never knew I could run so fast.'

At any other time, the image of Em's running, of Em on a motor bike, might have made Lily laugh. Now she didn't, not while Richard Chote was listening with a quizzical look, not while Em was heavy with reproach. 'How could you?' Em kept reiterating – 'be so stupid, be so thought-less, be so cruel?' – those were the things she didn't say but Lily felt them. As before, like a child, she wanted to protest that it wasn't her fault. A second time she bit the words back.

'And how did you know where she'd be at?' The owner of the hut's voice was innocent but his glance was keen, waiting for Em to give Lily away. And Lily saw the words trembling on Em's tongue, 'Because I knew she'd come, she's like that. Latched on to something, she never lets go, no matter what.'

Again these were things Em didn't say, but her cheeks burned. And Lily felt her own face flush as red. He's quick, she thought, angered that he'd proved his point. Botheration, she said to herself. And bother Em. Wish she'd mind her own business! But those thoughts too were for hiding. Instead, deliberately proud, she gathered the folds of the blanket about her like a queen and, keeping her back as deliberately turned on Richard Chote, spoke brightly to Em, in that artificial tone which had already caused so much trouble.

'No need to fuss. Wait a minute and I'll dress. Then we'll go home.'

The owner of the hut laughed. 'And where's that?' he asked. 'At the bottom of the sea? What about the poor chap in there? What about your boat?' He jerked with his finger, showing contempt. 'Or didn't you think of that when you cajoled him into bringing you?'

'Will's never still here as well.' Em's own voice raised. 'Fresh out of hospital. Oh, Lily Polleven, 'tis too bad of you.'

Lily was about to retort, 'And what should I have done with him, make him swim back?' when Richard Chote interrupted, his face darkening. 'What name?' he barked at Em. 'What's that you called her?'

He was almost shouting, pointing at Lily. 'You, who are you?'

Lily drew herself upright. 'No need to bellow,' she said in the voice she reserved for inferiors. 'I told you my father owns this cove. I'm Miss Polleven, and she's my cousin, Emma Trevarisk.'

'I'll be damned.' Richard Chote leaned against his door frame and stared at them. 'I'll be damned,' he repeated, 'the very people I hoped NOT to meet. Well, I told you who I was.'

Rage had begun to fill him again, he brimmed with it. It made Em back away but not so Lily. On her high horse now, she outfaced him. 'Yes,' she cried. 'But it makes no difference. I've never seen you before, never even heard of you.'

'Probably not.' The tone became dry, sarcastic, anger held in check. 'But *she* might have.'

Again the finger flick, this time at Em. 'And her father certainly would. Ask Ben Trevarisk who Beth Chote is. Beth Martin that was. The Beth Martin who lived here and sheltered your mother, Miss Know Nothing. Whose brother was drowned saving of your father's skin!'

He straightened himself, breathing hard. 'Funny how the past repeats itself,' he said in the same sarcastic tone. 'If I'd known who the sea'd washed in I'd have left well alone.'

Had he fired off his rifle a second time he couldn't have achieved a better sensation. 'Oh God,' Em said in a queer breathless voice. She clutched at Lily. 'It's Jeb Martin's nephew, Beth Martin's son. I knew we shouldn't have pried.'

Her legs gave way, she sat down with a thump, her boots sticking straight out over the ledge. 'And him risking his life just as his uncle did,' she said in the same breathless way. 'And me like a dummy without a word of thanks.'

Useless for Lily to protest that the danger was minimal, nothing at all; useless to argue she could have coped. Thought now of William Pendray's danger made Em forget all else. She tried to scramble to her feet. 'Is Will all right?' she asked, her voice even more shaky. 'I'm that upset I can't think straight. My brother Tom'll fetch him later, if he could just stay here quiet 'til then. But what about the "Seagull"?' She wrung her hands in indecision.

Then she said, suddenly proud, 'The "Seagull" doesn't matter. But Will does. You be good to him. You've been a soldier, haven't you? That's your uniform in there. You'll understand how it is with him.'

Richard Chote smiled. The smile lightened his face, made him younger, made one see what he must have been like before war and experience had hardened him. 'I'll look after Will,' he said quietly. 'I'm only glad that somebody's thinking of him. And his boat's safe enough where 'tis, no need to worry. As for Miss Polleven,' again that hateful, sarcastic sneer, 'I suggest you clear off with her. Keep her caged up, where she can warble away without causing more harm.'

Lily almost stamped her feet although since they were bare no one would have noticed. 'It's not fair,' she started to defend herself, 'it was all a mistake. I never asked . . .'

She stopped, forced herself to be quiet. Even to her own ears her voice whined. And how could Will Pendray be blamed, unable to explain, unable to do anything? Never in her life had she felt so accused – for all the wrong reasons. 'It's done with,' she heard herself say, 'I shan't say more. Except that even if the hut is his, he can't block off this cove.'

She ignored Em's deprecating gestures, again faced Richard Chote, eyes defiant, hands on hips, holding the blanket up like a shield. 'And I mean to continue coming here,' she told him, 'whenever and however I choose.'

On that uncompromising note she stamped inside, ignored Will Pendray's huddled form, snatched her things and went upstairs. Her clothes smelt of smoke and were still so damp they clung salt-sticky to her skin, soot from the fire smearing them in long black lines. By the time she had come down, Will too had gone outside, was standing beside Richard Chote, Em in between. All three had climbed down on the beach, heads close together as they bent over the boat. Lily watched them for a moment. As when she had first heard Emma speak of Will, she felt a pang of jealousy. Yet whatever Will and Emma meant to each other was nothing to her. Nor was Richard Chote. She had no feeling for him, would have nothing more to do with him. Don't pry, Em had said. Well, what she had found out meant there was no more point in prying. But even so she still didn't like Em to stand so close to either man. Em was her friend; Em was on her side, not theirs.

But when later she and Em had left the cove and begun the climb back up the valley, it suddenly came to her that for once Em was not so docile as she usually was. Uneasy at Em's reproachful looks, not sure what they meant, she began to question her cousin, using Jeb Martin as subterfuge; she had often wondered about Jeb, she said, what had he been like? Half hoping to be contradicted, wanting Em to join her in criticizing Jeb's nephew, she asked if Richard Chote resembled him.

'Not in the least,' her cousin's reply was encouraging at first. 'Jeb was a giant. Big. Strong. That's why they used to say how strange it was that he was drowned and the others weren't. By rights it should have been the other way round. But Lily,' she stopped to catch her breath, turned to the attack, 'what made you talk and act so rudely, adding insult to injury?'

'I wasn't rude,' Lily cried. 'He was.'

'Only when you provoked him.' Em was stern. 'You treated him, well, I don't know, like some servant. You didn't even thank him, let alone apologize. I did both for you.'

'So that's what you were whispering about.' Lily's discomfort broke out. 'That's what made you his champion. I'm surprised at you, Em, I thought you'd stand by me. As for what I think,' she tossed her head, 'I say he's an interloper and a thief.'

At Em's shocked denial, 'Yes, stealing what's not his.'

Em said, 'I don't see it that way at all. And I'm sure not many people would. And we were just discussing ways to get Will home. 'Twould be difficult for Mr Chote.'

Ignoring Lily's mutter of disgust, 'Mr Chote, indeed, as if he's a prime minister!', Em added, her voice still full of reproach, 'Didn't you see how crippled he is? His kneecap was blown off in one of those attacks, like the one Little Ben died in. He's been in hospital himself for the longest time. The last thing he needed was to be forced to go wading through the surf. And it was the last thing Will needed!'

She stopped, her feet firmly planted on the slippery turf, her arms crossed, her own eyes fierce. 'I've never said so before,' she cried, 'but you are wilful, Lily Polleven, a spoiled child. You should be ashamed.'

With her reddened cheeks and her hair fluffed out, Em

looked for a moment like a little hen, and for a moment once more Lily was tempted to laugh. All the conflicting arguments again surged up until she beat them down. She pretended to listen while Em continued to scold, the very act of scolding itself a new and uncomfortable experience. Beneath her own bland exterior, unrepentant, Lily hardened her heart. Don't care, she thought, you can bleat to Kingdom Come. Cove's ours, even if I have to fight him for it.

Unbeknownst to her, another member of her family had come to the same conclusion. How Michael Polleven reached the decision that Richard Chote must be got rid of was roundabout and tortuous but the main reason was simple. Michael was in love.

The way that had happened was equally simple, although unexpected. The night following Farell's original attack, the night Michael had got drunk and quarrelled with Emma and Lily in some distorted attempt to get even with them, when to bolster up his courage he'd forced himself to appear at the Club dance so no one would guess he feared rejection, he'd had a pleasant surprise. Instead of ignoring him Farell had actually been waiting for him in the vestibule, had greeted him effusively, and had gone out of his way to be pleasant, much to Michael's relief. Moreover, ever since, with an uncharacteristic show of determination, Farell had taken Michael under his wing as it were, had insisted that he and Michael still were friends, had not exactly apologized for his previous remarks but in every way shown he felt apologetic. Most surprising of all, he had insisted Michael and Iris should meet, had persisted in showing Michael off in a good light, a 'genuine Cornishman', he boasted, as if that was something special.

Although Michael remained suspicious of Farell's change of heart, remembering from school days how Farell liked making fools of people, nevertheless he had endured this fulsome attention. It was worth embarrassment to have Iris Duvane show her reputed interest. A gift from the gods, or goddess, how did the tag go, meant he'd no call for complaint. And to Michael's thinking Iris was a goddess, a superior being, whose large blue eyes, short black hair, round bright cheeks and bright painted mouth proved even more desirable close to than from a distance.

True, the cropped head of hair, when tossed, had a very commanding appearance; the lips, if bright, were thin, capable, when not amused, of being compressed in very dominating fashion. And the eyes, if large and blue, were alert with a kind of sharp shrewdness that reminded Michael of Farell himself. In short, as well as falling in love, Michael was in awe of Iris, not least that she was older than he was.

Yet for Michael this difference in age afforded him strange satisfaction. Against Iris's sophistication his own youth was enhanced rather than diminished; the very words 'older women' gave him a thrill, as if he were conferring a favour as well as receiving one. He decided that this added to her mystery and made younger girls appear shallow, not worth the trouble of pursuing. And Iris certainly gave the impression that she wanted to be pursued, more, that she was perfectly capable of doing the pursuing herself if she had to.

Farell's apparent function as Cupid had been richly rewarded. On two consecutive evenings, Iris had sat opposite Michael in the bar of the Club. Drink in hand she had gazed at him intently, her red fingernails, attached like vines, clasped round the stem of the glass. It was by sheer accident that the day she decided she had grown weary of waiting for Michael to make the first move was the very same that Lily had determined to find out about Richard Chote, and Richard had fished Lily out of the sea, thus completing a circle of events that had started before any of them were born.

Michael had taken the afternoon off from work, a luxury he felt guilty about but was becoming used to. As soon as he entered the Club, on the pretext of looking for Farell (who he knew would never be there at that hour), Iris detached herself from her group of friends, crossed the room and came to sit on the arm of the easy chair where Michael had hidden behind a newspaper.

'Tell me all about yourself,' she demanded above the hubbub of general conversation as they now sat close together, separated from the rest of the crowd by the high back of the chair. And when, blushing, Michael muttered something incoherent, 'Nonsense,' she said, rounding on him sharply. 'Don't be so diffident. If Hugo Farell says you ride like an Alexander, you do. A Cornish Icarus, he called you, overleaping the clouds.'

If Michael understood the classical reference he certainly didn't understand why she repeated it, or why Farell had uttered it in the first place. It was true, exasperated with his bike and anxious not to waste so much time away from the farm, he had taken to riding his pony to the Club, especially during the day as now. And it was true he felt more confident on horseback, even on a beast he had outgrown; a horse certainly looked more romantic than a metal bike which rattled ungracefully over stones and whose tyres were always needing pumping. But Iris Duvane's repetition of over-exaggerated praise made him uncomfortable, as if she were secretly laughing at him without his knowing why.

As if aware of his doubts, Iris leaned back, crossed her legs and blew cigarette smoke into the air in rings. He'd never seen a woman smoke before and couldn't stop staring.

'I know Hugo's always exaggerating,' Iris said, dismissing Farell with an airy wave, apparently unaware of any inconsistencies in her remarks, a failing that Michael found attractive. It was nice to find someone who wasn't always right. 'But I'm not like him. He's a real "townee". Me, at heart I'm a country wench.'

As if this revelation wasn't startling enough she followed it with a second. 'I've always seen myself as a farm lass, don't you know,' she'd said, bending towards him as if to whisper. 'Up at first light, cutting hay in swathes through dew-drenched fields, Merry Olde England.'

Then, as if she'd guessed he'd think she was making a joke

at his expense (for the thought came to him of how she could wade through mud in those high-heeled shoes and those short, almost scandalously short skirts, how she could grub in the earth with those long pointed nails), 'Honestly, if you don't believe me, just try me with a scythe or hoe. I'll prove how good I am. I did landwork in the war in East Anglia. Ask anyone.'

Her voice held a note of entreaty which again appealed to him. He found that he was outraged that her veracity might be challenged. He watched her hold up her glass and twirl it, looking at him through the contents as Farell had done. 'I know all about farming,' she said. 'Lead me to a real farm in this beautiful, beautiful, Cornish countryside, and I'd be in heaven.'

Again he wasn't sure what she really meant. But when with awkward skill he turned the conversation away from farms, for the thought of Iris Duvane at Nanscawn put him in a dither, she pulled her mouth down as if chagrined, as if she expected a different response, as if, in fact, she had been angling for an invitation.

The thought made him panic. Instinctively he felt it inappropriate. In the normal way of things such an invitation would never have occurred to him. No other girl he'd known, not many, had ever asked to be brought to his home. And for him to have invited her would be paramount to what, becoming engaged, becoming married? He blushed again at the idea.

She moved then to other things, spoke long and passionately about Cornwall, 'this Celtic outpost,' she called it; confided her own immediate goals in life, 'just to get away from crowds, lie on a beach, listen to the birds, gulls, aren't they? And dream'. And finally talked of Lily. Why didn't he bring his sister with him, what was Lily like; was Lily shy – she liked quiet, reserved girls – again a jumble of inconsistency which he found endearing.

'They say your sister likes walking, perhaps she's good at sports,' Iris said at last, in a voice that among her crowd was known as 'jolly'. 'Our villa, or rather Hugo's villa, has got a tennis court attached. Lots of people gather there every afternoon. She must come and play sometime.'

And when instinctively he had frowned at the idea of who the 'they' might be and what else might have been said, hastily, as if to put his mind at rest, 'I'd love to meet her, honestly.'

A little moue crossed her face and tightened the red lips. She leaned towards him in confession. 'I'm not one to gossip,' she said. 'And I'm no prude. The ordinary is boring, all the old familiar ideas are past. And I'm tired of familiar people, all those one meets in town, swarming down to Cornwall like bees. It'd be fun to discover someone different.'

And she'd raised her glass as if in unconscious salute to the 'difference', as if world-wearied by familiarity, as if worn out by it – all proof, he'd felt, of her sincerity. And proof also not only of what gossip about Lily might have been but her generosity in ignoring it.

By the end of the conversation Michael was caught. Over-whelmed, smitten, dazzled. In a daze he rode home. Anything the goddess wanted must be catered for, even to bringing her to Nanscawn. Not that there's anything to be ashamed of there, he'd thought, one look, and anyone would know its worth. And my stake in it, although that was a new idea, one he'd never had before. But if Farell's told Iris about Lily, what does Iris really think? It isn't that I can't keep Lily in line if I have to, although she can play up if she suspects she's on display. It isn't even that now mother's away Em's acting as hostess, although I don't like that. But I don't want Iris to be embarrassed by my relatives. I don't want to be embarrassed myself.

And so there it was, he was still caught in the same dilemma. More, it's the crux of it, he thought, perplexed, for thinking didn't come easily. By inviting Iris to my house I'm showing how vulnerable I am; I can't keep her world and mine apart.

That the embarrassment was of his own contrivance didn't

help. Once more he began to blame Lily. But Lily was his sister, he couldn't get rid of her. It was then that it came to him that all these difficulties had come to a head, or, if not to a head exactly, were intertwined with and exacerbated by the intruder in Polmena Cove. Surely equal blame lay with the intruder. And he could be got rid of.

Michael knew he had no reason for disliking a man he'd never met, who had done him no harm. All stemmed from Farell's original sneer which Michael could not forget – how could he, when it filled his waking hours with mortification. Gradually as he brooded, it appeared easy to blame Chote. Chote's very presence became a link with his mother's past, reviving a period of her life which Michael wished to forget, more, wished to drown as many fathoms deep as Jeb Martin himself. With Richard Chote gone, things would simmer down, revert to normal. In that way at least, Michael thought, I'll be free of further embarrassment. Or so he convinced himself.

On his return to Nanscawn he didn't even notice how subdued Lily and Em seemed, as he was much too engrossed in his own affairs. And even if he had noticed, he wouldn't have questioned them, out of pride. Let them go their own way, he thought, they're nothing to me. Instead he decided to make it his business to find out the intruder's name; easily done, he'd only to ask in the village. But when he did so, no one told him of his sister's latest escapade, although again, had he bothered to show interest, he would soon have heard of it.

On learning who Chote was, he understood at once what Lily had failed to appreciate, that ousting Richard Chote would not be easy. In local eyes Richard Chote was the nephew of a hero, most of the villagers would welcome him, would be horrified at any attempt to drive him away and would certainly swear that he had the right to the hut, since his uncle and his mother had once lived there.

Michael knew of only one person who would have no qualms in making short shift of squatters, who would even relish the task. That was his grandfather, the Sir

Robert Polleven whom he so admired, whose knowledge of landowning and possession was unrivalled, and whose grasp on his own lands was maintained with feudal tenacity. The very next morning therefore, Michael paid a visit to Polleven Manor to ask his grandfather's advice. He knew of course in doing so he went against his own father's principles, Socialist twaddle his grandfather would call them. 'It doesn't do to be greedy,' he could hear his father's voice. 'We have enough, there's room for all.' Michael had never openly opposed his father before. Now he steeled himself to opposition.

Since by his grandfather's standards gentlemen travelled only on horseback, Michael rode his pony, although he knew he had outgrown it. His grandfather, a fine horseman in his day, would be shocked if his grandson wasn't well mounted. But he would be even more shocked if Michael appeared on a bike. Crossing the main roads by bridle paths that wound in and out among moorland patches, twice Michael disturbed nesting pheasants and once a rabbit, which scuttled from the path. Today he noticed them. Next time he came this way he'd bring his gun. He also noticed where burned grass and a circle of white stones marked a former gypsy encampment, another sort of encroachment which his father would have and his grandfather would never have permitted.

Such blatant trespass made Michael suddenly angry. He dismounted, stamped at the burned areas, grinding the ashes with his boot. Allow one, he thought, allow all, might as well open the front gates and be done with it. Remounting, he rehearsed the arguments he would use to tempt his grandfather to intervene. Even to his own ears they sounded weak.

By now he had persuaded himself that it was getting rid of the trespasser in Polmena Cove that was vital to Polleven interests; any discomfort surrounding his own origins and the possible effect of them on his courtship of Iris Duvane had retreated conveniently into the background, although by now too the idea that he meant to court Iris Duvane, perhaps even marry her, by God, had become firmly fixed in his mind.

But he had the sense not to mention that to Sir Robert, it was too big an idea to share with anyone. Like his sister he would concentrate on Polmena Cove, find out for sure if it belonged to him and his own family. And then, when he'd established that, come hell or high water Richard Chote must move out, if he knew what was good for him.

Sir Robert was leaning over the veranda at Polleven Manor, when Michael came galloping up the drive in approved hunting fashion. The old man nodded with satisfaction. Impeccably dressed in clothes fashionable before 1914, his shoulders still stiff in military fashion, his white hair smooth, cut to perfection, except for the slight tremble of his hands on the rickety railings he looked little different from the Sir Robert who had refused to help Michael's mother in her time of trouble. Yet he was different. There were differences, great and small, in the old man, caused by more than age. And Michael was aware of them, although as yet he had no name to put to them.

'Haven't seen you in a while.' Sir Robert let a hint of sarcasm show. 'To what do we owe this unexpected pleasure?' For your own benefit not mine, I'll be bound, was what he meant as he reached out a fine-veined hand with its tracing of liver spots to pat Michael's pony. And as it snuffled gently into his palm, searching for sugar, 'You've grown too heavy for it,' Sir Robert said, critically. 'What's your father up to, not getting you a new horse?'

Again a malicious flash. Your father won't give you a new horse, the glance said, but I might. If you behave as I want you to, that is, if you do as you're told.

Michael pretended to be busy with stirrup and reins. He knew what his grandfather hinted at. He could never be certain if his grandfather touched sensitive spots by chance or had an uncanny instinct for guessing what they were. Michael had long been aware that his father and grandfather did not see eye to eye about many matters. He knew for example that the old man was disappointed in his son and had fixed his hopes upon Michael as his true successor.

But being favourite takes its toll, and Michael sometimes resented it.

His grandfather noticed his reticence. 'Come on, boy, no sulking,' Sir Robert chided. 'No need to keep pretences up. Trouble's written over you. Tie your nag to the railing there and walk with me. I'll be glad of company.'

He climbed stiffly down the front steps, leaned on Michael's arm as the two of them wandered across the park towards the bridge. The river wound here in wide lazy loops fringed with rushes where duck and moorhen bobbed and paddled. But the deer that had once grazed were gone, as were the trees; since the war the park had reverted to pastureland where cattle hooves dug up river banks and left muddy scars across the turf. If Michael turned to face the house, even from a distance he could see how its lustre had faded. Paint peeling from the woodwork, railings rusted, the gardens of which his grandmother used to be so proud fast reverted to weeds, all evidence of grandfather's diminishing fortunes. What's the use of being heir, Michael thought, even more depressed, if there's nothing left to inherit?

This was another reason why, in the past months, Michael's visits to Polleven Manor had been so few. He preferred to keep intact the image of the Manor when he'd been a child, when there had been grooms to take horses to the stables and gardeners to trim lawns, when the whole house had been open and brimming with lights and flowers, when his grandmother would hurry to welcome him, not sit listless by the window in one wing, looked after by a single servant who was nearly as old. That the war was responsible didn't help any, nor that Michael's father casually accepted the change. 'Can't be reversed,' Julian had said, 'all through history families wax and wane. We've had a good innings, time to move ahead.'

All very well for him, Michael thought, suddenly irritated. But not for me. Julian Polleven may have broken from the mould, may enjoy owning and running a farm. On other counts Julian Polleven's wrong. In the real world where

I've found myself, the world of bankers and businessmen, a Cornish farmer and his son are pretty tame stuff. And where there's money, real money, any man, lowborn or not, can swagger as if he is a real squire and spend his days in real squirelike leisure without a flicker of regret.

As they walked, the old man probed, a surgeon feeling for a bullet. And like a patient drawing back from pain, so Michael resisted, drawing away from his grandfather's questions as he did physically from his touch. He knew he loved his grandfather, he knew his grandfather loved him, and yet there were things one mustn't divulge for grandfather to use, for grandfather to turn and twist. But as a patient comes to a doctor for relief, so Michael couldn't resist the temptation to ask Sir Robert for help, even if he had to pay a price for it.

For his part Sir Robert was good at digging out bullets. Gradually, without meaning to, without knowing how it happened, Michael began to explain not only what he'd heard about Richard Chote and why he should be ousted without delay, but also why Chote's presence was an embarrassment to him personally. He didn't actually mention Lily, nor what Farell had said of her, and of course he said nothing yet about Iris, but even as he spoke he felt his grandfather searching for these secret thoughts.

Sir Robert listened with flattering attention, he was a good listener. Like a leech he fastened on the first difficulty. 'Chote, eh? Nephew of Jeb Martin? Then there'll be problems.

'No doubt the cove belongs to us,' he went on, 'of course it does. Any old map will prove that Polmena Cove's part of the Polleven estate, always has been. But I'd heard someone'd been rooting round Wheal Marty, and didn't like the sound of that.'

He tapped with his stick, uprooting docks, coughing slightly to impress Michael with his reasoning. 'Don't like the idea of working a mine so close to our property,' he said. 'I'm not really worried, mind you, it's been closed for decades and as a mine it's finished, had men down myself once to look, no likelihood of finding anything. But best to cover all eventualities.'

He tapped with his cane again. 'We're dealing with a bolshy malingerer, boy,' he said, 'squeezing what he can out of us, so we'll squeeze back. I'll have a word with my solicitors in St Marvell, make the blackguards work for a living, warn them to chase Chote off if he comes sniffing about. And warn old MacDougal at the bank to cut off any money supplies at source.'

He moved on, quicker now, as if new life was flowing into his limbs. 'Now not a word to your father, boy.' The old man grew crafty. 'Not a word to anyone. Secrecy, that's the ticket. The cove still belongs to me. I've the right to handle it, I'm not too old. But 'twould be a serious setback if Chote turned nasty and tried to entrench himself. If I were you, I'd thrash him out without waiting for the asking. Had I been your age I'd have done it long ago.'

The snap of his fingers suggested how weak Sir Robert thought Michael, how strong himself in comparison. It made Michael feel even more incompetent.

Then Sir Robert added something else, the thing that Michael had been dreading, just as if, Michael thought bitterly, he's been holding it back all this while to savour it, teasing me with it. 'What's this about your sister, heh? You know what she's been up to.'

He never called Lily by her given name, it was always 'your sister'. And these weren't questions, they were statements. He likes his little triumphs, Michael thought, he likes catching me out, as if the world owes him something. He used not to be like that.

'Don't say there's anything to it either,' Sir Robert went on, still speaking of Lily. 'Don't say there's anything wrong, yet. But there's talk. She's been seen at Cove in Chote's company and men like Chote aren't to be trusted. And your sister's of a susceptible age.'

He gave his secret, bitter smile. 'If the visits continue,' he said, softly, conspiratorially, making Michael part of his way of thinking, 'who can tell what might happen. She's wild enough. As for what to do with her,' he smiled again, 'I warned your father there'd be trouble, years ago that is. But Julian'll never listen. Soft as butter. I sometimes think it was his brains he lost out there in Africa.'

Harsh words, but he had harsher.

'I'd nip it in the bud,' he said then, as outspoken as Farell. 'Like mother, like daughter. Bad blood will out.'

The unexpectedness of Lily's behaviour cut Michael to the quick. But his grandfather's choice of phrase cut even deeper. All those hidden humiliations once more boiled to the fore. As he opened his mouth to defend himself, Sir Robert abruptly dismissed them.

'Don't worry, boy,' his grandfather, having made his point, could afford to relax again, could become assuring, sensing Michael's fears, unerringly putting a finger to the sore. 'You're unadulterated, no taint of Trevarisk, pure Polleven. And I've plans for you. I've had my eye on Polmena Cove for a long time. It'll make your fortune, boy, when I'm gone.

'I'm doing this for you, boy,' he added, standing very upright, at attention, as if his shoulders were bent to touch his backbone. 'You must know that. But damn death duties'll swallow most of what's left if we don't take care of it.'

And when he'd told Michael what his plans were and sworn his grandson again to secrecy, 'Got to get on in this modern world, got to be bloody business-minded,' he added after a pause, when, like Michael, he seemed overwhelmed by the magnitude of his proposal. 'Take chances. All the world on pleasure bent, even workmen expecting holidays. Pander to the visitors, boy, there's success.'

He smiled at Michael, his bitter smile, as if astounded by his own cunning. There's affection for you, it seemed to say, see what I stoop to doing. And for a moment Michael's heart leapt at the prospect of that vision.

'I say, you're going it, Iris, aren't you just.'

Several days later Hugo Farell was lounging under a large

61

fir tree while Iris, along with some members of the Club, was playing tennis on his parents' lumpy grass court. He looked at his cousin with a mixture of mild affection and spite as she threw herself down on the lawn at the end of the set. Iris wasn't his actual cousin of course, was some distant relative of the mater's. Orphaned young, 'without a bean,' as she herself put it, Iris had been brought along to keep his mother company during the season. And as such was invaluable to Hugo to occupy the old lady when the pater was off with golf and fishing, thus freeing Hugo from the role of nursemaid.

He had been watching Iris from behind the smoke of a cigarette he was almost too lazy to puff. Overhead, between the trees, the blue sky made jigsaw shapes and sun motes danced on the lawn beyond. From the veranda of the bungalow his family had taken for the summer there came the comforting rattle of china, and presently the tea trolley would be drawn round by the little Cornish maid who, for all his mother's hectoring, could never keep her black uniform clean, and whose thick brown hair under the white cap stuck out like a fire brush.

Iris's white dress was uncreased and she appeared cool, but she was panting slightly from effort. She doesn't look her age, Hugo thought critically, must be close to thirty now; it was only he who was getting stiff and puffy at twenty-three as if he were already fifty! But on a day when the looked-for invitation to Nanscawn Farm had finally been given, and accepted, Iris had reason to be perky.

It wasn't Iris's tennis-playing skills Hugo Farell was commenting on. In his nonchalant way he was proud of her athletic prowess and glad, as much as he could be bothered to be glad of anything, to have her part of the family scene. Besides, his mother had explained Iris was bored with town, and was at loose ends what to do with herself. It was to make Iris happy that Hugo at first had set her on to Polleven.

It amused Hugo to keep Iris amused. Hugo knew Iris better than Iris herself; knew how she fed on the bizarre but had a short-lived attention span. Polleven had seemed a good joke at the time, one he and Iris could share. Polleven was such an ass, Hugo thought, panting for acceptance like one of his stupid dogs. Throw him a titbit of attention, Hugo had told Iris, he'll lick your hand.

What Hugo hadn't banked on was Iris's interest lasting more than an evening. Or that her desperation for a husband made even a young Cornish squireling seem appropriate. As Hugo loved to do, he had put a game in motion; now he was piqued that the game was becoming too complicated for his taste, might even turn dangerous if it developed into anything serious.

Iris showed no resentment. Leaving her tennis partner to wander off and fend for himself, she nudged Hugo's knee with her hand, her fingers opening and shut, meaning she wanted him to light her cigarette. Then she too leaned back against a tree trunk and inhaled deeply. But when Farell, determined to make the point prick, added, 'Of course, he's too young,' 'Oh, I know he's young,' Iris broke in, 'they're all too young. Who of my age is left?

'They're dead in France,' she added, bitterly for her, it wasn't the sort of remark she allowed herself. 'Or France's made them cold and . . .'

She turned on her side to finger the fronds of tamarisk dangling over the hedge. Hugo had the feeling that she was about to say 'cold and impotent', and for once was surprised. He hadn't expected such sexual candour from Iris, although she never minced words about anything else.

Then Iris turned back, made a little face, smiled her brilliant smile as if reminiscing. 'But a bit of a dear,' she said, returning to the theme of Michael Polleven. 'Something for me to do. All very well for you,' she went on, 'asleep all day. I don't know how your mother stands it. No chambermaid will work for her, you stay in bed to noon. But I've got more life in me than that. And,' this last defiantly, 'I find him interesting.

'Or rather his type is,' she continued quickly – Hugo was sure she was inventing as she went along, she was good at that – 'a Cornish youth, untrained, untaught, fresh from public school, with a title on one side and fish on the other!'

'Perfect inverted Victorian class snobbery,' Hugo said lazily but his glance was sharp. 'So which side are you on?'

Iris ignored the question. 'It's all your fault anyhow,' she said, batting her eyelids. 'You shouldn't have tempted me.'

She tapped Hugo with a broken-off tamarisk frond. 'And why should you care? In London it never bothered you what I did in my spare time.'

Hugo had to laugh. Although she was so much his elder, Iris never failed him. Such bounding enthusiasms, such reversals of opinion, such highs, such lows, even listening to her exhausted him, yet kept him amused. London's not here, he wanted to say, you can't behave here as you did there.

'The season's young,' he said, 'I don't want you burning out too soon. Or flouncing off because you've outworn your welcome. Not that I've fears for you. You can look after yourself. But if you gobble Polleven up, what will you play with afterwards? It's not that it interests me,' he added with something of a sneer, for the thought of loyalty struck him as old-fashioned, 'I've no interest in either of you. Polleven's no friend of mine. And if he's taken in by you, well then, by definition he's an idiot. But I've expended a lot of energy on him for you; I expect some return.

'Of course he's got prospects,' he couldn't help adding, stirring things up again, 'how much, that's for you to decide. Or if what he's boasting of now is worth bidding for.'

He'd gone too far. Iris threw her cigarette aside; in one fluid movement she got up and shook the grass from her skirt. 'Beast,' she said, her voice sharp, 'anything for a laugh, that's our Hugo. Well, for once you're laughing on the wrong side of your face.'

She flounced off and could be heard calling for a fresh set with a fresh partner, what was the matter with them all, the day was young. Farell sank back again, a little smile curling round his lips as quickly suppressed. He couldn't resist the pinpricks, they made for such lovely reaction. And although it was true that he had no feelings at all for Polleven, he could pity a chap once Iris had her teeth in him. Except, he had a sudden uneasy qualm that perhaps this time he had overstepped the mark. And that, despite Iris's sophistication, if she toyed with Michael Polleven, in the end it was a game they might all regret.

CHAPTER 5

Michael Robert peered in the hall mirror, smoothing his hair, listening to the wind and rain. Damn, he thought, why had the weather changed today? He'd chosen Saturday. He couldn't be faulted then, or accused of neglecting the farm; had made a point of going early to the bank to withdraw double the usual wages. Paying the men for just one week as his father always did, he'd kept the rest in hand – 'Just in case,' he told his sister when she'd questioned him.

Equally to avoid criticism he'd not mentioned the invitation until it was all arranged, until it was too late to back out, although it gave Em twice the work and annoyed Lily. For the umpteenth time he straightened his tie before going down into the kitchen.

All was a bustle of preparation, Em cleaning silver spoons, Hetty baking her famous saffron buns. A sponge cake, smooth as velvet, was already cooling on a plate and Em turned triumphantly to show him it. Michael ignored her, like a general surveyed the scene, left again. He'd already given his orders, they'd be obeyed.

'For God's sake,' he'd told his cousin, 'Hetty's not to serve. Bring the tea in yourself. Make sure Lily's dressed right. And use the best cups.'

He hadn't had the nerve to tell Em to leave after pouring the tea, taking Lily with her, but he'd shown that was what he wanted, scowling at everything she said and refusing to talk to Lily. He'd not yet confronted Lily, that'd come later. Later he'd have things out with her.

'Botheration,' he'd overheard Lily say, 'whatever does he want them for? I've heard of Farell, even at school he sounded mean. But who's this Iris Michael's always talking of? We don't know her.'

Michael had grinned to himself. You will, he thought, and when you do, you'll be surprised. You'll get your comeuppance then. And serve you right.

Since his return from Polleven Manor, he'd hugged his secret to himself, obsessed with the prospect of Iris's visit, equally obsessed with what his grandfather proposed. But 'Mum's the word,' his grandfather had warned again as he left, and Michael had kept mum, hiding it from his immediate family. If the opportunity to boast a little to Farell, and through Farell to Iris, had proved irresistible, he told himself he'd done no harm. He'd only dropped hints and suggestions, nothing explicit, enough to tantalize Farell, enough to show that in business matters the Pollevens were Farell's equal. That idea alone gave him confidence. And he'd issued the invitation Iris angled for.

When at last his guests arrived, Farell in a pale grey suit, Iris a vision in pink and cream, Michael dashed out to herd them in. How proud he felt as he ushered them inside. In spite of the rain the farm showed up well, he'd worked hard all week. The hayricks were neatly stacked, the courtyard swept; although other tasks were more pressing he'd had the drive and hedges cleared. 'Come ye in, enter, sit ye down,' all the new expressions so much in vogue bubbled freely from his lips. He flapped a deprecating hand as he'd seen Farell do, when Iris murmured, 'How nice this is.' A 'nice' from Iris was a superlative. When she added, 'I love the house, all that ivy, all that brick,' his chest swelled. He hadn't the heart to correct her mistake, but Lily did.

'It's granite,' Lily said. On seeing Iris, Lily's suspicions had been aroused. Watching her brother's solicitude, Like a sheepdog, Lily thought. And on actually meeting Iris, on shaking Iris's white-gloved hand, Lily had been even more amazed. Lily had never thought much about her own looks, certainly not much about fashion. Now she sat in the parlour and tried not to stare, while Em, equally ill at ease, passed Hetty's cake, avoiding noticing their guest's lace-stockinged knees.

The first part of the tea-drinking was not a complete success, but neither was it a disaster. No one upset the cake stand or dropped the cups and Hetty's cake was 'fabulous' (Iris's word). Although the guests did most of the talking – Michael too overcome, Em too busy, Lily too critical, to play more than a minimal part – conversation stuttered along. But after that first moment of suspicion, Lily listened carefully. She didn't like what she heard. They're not our type, she thought. If these are Michael's friends no wonder he lets the farmwork slip.

When Farell made one of his jokes, and Iris laughed, she sensed the cruelty beneath the joke, the insincerity of the laugh. Farell's as I imagined him, she thought, with his straight black hair and pointed nose like a bird of prey, hovering to pounce. But it was Iris Duvane's gushing that put her most on guard.

Iris continued to love this and that, loved the view, loved the furnishings, wasn't the farmhouse quaint? 'Aren't you lucky?' she said twice. 'You don't miss much, here in the heart of country quiet.' She sighed, as if deprived at not having it. 'Who'd want to live in London if they had a place like this?'

She glanced at Michael. 'I must, simply must, explore your beautiful garden,' she said. She flung wide her arms. 'I'm imagining a vast lawn, edged with flowers,' she said in a dreamy voice. 'Herbs, I smell lavender and sage, rosemary perhaps. Rosemary for remembrance. So I'll remember this.'

She closed her eyes, the long lashes resting against her pink cheeks. Like a doll, Lily thought, how can Michael stand it, she's so old!

'I'll show you now.' Exasperated, Lily jumped up. Before Michael could stop her, she opened the French windows, letting in the rain. Water had puddled on the paving stones and the wind was chill. A gust of air swept into the room making the fire smoke, and for a moment the cold grey outside the house seemed to invade its placid interior.

'Whatever are you doing, Lily?' Michael was scandalized. 'Miss Duvane'll get wet.'

'Oh,' said Lily, smoothly sweet, 'she won't let that worry her. She knows we're used to rain in the countryside.'

Miss Duvane herself, after peering out hesitantly, bravely declared she didn't mind at all. The rain was another Cornish thing she loved, wasn't West Country drizzle soft, gentle on the skin like rosewater. Leaving Em and Farell hovering on the doorstep, and taking Lily's arm, a gallant soldier, she trooped outside, while Michael, smiling like a Cheshire cat, dashed after her with a bundle of wraps and shawls.

'Lovely,' Iris cooed, admiring the flowers. She wiped the drizzle from her eyes. 'Who's the gardener with green thumbs?' She turned her face up to the sky and breathed deeply, letting the rain bead along her close-cropped hair. For a moment, her frantic enthusiasms stilled, she almost looked at peace, her features relaxed. Perhaps for once she's being honest, Lily thought, for the garden was lovely, its colours more vibrant against the grey of mist, the outlines of bush and tree suddenly clear and vivid. And perhaps I've been too cruel, she thought, perhaps she isn't as bad as she sounds.

As reluctantly she prepared to amend her opinion, willing herself to give Iris the benefit of the doubt, Iris opened her eyes, turned to Michael and said something which hardened Lily's heart for good – something which Lily was immediately sure Michael hadn't wanted spoken of and Iris had made a mistake in mentioning.

Heralded by a bright smile, a cheerful determination to please, Iris's question was of the sort that superficially sounds innocent – underneath are implications that reverberate, perhaps for years.

'Do your grandfather's plans for Polmena Cove include a place like this?' Iris asked, smiling at Michael conspiratorially. 'Will there be real Cornish gardens and real Cornish food, served by real Cornish maids? Will it be a true Cornish resort that we who love Cornwall can truly take to our hearts?'

There was a silence, again the sort that reverberates. Iris's expression didn't change but something in Michael's look must have made her sense her blunder. Suddenly she shivered. 'Let's go in,' she said. Before Lily could repeat, 'What plans?' she turned abruptly and hurried back indoors, Michael shielding her from the rain with his jacket. When Lily caught up with her, Iris had already changed the subject.

Cleverly focusing her attention on the younger girl (as if to fob me off, Lily thought) she began to praise Lily's eyes and skin, much to Lily's embarrassment.

'Bring her to London, she'd set the city world afire.' Iris was determined. 'She'd be a huge success, wouldn't she, Hugo?' – appealing to Farell to back her up, Lily thought, so I can't ask what she means, expecting him to cover for her so I won't notice. But if Iris expected Hugo to co-operate, Iris made a second mistake. Hugo Farell seemed to take pleasure in doing the very opposite.

Despite Michael's growing discomfort, despite Iris's tugs, Farell began to elaborate, refusing to be interrupted, revealing in all its sordid detail what Grandfather Polleven's secret was. As if he's revelling in it, Lily thought, too startled herself to interrupt, as if he's enjoying the effect he's caused – how thrilled everyone was, what a bully idea, the best access, the best beach, the safest stretch of sand, Polmena Cove the perfect place. And what a great investment plan! His own business friends were full of it, there'd be no lack of support, he'd vouch for that.

Finally, as if to put the finishing touch, 'It's what's needed,' he said. 'It takes a modern-thinking man to come up with it. I congratulate you, Polleven, in having a relative of such modern ideas. A resort that caters for the masses, the mind is dazzled. Myself,' he drolled sarcastically, 'for my taste, like Iris I'd prefer a perfectly run hotel where people can be made welcome with Cornish hospitality.'

He too waved his arms like a Merlin, parodying Iris. 'I see a granite building, square, solid, rising from the stones,' he intoned, 'a castle on the cliffs. A new Tintagel. And we, its defenders, like the knights of old, riding up to it.'

Usually her cousin's extravagances made Iris laugh. Now, when at last he stopped, she grimaced at him and a second time changed the subject. 'You can't know how horrid those bungalows we stay in are,' she said, 'so tasteless, so much alike. It's true, Hugo, don't be difficult. You're always criticizing them.'

She addressed her cousin directly, this time partly because she's remembered she's his parents' guest, Lily thought, suddenly shrewd. And partly because she still thinks I'm too dense to notice what she's doing.

'I even hate the names they have.' Iris was warming to her theme. 'Bide-a-Wee, and Bon Repos, and Bluebell Cot, well, they are dreadful, aren't they, for boxes of wood and stone.' She shuddered as if to show how sensitive she was.

Farell laughed. 'Call it Hotel Camelot,' he said. 'Bring down the London trade and pour the lucre in. So get on to your solicitors, old boy, and prove Polmena Cove is yours before that fellow Chote steals a march on you.'

He rubbed his fingers together as if adding that lucre up, then winked at Lily, as if she knew what he meant. And all the time underneath they're both assessing us, Lily thought, assessing Michael, like bankers calculating how much we're worth.

She jumped up. 'We don't need visitors charging down our cliffs,' she said. 'Better for us if they stayed at home where they belong.'

She turned to her brother. 'And you should have more sense,' she rushed on, 'aiding and abetting grandfather in foolishness. He's no more right to Cove than you have.'

With that broadside the party ended, Iris and Farell discomfited, Michael again furious, Lily in disgrace. When the first three had left (Farell having invited Michael to come with them), Lily and Em once more sought refuge in their own room.

'How dare he!' Lily, at first almost speechless, was recovering. Quicker than anyone she had grasped at once the possibilities of Cove's potential and was horrified by the thought of its misuse. She wasn't clear what exactly Grandfather Polleven had in mind, a beach resort with ice-cream carts and tea rooms and bathing huts, or a hotel like the others sprouting up along the coast, or perhaps even a development like the one where Iris and her cousin lived – the prospect of any of these, so close to Nanscawn Farm, almost on their own doorstep, was overwhelming. 'We'll be overrun,' she cried. 'Swamped. Isn't that like grandfather, always thinking of money these days. Father says it's the effect of the war that's turned him into a money-grabber. But he's no right to destroy Cove just to satisfy strangers. He's no right to tear beauty down for those who don't know what beauty is.'

By now she was close to tears. 'Father'll never allow it,' she said. But she wasn't sure. Father always thought differently from most people, he might think sharing was better than keeping to oneself. And what control did father have over Polleven land anyway; if it were part of the estate it would still be grandfather's.

Em didn't reply. Like Lily she was horrified. She hadn't liked their guests either, but Lily's impulsive rudeness hadn't made things better, might be more damaging than helpful. Moreover in her more practical way she couldn't help thinking of the jobs any building project would create. With the mines shutting down, with the fishing so poor, with her own brothers out of work, it might prove a godsend for many Cornish people. But she didn't say so to Lily, only listened until Lily had finished her outburst against her brother, against her grandfather, against the visitors who had seduced her brother into betrayal of his birthright. It was only when in turn Lily fell silent that Em felt constrained to point out how strangely things reversed themselves without anyone's trying. 'For have you considered,' she wondered, 'that if your grandfather does go ahead with what he says, the only person to save Cove will be the man you've so attacked for having trespassed there?'

And when Lily looked at her, 'But of course, Lily. If it belongs to Richard Chote, your grandfather can have no claim.'

She didn't have to add, 'So if you want to keep Cove intact, you'd better hope Richard Chote does own it.' The thought had already sprung into Lily's own mind.

'She didn't mean it.' Michael, angrier than he had ever been, furious with Farell, furious with Lily, found himself defending Lily, because not to do so would make his sister's outburst even worse. 'And it doesn't matter that you told her, she'd have to know sometime.'

At least, he thought to himself, I hope it doesn't matter. If grandfather doesn't find out, that is, if Chote doesn't hear and be on guard. For the first time it occurred to him that true businessmen don't boast of their business ventures to impress their lady friends.

He and Iris were again together in a back room of the Club where they could find some privacy. Without a word of apology, without even an excuse, Farell had gone off to play billiards, had left them with a sly glance that showed he was perfectly aware of the dilemma he had placed them in. 'Well, he's as much to blame.' Iris was equally indignant with her cousin. 'He led us on. He's a pig like that.'

She made her little moue, pursing her lips together in a way that made Michael think only of what it would be like to kiss them, to feel their cool redness against his own fevered skin. As if she knew what he was thinking, she pressed her hand over his. 'And in all this empty countryside,' she said with a little sigh, 'with all these vast plans for turning it into a resort for more people, wherever shall we find space for little us to be truly alone?'

She pointed her long fingernails to the open door leading

to the next room, against whose light the silhouettes of other Clubbers could be seen. 'Trapped,' she whispered dramatically in his ear, with another delicious moue, 'like animals in a den. No escape. Surrounded by a sea of gossip. Poor us.'

Her muddled metaphors didn't worry Michael but he was worried how to answer her. He disliked the image of being caught like an animal in its den, he disliked even more the idea of fresh gossip, and he had no suggestions where they might go together. Iris might have been joking about that but beneath the exaggeration he sensed an urgency. Dimly he remembered what other chaps talked about, hinted at, wayside inns where no questions were asked, rented rooms for an hour or so, for a night even, but how could a fellow expose a goddess like Iris to such low vulgarity, even if he had the means of getting her there?

The fragrance of Iris's hair, brushing his cheek as she leaned towards him, the closeness of her body in its flimsy pink-and-white dress, the perfume she used made him dizzy. He hardly heard her next whisper, 'Hugo's left his car key, look, I've got it here.'

She dangled it before him, it swayed to and fro in the light. He watched it, mesmerized. In his pocket he felt his wallet where he'd put the rest of the farm wages. 'Come on,' she whispered again; was it her whisper or his? 'Come on, do. We've plenty of time.'

Em lay in bed, waiting for Michael to come back, he'd never been as late as this. She wondered if there had been an accident, should she telephone the police? But surely his friends would let them know if there were any difficulty. As when she was a child she wrapped her arms about herself, like a ball, a defence she'd always had from the bad times that darkness brought, when her father returned home drunk and her mother prepared to do battle with him. As if in the present, she still heard Ben Trevarisk's drunken mutterings and Charity Trevarisk's curses in reply. 'All these children, every mouth to feed, where's the money coming from if you drink it dry?'

Drink had ruined her father, had embittered her mother, had made her, the only girl, a burden no one wanted. Desire would ruin Michael, she thought, lose him to lust, render him incapable of withstanding it, render him incapable of restraint. Dreaming now, she saw her cousin wandering like the knight of Keats's poem, pale, drained, the knight Farell spoke of, seduced by the Lady of the Meads. She saw the meadows at Nanscawn, the stooks of hay left to dry, fragrant in the sun.

Will stood on the wagon, his shirtsleeves rolled up, the hairs on his arms golden.

'Toss it up,' he called down to her, teasing her, laughing at her because that wasn't a woman's job. And she, laughing back, took up the fork with its heavy pile of hay and heaved until she had lifted it above her head. 'There, now,' she said, panting. 'Does that do?' But Will had already turned away, she couldn't make him hear, although she called until she was hoarse. And when she woke it was morning and the sun was shining again and Michael was letting himself in the front door, like a cat on the tiles all night.

CHAPTER 6

*T*he last person to hear about the threat against him was Richard Chote, although he was not left long in ignorance. The weekend's rain had gone as suddenly as it had come, like fog seeping up from sand, and he was sitting outside his hut, in shirtsleeves, hair plastered flat from a quick dip in one of the rock pools, when he heard the sound of someone coming down the incline. Despite the rain, or perhaps because of it, the sea was warm, smooth. He felt it like silk upon his skin. He was tired and his leg ached, but he was used to that. Now, at the day's end, the sense of calm, of physical and mental content, was so complete, had become so familiar, he hardly noticed it until it was rudely broken.

The progress was noisy, deliberately noisy, as if forcing itself on his attention. Immediately his mood was broken. He felt anger, that sudden uncontrollable anger that came so easily these days, as if after years of holding it in check it came flooding out. No one has the right to invade my privacy, he thought, least of all a Polleven. What can she want of me? Then, angrier still, why can't she leave me alone?

He was sure his unwanted visitor was Lily Polleven. Lily Polleven had made no secret of her determination to return; her farewell had screamed defiance. It would be like her to seek him out again, to tackle him head-on in his own home. She'd done so once, why not again.

He began to limp up and down the ledge. Every day now he went to the mine at first light, following what must have been a pony track halfway up the cliff, part buried in the undergrowth, part completely lost after a landslide. He'd found his way up it, idly, attracted by it as he had been attracted by Wheal Marty, because it existed, he supposed, because it gave him something to do. Only gradually had it become a challenge – to show what he was capable of. He even found pleasure in learning to balance on his sound leg, relying on his back and shoulders to keep his balance, bracing himself against a wall and using pick and shovel so he didn't fall over as he'd done at first. He'd had to adapt the pick – slow work all this, but being slow didn't trouble him. After years in the trenches, risking death to gain mere feet of mud, the placid inches he fought for here seemed well won.

And once these first objectives were achieved he'd found practical problems that he enjoyed trying to solve. The rubble that blocked the entrance, for example, the draining of the water that pooled inside, the efforts to dig and clear, 'delve', his father would have called it with biblical accuracy – these taxed his concentration as nothing else had ever done, as if all this time the mine had been waiting for him to come and discover it.

Richard liked the word 'delve'. He liked working where, over years, perhaps centuries, men had worked, patiently, enduringly, nothing grand here, a small mine, suited to a man and his son perhaps, the pair of them labouring in unison. Possession wasn't what those earlier workers had in mind, he thought, having it belong, owning it, keeping others out. It hadn't been in his mind either until Miss Polleven put it there.

Actually he'd never thought about mining until he'd come to Polmena Cove, never even knew what mining was, for all that Cornwall was a mining county. When he was a boy his mother, Beth Martin, had spoken so often of Polmena Cove with such intense longing that, like her, he had always felt an exile in the small inland village near Truro where they lived. The sea's in your blood, Beth Martin used to tell him, as it's in mine. But it wasn't the sea, he'd no wish to be a fisherman.

Since Lily's last visit he had deliberately not thought of her. I've never heard of you, she'd said. Well, equally, he'd never heard of her! His mother, naturally enough, had never mentioned any of the Pollevens, her memories concentrated on her poor dead brother, but his father had spoken of the family with contempt. Landowning aristocrats, he'd called them, with an overlarge opinion of themselves – a description that fitted the daughter, Richard thought, vain and full of self-importance. He was surprised how the memory of her arrogant voice still grated. She'd better not order me, he thought. I've had a bellyful of ordering, a lifetime of it, a wartime of it, enough's enough.

Lily, if it were Lily, came on fast without any attempt at secrecy, moving quickly as if running. He imagined her forcing her way through the brambles which were already springing back across the track (a mistake to have cleared them, he now decided, an open invitation to investigate). In spite of himself he remembered her singing last time, a thin thread of song above the surf, like a far-off bird. Fond of music himself, he had been touched by that sound as by few things in recent years.

The song she had sung, 'Over the Sea to Skye', was on that most sentimental of themes – a battle lost, followers dead, a young prince on the run through stormy seas with only a loyal woman companion – he couldn't help remembering when he'd heard it last, when, before an attack, a young Scottish lad had leaned against the trench wall, whistling it softly under his breath, over and over, to give himself courage.

And he remembered too, how on seeing the boat and its two frightened occupants, his own romantic fancy had taken hold, and for a moment, a second, he had been deceived by it – until he had realized what the girl must be after. It was partly disappointment which had made him fire off a warning shot, as much a reminder to himself not to start dreaming the impossible as to keep intruders off. Perhaps he should use his gun again.

But there was another side to the picture and that also coloured his memory although he didn't want it to. First was Emma Trevarisk's defence of her cousin. 'Lily's kind-hearted,' Emma had said while they had waited on the beach, 'she won't take advantage.' Em had smiled. 'A voice like an angel,' she said, 'charm birds from trees. When she's had time to think today over she'll be that cross with herself.'

She'd grasped his arm. 'Twist you round her finger,' she'd said. All the while her own eyes had been fixed on Will Pendray. Look at me, answer me, her eyes had pleaded. Will had turned his head away; Lily had reappeared, the conversation had ended. But Emma's look and Emma's words were ingrained in Richard's memory.

Then, when the boat was about to capsize there was the way Lily had held Will in her arms; not a selfish act, he had to admit, not the action of someone intent only on her own safety. Nor had she panicked, or given way to hysterics like lots of girls. Despite the loss of one oar, she'd pulled with the other as strongly as a boy, had afterwards dragged the boat from the water, handled the heavy buckets as if she were used to hard work, bending and bailing without complaint. I could have managed, was all she'd said.

As for her appearance, with her windswept hair, her dirty wet clothes, she looked as scruffy as any village urchin. He found he was grinning at the thought. If fire had darted in the eyes when he'd told her off, if beneath the clinging material the lithe body had moved with grace, if he sensed the passion held in check – these were images to put aside, having no relevance. But they made him decide to sit quietly back and see what would happen.

Sure enough after a while Lily emerged from the under-growth, stood still for a moment, catching her breath, like a deer he thought, then came on straight towards the hut.

He thought her more pretty even than in memory, cheeks flushed, hair flying. Beneath a dark coat he glimpsed some lightweight material, a faint grey-blue, shot with silver, a dress that itself seemed meant for twilight.

She stopped underneath the ledge and stared at him. Not out of guilt as she might well have done, not even out of awkwardness after their last meeting, but directly, summing him up. In a strange way she reminded him of his mother; Beth Martin had the same knack. Perhaps I've been overharsh, he surprised himself with thinking. In a household dominated by women he'd never been hard on a female before. When she spoke it wasn't the high, classy voice he heard but the directness, that almost child-like way she had of stating things without bothering about consequences.

'Two days ago my brother let slip a secret, or rather Iris did. What he and my grandfather plan for Cove. And since it's worse, far worse, than having you here, I've come to warn you, if you'll take notice.'

He found himself laughing. 'Depends what the warning is,' he said. And, as her face clouded and her eyes began to spark, 'Come up and make sense of it.'

For a moment he wasn't sure she would accept, he could see indecision contending with what no doubt she would think of as 'proper'. But again he misjudged her. Ignoring his offered hand she climbed nimbly over the ledge and seated herself at one side, letting her feet dangle as Em had done, spreading her cloak to make a dry place and arranging her skirts in a belated effort at dignity. A scratch on one arm was bleeding and, failing to find a handker-chief, she dabbed at it with a corner of her sleeve, saying, 'Oh rats,' under her breath as the stain spread. He stifled another laugh.

'I shouldn't have come here like I did.' She spoke abruptly, again no real word of apology or explanation, a simple statement of fact. 'Even if the beach belongs to my family, that doesn't mean this hut does. But everything else is ours.

Michael Robert confirmed it's all part of the Polleven estate. And instead of making me glad, it's all gone wrong. So I missed the music rehearsal and came here instead.

'The rehearsal for St Marvell's Festival,' she added impatiently when he looked blank. 'You know, the Festival at the end of summer. I'm singing in the Women's Choir, their lead soprano, but they'll have to manage without me tonight. Michael Robert may exaggerate,' she continued, 'but Grandfather Polleven doesn't. My grandfather's obstinate. When he wants something he's not easily put off. And he can always persuade my brother into helping him. In my father's absence they've decided to drive you out so they can start ruining Cove.'

This spate of words left her breathless and him utterly confused. 'Hold hard,' he said. 'Start from the beginning. Who are these people, this grandfather who sounds so frightening? And how do they plan to ruin what is mine?'

While she told him, in equally breathless detail, a confused story where names like Michael Robert and Iris Duvane and Hugo Farell mingled with Sir Robert Polleven's, he let his thoughts wander. The tide was halfway in, the smell of seaweed and salt and fish fresh and pervasive, the setting sun touching the sand with gold. Above the murmur of the waves he could hear the piping of oystercatchers as they skimmed the surface, their black-and-white wings flashing. Suddenly he had a picture of a beach covered with litter, a stream-bed dammed and tarmacked, a valley floor turned to parking for cars and caravans.

Only when Lily too became silent, as if she'd run out of words, did Richard sit back and sift through all her information. Suddenly his brain didn't function. As he had taught himself, he wanted to blank the unpleasantness off, make himself impervious to it, make it not matter. He had to force himself to ask the questions she so obviously expected: was there any truth in what she had been saying, how did she know it wasn't exaggeration; couldn't it be wishful thinking on one side and old age dreaming on the other? You didn't show such concern when you accused me of trespass, he wanted to add but didn't.

Lily bit her lower lip, out of impatience. 'There's no mistake,' she insisted. 'It may only be a matter of days. I don't trust Michael. He may try to take the law into his own hands. You should be ready to defend yourself.'

Not meaning to, again he found he was smiling. 'What with?' he asked. He pointed to the ledge where the pile of discarded bits of sample core from Wheal Marty were piled. The rocks were threaded with silver and red and studded with crystal, prised up from the mine entrance. 'Shall I use them for bullets,' he said, laughing, 'or build the wall higher? There's more where they came from.'

When she started to say, 'It's serious,' he laughed again. 'Well, seriously then,' he said, 'I've plenty of experience of sentry duty; I can withstand a siege. A farmer leaves me bread and milk, I've water and tinned food, I'm well supplied. There's the mine to retreat back into, and all the mining supplies, blasting materials, flares, things like that. As a last resort I could always drift away in Will Pendray's boat.' And, not smiling now, he thought, for that matter I still have a gun – although since the war I've vowed not to use it and certainly don't want to be provoked into firing it at your brother as I was provoked into firing it at you. I'm laughing at myself, he wanted to tell her, a make-believe war, a make-believe attack, a make-believe defence. Remember, I've known what real war is. I'm tired of fighting, that's not what I'm here for. 'Why should it matter to me?' he wanted to say, and then did say, the question slipping out without his meaning to.

Lily's impatience broke out. 'You're the key,' she cried. 'You must have a deed, or whatever it is, to prove Cove's yours. You're the one to stop them.'

'And why do you think I'd want to?'

'Because you've got to,' Lily said, 'because you wouldn't be here unless you loved it. Because you must love it as I do.'

She turned on him, with a sudden fierce protection. 'Look

82

at it,' she said. And for a moment Richard saw Polmena Cove through Lily's eyes as perhaps he'd never seen it. Why, she truly cares for it, he thought almost in surprise, it isn't just about possession, the haves against the have-nots; it isn't only wanting to keep it all for herself.

'It's not the people,' Lily was saying passionately. 'They'd be bad enough, although I wouldn't mind the children. But it's what the people'd do and want, and the way we'd have to cater for those wants. Cove'd become like a second Blackpool. Or like that club Michael goes to, with its cocktails and gramophones. And instead of the stream and the valley with herons and foxes, there'll be a great big hotel and a new golf course, and red-faced men in plus fours. So it's up to you,' she repeated. 'You're the only chance we've got.'

And for a moment she closed her eyes as if the contemplation of all those horrors was too much even to think about.

Her passionate conviction almost touched him. But he was leery of convictions and had had passion leached out of him. Suddenly weary, he almost closed his own eyes. It's all very well for you to come running when you're in trouble, he thought, expecting, no, commanding me to help. I've done enough.

'Michael's like someone possessed,' she was saying, as if trying to make him understand. 'First the Club, then Iris. My grandfather dotes on him,' she added as if that too explained everything. 'He'd do anything for Michael. I'm sure he's thought of this scheme to make Michael happy. Grandfather's disappointed in my father, you see,' she said, the first faint awkwardness showing in her voice. 'Hates my father even, because he's crippled.'

She blushed suddenly. 'He was in the Boer War,' she said after another awkward pause. 'He's awfully brave. But you mustn't think too badly of my brother. Em and I keep hoping this is a phase he'll grow out of.'

She jumped up. 'And now I must go before he finds I'm not at choir practice and has another reason to be angry.'

'And won't he suspect you've warned me?' Richard asked.

'It's a real about-turn for you, isn't it, hobnobbing with the opposition?' His voice was deceptively gentle.

She had the grace to blush. 'It's no good dragging up the other day,' she said. 'I've said I'm sorry. And if I give the wrong impression now, well, I'm sorry about that too. But I've got to rely on you. So let's call a truce.'

She held out her hand. It lay brown and hard in his. Suddenly he wanted to hold it and not let it go, feeling a pang, what, of regret, that he could not share her innocent optimism. 'Stay,' he wanted to tell her. 'There's stew in the pot, the table's laid. We could make plans ourselves.'

He let the moment pass, felt it slide away, regretted its passing, then closed it off. He had no wish to make friends with a girl who would drop him like a bad penny when he was no more use to her. But when she had gone, climbing as quickly as she had come, once more he gazed round him.

The sea waves beat, the surf surged on the sand. Almost with exasperation he realized that something of her passion had touched him. Not passion for himself, but for this place, as if in truth it were part of him. She'd not exaggerated, he thought, surprised and then almost pleased at the revelation – and I imagined I couldn't love anything again.

Suddenly all the implications of what Lily had been telling him came home to him, how other people, who had never known what wanting was, who had everything their hearts could desire and more, had designs on his place of refuge. My uncle drowned for this, he thought, and I nearly died in the war. If here is battle then I draw the battle line.

He paced up and down the ledge as if on watch, every so often pausing to survey the view, much as once, long ago, Jenny Trevarisk must have done. Other thoughts came crowding fast, memories, both happy and sad. He was the first child, the only son. While his father lived, there was no way of escape. Leaving school at fourteen, reluctantly he had followed his father into the shoemaking trade, but every day had chafed at the waste. What his real talents were then he didn't know, but he had not seen himself as a village cobbler. Then war had come and so had belief that here lay his purpose. That was the biggest mistake he'd ever made.

When the recruiting officers came to Truro, he had been among the first to enlist although he was far too young. But it was not for patriotism, albeit family and friends may have praised him for it. Only his mother had seen through him. Small and plump, her hair turned grey, Beth Martin was never one to shirk truth even if it hurt.

'You're under age,' she said. 'You don't have to go.' She sat by the window darning socks. Her eyes beneath the spectacle frames were black, bright as a robin's, fearless. She stuck the needle in, rolled up the thread, put the sock back in her sewing box. He knew what would come next. 'The shop needs you since your father's heart went bad. If he can't go on, who else is there? The girls need you. I can't keep them steady on my own.'

She didn't say, 'I need you too. How shall I endure it if you're gone?' She wouldn't ask for herself as she could for them, the gentle shoemaker father for whom she had left this sea existence; the sisters, bright and flighty, unlike either parent and growing up in a changing world where they were determined to 'get on'.

He didn't want that sort of success, that wasn't the change or excitement he was looking for and his mother knew it, knew there was something more he wanted – call it a cause, an intensity, the lack of it made his life seem too small and confined. Well, perhaps he'd never know what the real cause was, what the intensity, but the war had not satisfied him. His mother had let him go, although a word to the authorities could have prevented him, did endure his father's death and his own maiming. And after the war was over and he returned, when his father's shop was sold she gave him his portion of inheritance and let him leave again without any further hindrance. If she knew of one other, more personal, reason for leaving, she never mentioned it but she must have felt it as deeply as he did. And of the whole sorry business, the only thing that must have pleased her was his choice of refuge.

That he had survived the war, when so many hadn't, still amazed him. Sometimes, sadly, like William Pendray, he felt that survival itself was a random gift, denied as equally randomly to so many others. He made himself push those thoughts under. As with all memories of the past they must be buried. But no matter that like William he was scarred, crippled for life; if he had been spared, there must be some reason.

The too familiar sense of irritated exasperation returned, that for all his trying the outside world wouldn't leave him alone. He had come here to recuperate, to heal himself. The last thing he wanted was to be involved in other people's affairs. He sensed, with that extra perception that had often kept him out of trouble in the war, that he wouldn't be left alone again. And that, like his sister, Michael Robert Polleven would be stubborn and direct.

CHAPTER 7

Michael lay under the hedge and watched Lily pass along the path from Cove where it turned away from the cliff. He'd just had time to scramble through the bushes on top and duck beneath. Nor did Lily see him in his hiding place. Head down, deep in thought, she was walking quickly back towards Nanscawn. If tomorrow I ask her where she's been, Michael thought, she'll tell me at her blasted singing, as if she's used to lying. For a moment he hated St Marvell, hated the Music Festival and everything about it, hated Lily with a raw and naked hate that couldn't hide the pain.

This proof positive of Lily's new wantonness was a blow, but one he had expected. He'd watched her leave the farm, presumably on her way to the practice, then, as suddenly sure where she was going, had gone after her, and waited. He lay still. He shouldn't have had to follow her, he shouldn't have had to skulk here in the damp grass, spying on his sister, suspecting her of the worst. Like a hurt he knew he'd have to live with, he thought, I'll never get over this, as if the division in his family were complete, as if he and his family stood apart, he on one side, they on the other.

He should have been with Iris. The thought of what he and Iris ought to have been doing set his heart thudding, brought a flush to his face as if his skin were on fire. But today he had been disappointed. Today Iris had been cool. 'Not so fast,' she'd said with her little laugh, tapping him on his cheek, 'caution, you know. A breathing space.' As if he were a child, he thought, as if having got what she wanted she weren't so eager again, as if each time she meant for him to beg and her to give or refuse, like throwing a dog a bone. Suppose Chote had been enjoying doing the same things with Lily? Suppose he didn't have to beg?

He jumped up, thrashing at the nettles with his stick, then, impervious of stings and thorns, pushed his way back through the hedge, and took the direction Lily had just come from, certain now that his grandfather was right. 'Like mother, like daughter,' Sir Robert Polleven had said, his old eyes bright. 'Bad blood will out.'

Another thought came to him, what had Lily told Chote about their plans for Cove. Of course Lily would tell, or Chote would worm it out of her. Again thought of Lily's treachery brought him to a halt. And once that fellow Chote knew, nothing would oust him, or stop him from using the idea to boost Cove's worth; he might even try to do the same thing himself. And then Michael would be left with the worst task of explaining the whole sorry mess to grandfather, of how Chote knew, and what Lily had been told by Iris, without revealing the existence of Iris herself.

'Who's Iris Duvane?' Michael could hear his grandfather ask in the drawl he used to show he wasn't interested. 'Not a Cornish name. Who's her family, her father, mother, brother? Make sure she's what you say she is. We don't want another mistake.' Grandfather wouldn't accept Iris, would dismiss Michael's lovemaking without giving Michael a chance to explain himself or even talk of Iris. Even more bitter, Michael thought, he means for me to marry at his choosing; he purposely won't like Iris because I found her for myself.

The empty wallet that had held the wages also burned in his pocket. That too needed explaining. He felt for the flask of whisky, brought at the last moment, not for drinking before, he'd told himself, but for celebrating afterwards; now he unstoppered it and took a drink, still uncertain what he should do, and yet certain he must do something that would call for celebration. 'I'd thrash him out myself,' grandfather'd said. At least, Michael thought, I won't be found wanting in that, at least I'll have that satisfaction.

He came down the valley just as the light was fading. From time to time he paused to listen. The dusk was closing fast, bats swooped among the bushes. Far off an owl hooted and some small creature shrieked. The stream chuckled in the undergrowth; the sounds and smells, even the peaty taste of it, were heightened by the evening damp, sucked up like nectar. Yet for all the past rain it never ran in spate at this time of the year, trickled through the twisted roots of gorse and ivy feeding into deep pools, dark and mysterious. When he remembered what his grandfather planned, its melancholy entwined with his, made him feel a pang of remorse perhaps, regret what he might be party to. Suddenly it occurred to him that its destruction was a real issue he should face, not the squabble over who owned a miserable shanty on a windswept cliff. More than that, by stressing the importance of Richard Chote he was doing the opposite of what he meant to do, putting his own future at risk by dwelling constantly on the past. And yet he couldn't stop himself. Suspicion hardening in him, thick as bile, forced him forward.

At the edge of the beach he paused a last time, parted the bushes slowly with his stick. He had dressed in dark clothes as a precaution and the stick was heavy, a cudgel; he felt its weight in his hand. So was the flask a weight. He took it out of his pocket, pulled at the stopper with his teeth, drank.

The tide was in now but he was not interested in the tide, or only in so far as the surf would drown any noise he made. Here on the beach it was not completely dark; the sky was some kind of silvery grey and far out in the bay the sea seemed to shine with a strange iridescence. He could just make out the shape of the hut lost against its background of cliff. No lights showed, no faint coil of smoke against the darker rocks. Michael's face creased into a smile. Sleeping then, he thought scornfully, blissfully unaware.

He took off his boots so they wouldn't crunch on the shingle, left them and the flask where he could find them, crept forward in stockinged feet, picking his way over the stone that formed the bridge, along the foreshore where the seaweed shifted at every step. Under the ledge where the old hut stood he paused again, holding the cudgel balanced. Strike with it against the door, he told himself, shake the sleeper awake, smash the windows, smash the walls, smash the place apart, destroy it once and for all, turn it to dust and ash.

He raised his stick, prepared to leap. Smoke billowed, a light flaring in his eyes blinded him.

Out of the smoke and flash, magnesium perhaps, he didn't recognize it, a figure rose up from behind the ledge, in places reinforced with bits of stone. A gun barrel pointed. As he dropped the stick and cowered, 'Up,' said Richard Chote. 'That's better. Now let's see what you're made of.'

Face to face they were almost of a height, almost the same age, a few months perhaps between them. Years of experience separated them, a lifetime of it, a gap of war experience that nothing in this century would ever cross.

'I thought it would be you,' Richard Chote said. He had an easy way of speaking, for a man whose house had been under attack, that is. And he had an easy way with his prisoner, if Michael could be called that, pushing him against the ledge while he took up his former position on the inside. 'I presume you've come alone.'

He put the gun down and waved an admonishing finger. 'First lesson of war,' he said. 'No night attack. Hard to see where you're going, harder to carry out. Second lesson. Never cross light background, stick to the shadows. Third, don't underestimate the enemy, always expect the worst.'

A hundred accusations, condemnations, excuses, swirled in Michael's head. What he said came bursting out like a gunshot. 'What were you doing with my sister?'

Richard reached down, produced a lantern, lit it. 'There,' he said, 'let's shed some light on the subject.' He leaned against the wall, obviously trying not to smile. 'Ask rather what was she doing with me,' he said. Then, as if seeing how angry Michael was, as if he hadn't the heart to torment him, more carefully, 'Before I answer anything, I've questions of my own. Namely, what brings you creeping here so late? Paying a social call?'

Suddenly his own anger showed. 'If so, I'm not at home,' he said. 'Isn't that the correct expression? Never will be. So don't come calling again. With or without your walking stick.'

He spun on his heel, went towards the hut, back turned contemptuously. That was a fourth lesson he must have known and should never have forgotten. It gave Michael the chance he had been looking for. Leaping over the ledge Michael seized up his cudgel. 'Damn you,' he cried, trying for a battering blow to the head.

Richard must have heard or perhaps even felt the rush of Michael's movements. Without seeming to alter direction, he ducked at the last second so that the intended blow took him on the shoulder, almost knocking him over. Even as it was, he would have overbalanced had he not had the sense to put up his hand so that his fist closed over the stick for support.

For a moment they strained with the cudgel between them in uneven contest. Michael was a fit young man at full peak of strength, determined to inflict punishment. Richard was crippled, wanting only to avoid trouble. But here again experience had its effect.

Richard must have known he was as strong as his opponent in some ways; there was nothing wrong with his arms or shoulders and if he could only keep his balance he could eventually get rid of the stick. Bracing his back against the closed door of the hut as he did when digging in his mine, resting his weight on his sound leg only, he wrestled until the stick came loose, then hurled it as far away as he could. It curled into the air and landed with a thud. 'Now then,' he said, panting, 'if you want a fight, let's start even.'

He must have known that he could endure for a while, provided he did not have to move from the one spot. And that, whereas his opponent hit out in a desperation born of some despair, as if sworn to some sort of vengeance, he himself was contained, muted down, concentrated on survival. He let Michael flail away, waited for an opening. He would keep Michael at bay, let Michael tire, then make his strike.

Knowledge of Richard's tactics made Michael redouble his efforts. He stooped, tried to force past Chote's guard, using his head as a battering ram. In twisting to avoid the blow, Richard's shoulders began to slip against the door. Powerless to stop himself, he slid sideways just as Michael's head cracked against the wall.

Both crumpled at the same instant, Richard falling awkwardly, defencelessly, hands over his face in an instinctive gesture of protection; Michael more heavily, like a log, on top of him.

Richard rolled over first. He had not lost consciousness, had been merely winded by Michael's weight. Clawing for purchase, he managed to drag himself up and reach for the lantern which mercifully had not overturned. Taking it up, he struggled back to the doorway, where Michael still lay senseless, huddled on the ground.

For a moment Richard felt fear catch in his own throat. He'd seen too many men slump like that, one moment alive, full of energy, the next, without any space of transition, reduced to nothingness, held together by scraps of clothes. He bent over Michael, at close quarters smelling the whisky. But Michael was not dead. He was breathing; the blood that seeped on the stones came from a cut on his forehead; the cut itself was not serious but bloody as such head wounds usually are.

Richard let himself sag then and struggle for breath, trying to ease the throbbing in his leg. Silly young bugger, he thought, showing off like that. After a while, when Michael in turn began to stir, he dragged out a bucket full of water which he dipped and splashed in the other's face.

With a sudden great gasp, Michael sat up and shook his head, like a dog after a swim. Water and blood splattered. 'What's up?' he said thickly, 'What's happened?' His gaze swung wide, then focused. He put up a shaky hand and touched his head, winced.

'Nothing serious. Nothing a sticking plaster won't mend.' Richard was taut-voiced but by instinct used words that he'd used many times before to wounded men unsure of themselves and frightened. 'Shift over a bit,' he said. And as Michael dutifully obeyed, he pushed the door open so that the inside of the hut suddenly was revealed. 'You'd better come in,' he said.

Catching hold of the other's arm much as he had caught hold of Will Pendray's, he steered Michael towards the same rough chair fashioned out of packing cases covered with old jackets. Slowly, moving painfully, he fed sticks to the embers until a flame caught and he could hang a kettle to boil. Then, rummaging into a sack hung on a nail, he brought out rough white material which he tore into strips, handkerchiefs perhaps, old ones, so fragile they parted like cobwebs. He handed them to Michael one by one to stem the blood. All the while he kept up a run of chatter, another old habit, the sort of talking men do when a danger is over and they want to find their own selves again.

'Don't know what your problem is, don't know what you're after. But all you'll find is here, all on display, nothing to hide. Look at it, it isn't much, is it, this hut you and your family seem to covet. Old wood, old stones, old roofs, old floors, that've not been touched in twenty years. A hut where my mother lived with her brother, far from everyone, doing no harm. And that's all I wanted out of it, see, an out-of-the-way place, a breathing space, a chance to put my thoughts together and decide what I'll do with the rest of my life.'

Michael heard him from a long way off as if from a fog he couldn't find the way through. It seemed to be part of the blow that had come from nowhere, then burst into a thousand yellow lights like the flash of the explosion which had so startled him earlier. He lay back on the chair, let the voice continue, weaving itself in and out, not unpleasantly, like the sound of running water.

'I'm a shoemaker by trade. At least I was. When they first told me I'd lose my leg, I laughed and told them a one-legged shoemaker wasn't good advertisement for trade. So I hung on to it and that's about all, that and a small pension. And the share of what my father left. No vast fortune, no luxury living.'

He stirred the fire, swung the kettle. 'So what shall I do, I asked myself, if I don't make shoes? I'd time for asking, months of time. I lay in that hospital bed and thought. But I didn't find out much. Only that I was tired of things torn down and destroyed without rhyme or reason. And that to some people a crippled man's a secret shame, to be hidden away in a corner and never brought out on view.'

He said to Michael, conversationally, 'Where do your fancies lie? What're your talents? We've all got them somewhere, however deeply hidden.'

Michael stared at this strange man who limped to and fro talking to himself. 'I need a purpose, see,' Richard was saying. 'I need to make sense of all that hideous waste.' Those weren't the words of a bolshy parasite, not the words of an enemy. Michael put up his hand again and touched his head. It ached still but with a vague unconnected throbbing. Suddenly he wanted to pour out all his own yearnings. 'I thought I was a farmer,' he wanted to cry, 'I thought I liked the land. I feel it slipping from me, like water. I don't know what I want.'

'There's a mine up there,' Richard jerked with his thumb out into the darkness. 'Funny name, Wheal Marty. I want to reopen it. I like its oldness and quiet,' he said. 'I like exploring in the dark. Sometimes, I imagine I can feel the ore there, the grain of it running under the fingertips. Mining's a Cornish birthright,' he added as if that explained everything, 'we've been miners since before Rome. And all secret, all underground, no rubbish or spillage, just as the last miner left it.

'I don't know anything about him,' he continued, 'except he was a careful man. All his mine props and pumps, horse-driven in those days, still in place, waiting to be refitted. I like his work. Shafts driven straight, galleries properly lined, nothing shoddy, all shored with stone and wood. Just needs clearing out. I don't know anything about that previous miner,' he repeated, 'but I like to think he was the original owner of Polmena Cove, the man who gave it to my mother's mother.'

He bent over the hearth, poured the water, neatly making tea in mugs. 'My mother spent all her life here until she married,' he said. 'Like your sister she was born here. Her mother never married, but whoever the father of her two babies was he gave the land as recompense. If it was my old miner, I like that about him too, all neat and tidy, fair return for fairness' sake. I'm beginning to think I'd like to pick up where he left off.'

He held out the mug. It was made of battered tin, a soldier's mug. Michael had a dim impression of a gesture made so often it had become a ritual. 'If you're tired of farming, why not join me?' Richard asked. 'Build up something instead.'

From the long way off where he'd gone, Michael dragged himself back to the present. He looked at his hand which held the mug. Compared with Richard's it was soft; for all his riding and farmwork, a gentleman's hand, meant for gentlemanly pursuits. Tin and pilchards. The words sprang in his head, buzzed there, tin and pilchards, the two staples of Cornwall, mining and fishing throughout centuries. I've had enough of fishing, he thought, fishing's been the root of all my trouble. One of two's enough.

He put down the mug, stood up. The hut walls seemed to spin in circles but he wouldn't show it. 'No, thanks,' he said. 'Not my vocation. I want more than that.'

'Living off others like parasites? Visitors like flies?' Richard mocked him. 'Tarred roads and motor cars?'

⸳ He stood rocking on his heels before the fireplace, his shoulders dipping. Like that you could see how he had to recompense for the shortness of one leg. An old soldier Michael's own age, a man who'd somehow been in battle while Michael had been playing at schoolboy; an old wounded soldier looking for peace who had bested Michael despite his handicap. Michael felt all the shame he'd ever known rise up and swamp him. He couldn't bear it.

'Damn you,' he cried, his face infused with red, 'damn you and all you stand for. I owe you nothing. The world owes you nothing.'

He started up, blundered to the door, pushed it open again. 'And don't think we won't smoke you out,' were his parting words, 'you don't have a chance.'

But as he ran across the beach, snatching for his boots, snatching at the flask which was to have been his victory toast, that wasn't what he thought at all, was the opposite of his real feelings. And the water that ran down his face wasn't the spilling from the pail, was formed from true regret that he hadn't the courage of his own convictions like that man back there.

CHAPTER 8

Lily and Em both heard Michael return but Lily reached him first. She had been sitting in the music room, thumbing idly through the scores, making amends for missing the practice. Her voice had not been in tune and her fingers fumbled on the piano keys. The discords seemed to echo the lack of harmony she felt about her, even in herself.

She had not liked her discourtesy to her brother's guests; she had not liked her deception of him. In retrospect it seemed unfair to have revealed her brother's secrets to her brother's opponent, but then, what Michael and Grandfather Polleven had in mind wasn't fair either. For the first time she saw that it wasn't the fate of Cove that mattered, so much as the man who now lived there. Somehow sympathy for him had supplanted her original intentions; somehow, without her meaning to, protection of Cove was mixed with protection of him – a strange situation she wasn't prepared for. 'A real turn-about,' Richard Chote had said. She felt torn in two – between ideas that shouldn't be in conflict, between people whom she certainly was unqualified to judge. Suddenly she wished she could confide in someone but knew instinctively even Em couldn't help her in this. I shan't go back there, she told herself, with one last decisive chord, shan't go back, ever. He must fend for himself.

It was then the front door opened and Michael came

inside, the stumbling steps so unlike his, she was suddenly frightened. He's drunk again, she thought. But when the footsteps stopped she realized something was wrong. At the door of the music room she stopped, terrified by what she saw.

Michael was sitting on the steps, she had never seen him so dejected, his shoulders bowed. Blood had saturated his jacket and when he looked up, his face was streaked with blood; the pad he held to the cut was soaked with it.

Behind her she heard Em hurry to the kitchen, looking for water and towels, she thought, as she herself went quickly towards her brother. The smell of whisky was overpowering, but he still knew her. He scowled, put his finger across his mouth as if to emphasize she must be quiet, put out the other hand to fend her off. 'Keep away from me.' His voice was rough. 'I don't need you.'

He let Em approach him, suffered her ministrations in silence, but when Lily tried to help, said, 'Go on, lie, tell us you've not been with him again.'

Lily didn't have to ask what he meant. But it was his way of saying it, not the actual words, that stung. Even his voice's different, she thought, and he's different. The boyishness had gone from his round face and in the faint hall light she could see the bruises, purple against the whiteness. She felt numb with pity.

Em stared at her cousins, realization dawning, until Michael turned on her too, pushing her away and spilling the blood-stained water on the floor.

'Don't bother to ask her,' Michael continued in the same way, a voice full of suppressed menace. 'She'll only lie. But I followed her to Cove. Boasted of it, didn't he, told me she was chasing him. And when I tried to fight him, look what he did to me.'

He levered himself upright, holding to the banister for support. 'She went there to reveal my plans. She's a traitor to her family as well as a slut. And she'll pay for both.'

He lumbered forward; for a moment Lily thought he was

going to strike her and flinched. A blow wouldn't do more harm than his words already had. But he stopped short of an actual blow and glowered at both girls.

'If that idiot Pendray went with her the first time,' he now said, shouting at Em, who after the original shock had moved forward to shield Lily, 'the more shame on you. He's your affair, not mine. If he's the best you can find, hang on to him if you want to, but don't get me involved. My family's honour's my responsibility and I'll not have my sister lowering herself. If Chote hasn't taken liberties with her yet, he will. That type always does. So keep her away from him, Em, do you hear, or I'll lock you out. As for her,' addressing Lily directly now, in a sudden ominous whisper, the whisper emphasizing the vulgarity of his next remarks, 'bitch. Whore. I'll not have a bastard sister with a bastard brat.'

He staggered off; they heard his door slam; they themselves remained crouched by the wall as if he had thrust them there. For Lily shame came first, that her brother would think of such things, would dare say them. Then came anger, at what he might have said to Richard Chote and what Richard Chote might have replied, must have hinted at, to have made them fight. But after anger came doubts. Why had Michael followed her, why had he gone down to Cove? What would Richard Chote have told, 'boasted' of, there was nothing to boast about. She knew she'd get no more out of Michael. Suddenly it became imperative to speak to Richard again even if that meant breaking her newly made resolve. If Michael thought he could frighten her away, then he was mistaken. Tomorrow she'd find out the truth.

'Michael trailed me,' she told Em. 'He spied on me. He lied. How could Richard pick a fight and beat him, that doesn't make sense. Michael hates me, Em,' she said, in turn pushing her cousin away as Em tried to comfort her. 'He hates me, and I don't know why. But if he quarrels with me then he's driving a gap between us, so wide that if he's not careful it'll never be made whole again.'

* * *

99

The next morning found Richard on The Cut at St Marvell. He was idly throwing empty limpet shells and pretending that his bad leg didn't belong to him. He watched the shells hit the water with a slight plopping sound, then sink to the bottom with its scatterings of rope ends and dead crabs and fish bones. The whole day's been like that, he thought, starting well, then ending in a litter of frustrations.

Taking a risk at leaving, as soon as there was light enough he had gone across the cliffs to the village, a labour of willpower. Hitherto he had visited St Marvell seldom, not anxious to intrude and in a way wary of its place in his family's past. That he'd succeeded in reaching it at all was a sort of triumph, he thought wryly, remembering all too clearly the steepness of the track.

He threw another shell, watched it sink. There went his first endeavour, he thought, the bank, where he had met with rejection absolute and complete, the possibility of any actual loan to open Wheal Marty as far-fetched as if he wanted to mine on the moon.

He leaned against the wall, threw another shell, and then another, a handful of them. There went the local solicitors, as fogged in prejudice as the glass windows of their inner office, all obscured in vague generalities, calculated to confuse. He tried to remember their long words, proprietary rights, mortmain, words he couldn't possibly know, and was clearly not expected to understand. No one asked if he had a deed; no one assumed he did. No one assumed he had anything of value and therefore it was not worth the time or trouble of finding out.

And that means, he thought now, someone's been here before me. Sir Robert Polleven perhaps or one of Sir Robert's hirelings, with advance instructions to shut me out. Well, damn them, they shan't.

He had only listened to Lily with half an ear; he hadn't expected such unyielding opposition. He cursed himself for his naïvety. Hadn't his father told him what the Pollevens were like? All right, he thought, stubborn himself, Sir Robert may have ways, official and devious, to twist the law; have money and influence to hire advice and stop my getting it; may have all the power of landed aristocracy weighted against a peasant – that doesn't mean he's going to get my mother's land. Or that I won't find ways to fight him. Although where they'll come from, he thought, ruefully honest now, where I'm to find influence and friends, here in the heart of Polleven territory, the devil alone knows.

As for young Polleven, he hadn't taken him seriously either, felt no real animosity towards him. Now perhaps he should. Funny to think of him as young, he thought suddenly; we're probably close in age. The difference is he avoided the war, I didn't. And he's a member of a vanishing world that he wants to cling to and can't, an anomaly and an anachronism at the same time. That doesn't make him easier to handle.

Thinking of these things made him remember Lily. He tried not to. He had begun to recognize that he thought of Lily Polleven too often. Her fierce abruptness, her casual assumption of friendship 'because she needed it', had made him smile, yet underneath it angered him. She's simply using me, he told himself. When the crisis passes, or what she thinks of as crisis, so will her need for me. Suddenly he could imagine her speaking of him as she had spoken of Will Pendray, in what he called her upper-class voice, a mixture of benevolence and condescension. Irritated, he thought, but suppose we had met in some other way, suppose she couldn't prejudge who I was, would she act differently?

He felt himself grow hot at the unfairness of it. All right, he thought, I know I give myself away in everything I do. My way of dressing, my speech, my very manner of thinking reveal my background as clearly as if it were stamped on me. It wasn't like that in the war. In the war a man was assessed by what he did, how he behaved under attack, how he reacted to danger and didn't panic – not by his family or his walk of life. Survival then was all, he thought, and survival's a great leveller. Of course there were officers, but they were often young, inexperienced poor devils. They died like flies.

And I've commanded men myself when I had to, when there was no one else left, and men followed me, not because I was richer than they were, not even because I told them to, but because we were together and had to rely on each other. I was wounded rescuing an officer, was in turn rescued by another officer – there's my final proof. No one cared then who was who.

So if equality's possible in war, he thought, it should be in peace. And if Lily Polleven's incapable of seeing it, well then, she's as prejudiced as her brother, as bound by class, as incapable of breaking out, as he is.

In his heart he didn't want to believe that. She's young, he told himself, untried, unformed. I'd like her to be different. I'd like . . . he was unable to say what he would have liked. He had so deliberately suppressed thoughts of women from his mind that he had had no room for them.

Shaking his head as if to clear it, as if to put all these things aside, he turned from The Cut and began to make his way back through the narrow street. Although he shied away from the idea, he knew instinctively that Lily's reaction to him would have effect, for good or ill wouldn't matter, there would be no going against it. Nor how he would react in return.

It was at this point his luck changed. Although he didn't see it so at first. When he first became aware of the burly man who followed him, he was alarmed. The man was big, advanced with firm decision, breathing hard. No coward, Richard shied away from unnecessary violence, knew how disadvantaged he would be in such a match. Sure this was one of Sir Robert's minions, sent by Sir Robert for some purpose, perhaps to get even for breaking his grandson's skull, he ducked off the main street, down the twisted lanes that branched off it, like vines, going as fast as he could.

The lane he had chosen ended in another square, surrounded on four sides by walls, festooned with posters which he pretended to study, the advertisements for the Music Festival in blue and gold, a week-long event of it, blurring as his breath came in gasps. The man still followed.

Backed against the posters, fists clenched, Richard turned to face him, shouted, 'What do you want with me?'

To his surprise, as the man drew near, a broad smile lit his face, revealing a row of golden teeth. To Richard's inquiry, 'Did Sir Robert Polleven send you?' 'Lord love us,' the other responded, with a hearty laugh. 'Not that bugger, not likely.

'Can't be two of you so maimed,' he went on, 'nor two in a soldier's coat. Be 'ee who I think? For if 'tis Richard Chote, yer uncle's my saviour.'

He thumped his chest. 'Jeb Martin saved me, my handsome,' he cried. 'My sins washed white, brought to the bosom of the Lord by that dear soul. And a better man ne'er lived nor died, or my name's not Ben Trevarisk.' And in a rush of gratitude he gripped Richard painfully to his chest, almost lifting him off the ground.

That this greeting was as unexpected as it was unwelcome must have been apparent. But even so, afterwards Richard had to admit it was not without recompense. Ben was not only froth and bombast. True, in middle age, Ben Trevarisk was himself monumental, a bulk of a fellow, whose broad shoulders and broader waist ran into legs like tree stumps. But on Richard's reluctant admitting of his name, Ben soon showed he had not lost his taste for the theatrics which had marked him when younger.

His bearlike embrace, his dropping to his knees to praise God, his deployment of the gathering crowd as witnesses of his effusive thanks, were part and parcel of his flamboyance and would have done justice to an itinerant preacher. But although, like his taste in stained-glass windows, his performance was overdone, and was something Richard could have done without, it was only Ben's methods that jarred. Neither in his religion nor his gratitude was Ben insincere. He meant every word.

'Now, then,' he said at the end, 'you mentioned Sir Robert. My sister's father-in-law, true, but naught to me. Tho' I grant you his son, my brother-in-law's a different kettle of fish. But if there's aught wrong, or some' at you need help with, if you'm up against the Pollevens like, as I do hear you be, why then, my dear, count on me. That's only fitty like.'

At this, Ben's once handsome wife Charity, for whom at first Richard felt a touch of sympathy, as dramatically made no bones about where her feelings lay. She stood at the top of her cottage steps, one hand on hip, the other clutching a frying pan, as if to repel invaders. 'He's at it again,' she said. When Ben thanked God she shrugged her shoulders and winced, went as far as to tug at his thick jersey sleeve to keep him quiet. In short, the more her husband enthused, the more Charity Trevarisk held back.

'What do us owe him?' Her grudging recognition of Richard seemingly set the value of the pilchard shoal, the wrecking of Ben's boat, even the expense of the window, against the loss or gaining of life, and somehow wound their way into her discourse, leaving the impression that, if Richard had returned to Polmena Cove at all, he must be well off; he and his family had already been sufficiently rewarded; she and her husband would have been grateful for half as much.

'As fer the rights of Polmena Cove,' she said, tossing her hair which once must have been luxurious black, 'don't know nothing about that. Doesn't do to cross the Pollevens, I do know that. And,' with a spiteful glance, 'they do say if they start building there'll be work fer all, which is more than he's offered.'

Richard was glad to remove himself from her discontented attack. Yet, despite the tasteless attitude of the wife, he was also left with the conviction that Ben Trevarisk meant what he said. As indeed might others in the crowd who afterwards shook his hand, telling him in their different ways how much they still remembered Jeb Martin. But how long their support would last if they knew how deeply Richard was pitted against Sir Robert Polleven; would Ben Trevarisk risk estrangement from his brother-in-law for a man who in truth was nothing to him – these were questions best not asked.

A second, equally unexpected, encounter gave Richard a

second line of hope. There was only one other person in St Marvell he was glad to see, apart from Lily herself, and escaping from the crowd he spotted Emma Trevarisk hurrying towards him. Em was alone; there was no Lily dancing by her side; Richard felt a strange mixture of disappointment and relief.

Em paused, reddened, came resolutely on, blushing and smiling at the same time. He had not seen her smile before. It reminded him of Lily. 'Mr Chote,' she said. He sensed a feeling of restraint, guilt almost. Consorting with the enemy, he almost said. Questions about Lily bubbled up, he had to stop himself from blurting them out, had Lily returned safely home, had she and her brother come to terms, where was Lily now, questions which he had no right to ask and which might get Lily into trouble. Instead, stiffly correct, he asked Em how Will was. He hoped Will'd recovered; obviously he himself hadn't seen Will, but he'd still got Will's boat, safely moored.

Emma smiled and blushed again; he could tell she was glad to speak of something neutral, something not connected with Polmena Cove and her adopted family's stand. Will was in the garden of his mother's cottage, she said, she'd just come from there. 'He seems so much better than before,' she said, 'almost as if . . .'

She stopped, put a hand over her mouth, that familiar gesture, as if she too wanted to prevent words pouring out. Richard recognized it. 'Almost as if he's normal,' Emma was trying not to say, 'almost like his real self.'

He thought, I've heard and seen hope like yours before, many times, too many to count, up and down until it wears itself out, until it kills even love. But he said nothing.

'Come and talk to him, do,' Em urged; like his mother she could plead for others if not for herself. 'He'll be that pleased.' Her eyes shone. 'Always speaking of you,' she said, 'good to talk to someone who knew what it was like.'

She retraced her steps, leading the way to the small weather-beaten cottage tucked under the cliff. There she paused for a moment, as if deciding whether she would come in. 'Don't want to wear my welcome out,' she said, hiding her own yearning under stoic constraint. Will was seated at a rickety table, his head bent and resting on his forearms. When he heard the hinges creak he looked up, but he only recognized Richard, only greeted Richard by name.

'Sit down, sit down,' he kept repeating, making ineffectual dusting motions on the table, obviously thinking up excuses to have Richard stay – mother would make an extra pasty, wait a bit, they'd walk down to look at the boats. 'By gum, 'tis good to see 'ee,' his constant repetition, 'someone who knows,' as Em had suggested, clinging to that thought as to a lifeline.

He paid no attention to Em who remained at the garden gate, even when his mother, sprightly as a hen despite her years, brought out a single bent-legged stool for a single visitor. The old lady also turned her back, as if she had no liking for either Richard or Em, ignoring them until her son repeated, as if continuing an ongoing discussion, 'I'll never'll go back to the mine, that's for certain sure.'

Then the old woman's watery grey eyes sharpened. Her reply was sharp too, with worry and indecision. 'That's no way to talk, a shame and a disgrace.' She flicked her oven cloth in the direction of the gate. 'There're people abroad. Don't do to let 'em hear 'ee speak like that.'

Not knowing what to say, Richard remained silent, hearing behind his back Em's feet tapping neatly away down the cobblestones. Her restraint touched him. He waited a while until he could hear her no longer, then sat down on the stool.

'What's to do then, how'm we to live? Just tell me that,' the old woman addressed her son, her voice a fretful whine. 'You won't have it said, but 'twas her cousin who near drowned 'ee.' She jerked with her thumb at the empty gateway. 'And what about the "Seagull"?'

She cast a second sharp look, at Richard now, fiddling with the cloth, her red knuckles dusted with flour. 'If 'tis lost, who's to pay for it? That's what I want to know. If he don't,' again a sharp look, 'will the Pollevens? 'Twere all Lily Polleven's fault.'

That too must have been part of some ongoing discussion, for her son pushed his chair aside.

'The boat's safe enough, he's come to vouch for it.' He nodded at Richard. 'But naught to do with Em. Nor Lily Polleven. 'Twas I who offered. If anyone be found wanting,' he said, 'I be the one. Always found wanting, there, can't be denied.'

He stood up, abrupt and gawky, a tall man whose strength was gone, went over to a corner of the garden. The name of garden was a courtesy to the daisy patch surrounded by brambles which smothered old lobster and crab pots. Nettles were growing through the slats and he now began to pull at the leaves, shredding them apart.

His mother watched him helplessly, wiping her hands on her pinny. 'Pity,' she said, close to tears, 'and him that were so good with engines, not one he couldn't fix. All set to be married, and to a good girl, though I won't say so in her hearing, what's the point of it now. Instead out here now 'til all hours, wanting to see things grow, he says, as if he'd never seen 'em afore, as if anything much will grow in these weeds. Don't make no sense. Why don't he take a spade and hoe to it then? Laziness, I calls it.'

Suddenly the image of the shattered landscape in France, the torn and blasted earth, rose in front of Richard but he couldn't speak of it. And perhaps the old woman guessed his feelings. 'Don't you go a-couraging of him,' she said, less severely, 'bad enough as 'tis. And don't you go forgetting that boat's ours, even if you did pull it in.'

With that parting remark she went grumbling indoors, leaving Richard sitting at the table, toying with a piece of wood. It was then the idea came into his head of a way of helping Will, and Em, and himself into the bargain, with no effort on his part. And when after a while Will recovered enough to return to the table, he put it to him.

It wasn't all contrived either. One of the difficulties facing Richard since he had thought of reopening Wheal Marty was the starting of the engines, now out of the question if he couldn't borrow money to have expert help. But some of the machinery was still in place, and as far as his untrained eye could tell, might be workable, although rusted with disuse. 'It's all small-scale,' he now explained, 'must have once been horse-operated. Don't know if it can be adapted to modern ways or must be replaced. And what the cost. But I'm thinking that if someone who's experienced could study the workings of the mine as I uncover them, he could advise me what to do.

'Won't be much pay to it,' he said later when he had found the right way to interest Will, gently leading up to the subject by degrees, 'won't be much work either, not to start, but 'tis a job you might, like.'

He spoke softly, for he knew Will's mother was listening behind the lace curtains at the window and he didn't want to raise her hopes, or give her another excuse for fault-finding. 'And if you don't care to come to the mine, why, who knows, perhaps you could make models of the engine parts here, for me to look over, like.'

Richard had made the offer on impulse, and for a second, a flicker, caught a glimpse of interest in Will's eyes. It was enough to make him stay on talking of engines in general. In speaking of them, Will showed none of his now habitual vagueness, even managed to draw sketches on odd scraps of paper, neat little drawings that an amateur could interpret. It was enough to make Richard suspect that even if Will were not capable of a direct answer on his own behalf, might in fact never be capable of direct answers again, he might still be brought closer to a rational living.

In thinking this he was aware of a strange feeling, as if a burden had lifted, a double burden in fact, as if in coaxing Will into supporting himself, at the same time he was benefiting Em. He hadn't thought originally how close Em and Lily were, but now he did. In helping Em he would surely win Lily's good opinion. Suddenly he wanted Lily's good opinion more than anyone's.

Even Will's mother, guessing something good might result, made amends for her earlier outbursts by bringing out the pasties, accompanied with pots of scalding tea that burned the mouth and tasted like boiled leather, as if to show she had accepted him – all in all a success.

Not a bad day's work, Richard thought later, as he came slowly down the last part of the valley, having cadged a ride on a farm cart most of the way back. Two good results to offset two bad. But when the euphoria died and he added up the results of his efforts, in practical terms he saw he had made little gain. In practical terms, unless his mother had a deed, as he'd already written to ask, showing that the beach and cliffs and hut were hers, unless he could somehow find financial support, he was still under great risk. On the stone bridge at the valley's end, his gadfly, his tormentor, was waiting to point this out.

CHAPTER 9

'What happened last night?' Lily's opening was not exactly hostile, was not exactly pleasant. Nor did she look at him straight on in the way he had become used to. Her hair was undone and her hat hung crooked by its broken string and she was sitting by the stream, her feet bare, presumably dangling them in the water while she waited. For a moment Richard let himself imagine her toes, dipping and swinging so that the bright drops scattered. He watched her, watched the slender ankles, the rounded calves, said nothing.

'There're bruises on your face too,' she said, more directly now, 'like my brother's.'

'What did your brother tell you?' Richard wanted to show the same directness. 'Did he tell you his purpose in coming here? Did you tell him yours?' Again he said nothing.

She waited until he had crossed the bridge, then, leaving her shoes behind, came running after him, quickly catching up as if to emphasize his lameness. 'Aren't you going to explain? Aren't you even going to try? And have you got the deed? Em said she saw you in St Marvell. Was that why you went there?'

She burst out, 'Is that what you and Michael quarrelled about? Or was it over me?'

'No,' he said, exasperated. 'No and no and no, to all your impertinence. Ask no more. For I'll tell you nothing.'

He faced her squarely then, her flashing eyes, her expectant look, her half-open lips. He hadn't expected thanks, realized in fact that Em wouldn't even know yet what he had been hoping to achieve on her behalf, had been stupid ever to think of thanks, but hadn't expected this persistent attack in its place. He put out his hand to close Lily's mouth, then, again without knowing, bent down and kissed it.

'That'll do,' he said, 'that's enough from you.' And kissed her again.

Lily jumped back as if she had been stung or as if he had hit her. Her hand went to her face like a child when it has been slapped. Her cheeks flushed. Then she burst out, 'Michael said you would. Michael said you'd . . .'

'Take advantage?' Angrily he completed the sentence for her. 'Well, you can tell him from me that I didn't. You asked for it.'

He reached up, pulled out the key from under the loose tile where he hid it, unlocked the door. 'That's finished her,' he told himself. 'That'll drive her off. Back she'll run, telling tales. And won't they make the most of them. Serve me right.' Telling himself he was an idiot, he went inside, slamming the door shut.

The fire was almost out and the hut was cold. He slumped down in his chair of crates, feeling more disillusioned than the day in hospital when they'd told him he would lose his leg. For a moment he heard her outside, then the noise stopped as if she had gone away. Suddenly he felt too tired to resent her questions or her presence. And as suddenly his knee throbbed so it seemed to swell and fill the universe. All he could think of was holding still and letting it gradually revert to its usual numbness as if it were not part of him.

After a while he heard her again, putting on her shoes he guessed, before she slowly turned the latch. She was standing at the entrance, her body in its flimsy dress outlined so that all the curves showed. A leap of desire transfixed him.

'Michael said it was your fault,' she said.

'And do you believe him?'

She considered. 'No,' she said. She cocked her head. 'It seems to me,' she added, factually now, without any hint of accusation, 'that if Michael came looking for trouble and if you hit him because he forced you to it, then that'd be all right. But if you provoked him out of meanness, or boasted, as he claims, then it wouldn't.'

He heard his voice come out as if from a long distance. 'Those are fine distinctions, too fine for me. And anyway why should you believe me? I could say anything.'

'I'd know,' she said, her honesty painful. 'Some things can't be lied about. But you owe it to tell me.' She added, 'To yourself more than me.'

'I don't owe anyone anything.' He wanted to shout it but kept his voice calm. 'I can't be bought and sold. If you want to think the worst of me, go ahead.'

A long silence followed. He heard his words echo round the hut, like a challenge. She'll leave for sure, he thought. To his surprise she moved behind him, there was a clink of spoons. He found he was being offered tea, black as he had come to like it, together with a currant bun from the paper screw she had in her pocket. 'Em's make,' she said.

She herself took the old stool and leaned against the door, mug in hand, looking out over the bay. The sun caught in her hair like a halo. 'When my mother lived here,' she said slowly, 'I suppose she sat like this a hundred times. And your mother and Jeb, they'd have done the same. Until Jeb fell in love.'

She added defiantly, 'It wasn't her fault my mother loved my father first. If you knew him, you'd see why. And it wasn't her fault she couldn't marry your uncle. She never meant for him to drown because she couldn't love him back.'

He thought, And it will be my fault I suppose if I fall in love with you. I'd be a damned fool if I did.

'Mother's always telling me to be patient,' she said with a rueful smile. 'But when you want something it's as if it's got to be right now. It's hard for me to wait as you're doing. It must be hard for you.

'But you mustn't waste time,' she went on, 'you oughtn't to hide away. You can't live all your life like a hermit. You should get about, be seen, before my grandfather and brother spread word what they are up to and undermine your claim.'

He would have laughed if she hadn't been so serious; the thought of trotting round, cap in hand, explaining who he was, was so ludicrous. And yet what else had he been doing in St Marvell? Again he was silent.

'People'll be sure to talk about you,' she chided him gravely, 'there'll be gossip. I told you my brother won't take defeat easily, and neither will my grandfather. There're lots of events, meetings, things like that you could go to, speak out, get opinion on your side.

'I've written to my father,' she continued, almost defiantly, 'although Michael doesn't know that yet. I've explained we can hang on until his return, but I'm not sure when he'll be back. And I wonder too, if your mother, might she help?'

She clapped her hands together. 'There, I'm done,' she cried. 'But we're still in this together, we're allies, aren't we, after all that's happened? Except,' and here an uncertain note came into her voice, perhaps unknowingly, puzzlement tinged with curiosity, 'if we aren't, you don't have to kiss me to shut me up.'

He sensed she hadn't spoken as any other girl might have done, provocatively, coyishly, out of a desire to tease. Despite himself, he was amused by her and immediately felt better. 'I wanted to,' he thought of saying bluntly, 'and your asking makes me want to all over again, so look out.'

She had scrambled to her feet, brushed down her skirts, put the mug back on the table all with the quick flowing movements that he admired the more that they were so different from his own cramped scrabblings. 'You can still count on me,' she said. 'And,' now she did blush again, 'I don't mind about the kiss, really mind that is.'

He heard her running across the shingle to the bridge. For a moment he imagined running after her, leaping the little stream as once he could easily have done, catching up with her. And imagined, if he now tried, her turning towards him with a look of pity only part concealed. He heard another girl's voice say in another place, in another world, 'I thought 'twould heal without showing. I thought no one'd notice. I didn't think you'd be lame for life.'

What's the good of it, he thought despondently, what's the point? Even if I win against her grandfather, it's she who gains. Either way, I'm left with nothing. But he couldn't get rid of her like that. Up came her image, everywhere he looked, flickering along the walls, like one of those films they showed in the cinemas – Lily running, Lily smiling, Lily young and enthusiastic, talking about title papers and meetings with strange determination as if, like her grandfather, she would always get what she wanted. But I won't be part of that game, he thought; she needn't count on me, a tame pet. To trot out for show, to prove how tolerant she is. And smiled at the thought, although again reluctantly. For he knew she was right in essence, if wrong in detail, and that if he were to do battle he had better come out of hiding and make a stand, as he had already started to do this morning, but with more positive result.

It was perhaps significant that, after she was gone, for the first time in many months, years even, he unwrapped one of the few possessions that he still owned, one that Lily for all her prying would never have found, for he kept it hidden under a slate stone set in the chimney, in a sort of clome oven, used once by smugglers. It was old flute, formerly his father's. Its stops and bindings were of silver, its mouthpiece ivory, the whole wrapped in his father's red handkerchief. He sat for a long while rubbing it with a clean cloth, dusting and polishing it. Once his father had taken pleasure in playing it in the evening when work was done, the music satisfying some deep yearning. As in a way it did, for it was the reason why his father had come to know Beth Martin and playing it had brought him to the St Marvell Festival Lily had spoken of. Now Richard couldn't help wondering how it would sound if it came as accompaniment to Lily's voice. If his father had been here to play and Lily had sung, Polmena Cove would ring with music again.

Lily ran up the valley until her heart thumped so loud she had to stop. Again a hundred different thoughts flitted in her mind but she didn't want to think of them. Or she wanted to think of them all at once: her brother's enmity, Iris Duvane's complicity, her grandfather's ruthlessness, her parents' unfortunate absence, Em's unhappiness – all together or each in turn, anything rather than remember Richard Chote. And what he had just done to her and what she had just said to him.

She was ready to admit that from the start she had offended Richard Chote, had gone out of her way to be offensive. And Em had been right, her insistence on ownership of Cove had been self-centred and stupid. Now she sensed that her efforts to back Richard Chote, although well meant, were equally futile, and did not really help. If anything they made her look foolish and shallow, fighting Goliath with a sling shot. And she was not even certain Richard wanted help. She was sure he laughed at her behind her back.

Michael's original anger at her 'flouting' of his supposed 'authority', as he'd called it, had seemed a family matter to deal with in her own time. She hadn't really taken her brother seriously; would have argued that if anyone 'flouted' authority, Michael did, far more than she. But Michael's outburst last night had changed all that, had brought other things into the open, not least her own position, which she had never doubted before. To be a 'bastard', to be illegitimate, had never mattered if you never thought of it. But to be called so, to be so named with venom, had somehow cast a cloud, a shadow which even Em's sympathy couldn't clear. And then to hint at disgrace, to hint at illicit lovemaking . . . how quickly Richard Chote had picked up on Michael's warnings; how quickly he had fixed the fault on her instead.

And actually to have embraced her – I won't think of it again, she told herself, I'll imagine Michael's words unsaid.

The image of her brother's fury, the grossness of his suggestions, kept coming in front of her – the more she pretended that she hadn't heard or understood, the more she knew she had.

No one had kissed Lily before, unless she counted children's games at parties, furtive little peckings in the dark, too silly to be worth the counting. Not like this, a man's embrace, an angry man. She hadn't liked it. Or in one way hadn't liked it, in another she didn't know, she wasn't sure. 'You asked for it.' That was what she really needed to think about and was avoiding.

Before she reached the road she climbed over a fence, close to the spot where Michael had hidden, made herself sit down on the grass and think clearly. She summoned up Richard Chote's face, thinned by suffering, its angry look. He always looks like that when I see him, she thought, as if I make him angry. But it wasn't anger like Michael's. It didn't come from disgust, or loathing, certainly not from loathing of himself. And sometimes when Richard was talking, with Em and Will for example, he looked happy. It's as if he's holding something back, she thought, hiding something, nothing to do with Polmena Cove, some secret in himself. As if, even in kissing, part of him doesn't want to.

It was all very puzzling, Lily decided, sitting there, her skirts spread on the grass. Life was so much more uncomplicated when all she had to worry about was her daily chores, her excursions with Em, her singing. Again she felt her world veering away from its quiet, well-known routines, spinning out of control. She sensed if she didn't stop and turn it back she would be too late. Yet she couldn't stop.

Her fingers busied themselves among the daisies, tearing them to scraps of yellow and white. 'He loves me, he loves me not.' She found she was chanting the old nursery rhyme aloud, and resolutely put her hands behind her back, ashamed, as if she had been caught out in a game that she had not even known she was playing, as if she were really in love and were trying to find out if the love were returned.

I don't want to be kissed in anger, Lily thought. And for a moment she let herself slide into the other forbidden thought she was avoiding, what it would be like to be kissed by a man you were in love with.

'In love with.' The expression gave Lily the strangest feeling. To be in love was something she had never had much time for. If she had, she would have imagined it coming in a great burst of sound and light, like an organ playing in church and the sun streaming through the stained-glass windows. Or she would be standing on a hill, singing very loudly so that everyone would listen. It wouldn't come creeping up stealthily as she sat in a meadow and picked flowers.

She looked about her. The sun was still warm on her face, the honeysuckle on the hedge had not lost its fragrance: a yellowhammer repeated, 'A little bit of bread and no cheese'; bees hummed busily among the clover. Her being or not being in love would not alter any of these things. Yet already she felt and smelt and heard them with unexpected clarity. And a strange relief possessed her that at least in her own mind she had had the courage to frame a possibility which certainly would alter everything – if it were truly so.

But, and here came a second revelation, suppose Richard Chote felt as she did? He might not admit it either. And further to that, and now there was no stopping her thoughts, they leapt ahead even to where she did not want them to go, suppose the first condition of love was not dependent upon the second; what happened if only one loved and not the other, what would it be like if both weren't in accord?

There's no way of knowing that in advance, Lily thought, not without a touch of wry humour, only time will tell. Just as Em says. Once more Em's stoicism surprised her. She knew she'd never be capable of stoicism herself. And in realizing that came close to admitting that perhaps she and her cousin shared more of a difficulty than they knew, both in love with men who, through no fault of their own, might never love them.

*   *   *

117

Iris was being equally philosophical about a completely different subject but for related reasons. 'I disagree,' she was saying. 'The Club shouldn't just be for fun.' She blinked, trying to look serious herself, a new image. 'We should allow the public in for debates and discussions.' And to Hugo, who was openly laughing, 'They've set up a committee and asked me to join. I'm to take the chair and organize it all. We're sending out posters, and inviting everyone to attend. It'll be a great chance for the locals to find out about us, and see we aren't so bad.'

'What locals?' Hugo pretended to be so overcome he had to wipe his eyes. 'The village women who do your washing, the carpenters, the gardeners who keep down the weeds on the Club driveway? They're not interested in debates, they only like your money. Besides you don't really want to "know" the locals, you want to study them. You won't ask them to dine, or dance, or become your friends. Except for one,' he added, 'if he's still going strong.'

She ignored him. It was partly to make sure she was too busy to see Michael that she had joined the Club's recently formed Round Table Discussion Group and had volunteered her services. But she wasn't going to tell Hugo that either. And when he now asked dryly what the first topic of discussion was, although he already knew, 'Well,' said Iris brightly, 'some of the Clubbers are always on about hunting and shooting, don't you know, how much they're against it, so we thought that would be the best thing to start with.'

'Especially since you know nothing about it and are never here in hunting season,' Hugo interrupted. He laughed, again struck a pose. 'Iris's Anti-Hunt Debate. Roll up and spout nonsense so that the local Cornish will change their ways. Particularly those whose livelihood depends upon it.'

He sank back into his chair, crossed his legs and picked up the Wadebridge newspaper where Iris's latest venture was given prominent notice. 'You do the daftest things, Iris,' he said. 'What does Polleven say?'

'Oh, he's agreed to be one of the speakers on the hunting side,' Iris said, not very convincingly, airily enough for Hugo to put down the paper and say in his shrewd fashion, 'Odd way to start being a country farmer's wife, I'd think. If he really is going to marry you. Or rather, if you are really going to marry him. But an amusing prospect,' he couldn't help adding, spurring her on, 'life's never dull where you are, Iris, even if misguided.'

Iris put on her little girl act and flounced away, refusing to listen. Hugo could be so irritating, she thought, you never knew how to take him. She wasn't going to confide in him that things had started to go wrong, she wasn't going to have Hugo say, 'I told you so.' Besides she enjoyed the publicity her new venture gave her. Even more she enjoyed the slightly bohemian tinge of impropriety at being the lady in charge. ('Look out, old boy,' the male elders of the Club now daily said to each other, ever so jokingly, 'here's Miss Duvane on the warpath.' They winked at each other, winked at her; one even tried to pinch her bottom.)

The tiff between her and Michael had gathered momentum after her visit to Nanscawn Farm, not because of the visit itself, she thought, although the sister had been such a bore, nor because she had enticed Michael into spending the night with her, but because Michael had been involved in some fist fight (which he refused to talk much about and she assumed he'd lost). She'd also assumed the fight had been about her, and instead of being pleased, had found she was annoyed. In turn Michael'd begun to sulk. Michael balky, Michael in a sulk, was a new phenomenon, not to her taste or liking.

Then too Michael's role as lover had become burdensome. It had been fun at first to do the seducing, to teach him things he'd never learn if she didn't show him; induct him into sophisticated habits that simple country girls wouldn't even know the meaning of. Now his clumsy pawing, which in the beginning had attracted her, seemed inept and his possessiveness (which at first she'd called 'sweet') appeared juvenile and cloying – as did his lack of caution and demands that they spend every moment together – to say nothing of her own growing awareness that he was of course still under age and neither his father nor grandfather had yet heard of her. In short she'd become tired of having to baby him along, and his insistence on marriage, in spite of her growing lack of interest, appeared both monotonous and childish.

For Michael's part Iris supposed the quarrel wasn't serious, could soon be mended if she cared to make the effort. For her own, she was growing bored and, as Farell had so often pointed out, an Iris bored was more dangerous than a runaway cannon. Hugo's right, I'll never marry him, she thought. And with a rare trace of honesty, he'll never marry me, he shouldn't.

Things, as she would have called it, between her and Michael came to a head when she asked him to be one of her main speakers – as a hunting farmer he'd do perfectly. I can easily persuade him, she'd told the other committee members, smiling to let them know how she would go about it. She was more than annoyed when Michael had immediately dug in his heels, saying he'd not be made look a fool.

'You're avoiding me,' he'd said. 'You're using this as an excuse.' He positively frothed disapproval. 'Hunting's a necessity.'

'It's fun for you,' she matched him, her eyes sparkling ever so brightly out of their blue shadows. 'But not for the foxes.' And, with a pout, 'Not for me either, if you aren't there on the platform to make my meeting go with a swing.'

If, once she'd got her way, if, once Michael had agreed, she didn't make a pet of him as he expected, if after his capitulation she didn't pat him on the back and tell him what a good boy he was, this was not only for her own fickle pleasure. She was discovering a sad fact: that holding a man just by smiling a little at him was as dissatisfying to the woman as it was demeaning to the man.

She herself distributed leaflets to all the neighbouring villages, driving from one to the next in Hugo Farell's little sports car, with a great deal of unnecessary laughter and shouting, only tapping Hugo sharply for impertinence when after a final bout of chauffeuring he'd said, 'I'll go along with this now, but you won't find me pandering to your vanity on the night as that poor weed Polleven does.'

The posters were pinned up, flapped in the sea breezes, tore eventually into shreds without rousing the interest or enthusiasm that the Club committee and Iris had come to expect. In fact no one really took notice of them, too busy with their own affairs to pay much attention. Only two outsiders attended. One of these was Lily.

Lily came for a purpose. She'd admitted to impatience; even more she disliked being idle, especially when she overheard Michael confiding in Em (as Michael often did these days, emphasizing his estrangement from his sister).

'Grandfather's only waiting for legal approval,' Michael had said, boasted, 'then he'll serve Chote a writ. And after that, he's already got surveyors on tap to measure for the road. We'll start with the road; it's most important. But we don't need the Clubbers, we'll do the financing on our own.'

Michael's talking big, Lily thought, just to impress Em. I don't believe a word. But whereas the old Lily would have rejoiced at the delay, the new Lily worried what might happen next and what she could do to meet this new threat. Shy about going down to Cove again, half aware of her own feelings, she felt self-conscious at interfering a third time, a new sensation. When she also heard Michael tell Em about Iris's meeting and his refusal to take part (although not about his change of heart), it suddenly came to her that she should follow her own advice to Richard, that is, go herself to see if she could interest the Clubbers in Richard's cause.

Lily had never been to the Club, although in the beginning Michael had once or twice tried to persuade her. When she also heard Michael complain about Iris, and saw the money Em offered him to replace the wages which he'd 'lost', she felt even more curious about Iris and the company she kept. The chance to see what Iris was like, on Iris's own territory, without the inhibiting presence of Michael himself, was too good an opportunity to miss. If she was hoping to persuade Iris's friends into saving Polmena Cove, if she hoped to convince these rich up-country folk of Cove's fragile beauty, even to curbing their own designs on it, she kept all these possibilities to herself.

Unlike Lily, Richard came to the meeting by accident. Left to himself he would have shunned it like the plague. 'Out of practice with crowds,' he would have said. But Lily's advice to him to go out and meet people had also struck a responsive note, and perhaps the truth was he was growing a little tired of being a hermit. It had occurred to him that he had confided more in Michael than he had ever in Michael's sister, and that didn't bode well for the future. He'd have liked to confide in Lily – if he could only have trusted her! In a strange sort of way his encounter with Michael Polleven and his subsequent visit to St Marvell had broken some reserve in him. He no longer wanted to be alone; when he was alone he thought too much.

He didn't hear of the meeting, or Michael's non-part in it, until he actually had come to the Club and by then it was too late to back out. And he would never even have gone to the Club at all, never have been invited, had he not taken himself into Bodmin one day on the pretext of consulting a mining engineer.

He brought a sack full of his best ore samples and, after a satisfactory discussion in a mining office, and a promise to look the pieces over, went into one of the local pubs, again something he rarely did at the best of times and not at all since coming to Polmena Cove. The pub itself was simple, a working man's pub, and, after a careful checking of his finances, he bought a pint of beer, warm and strong. He drank it slowly, listening to the other men.

Times were hard, they were saying, Cornish miners always the first to go. Mines were closing, Redruth and Camborne'd be ghost towns if something wasn't done. And what about the clay-workers, starvation money – he heard there a warning note for himself and was chastened. Suddenly he saw a face he recognized, although for a moment neither knew the other.

'Dick!' Hamond shouted. 'By God, Dick Chote in the very flesh.' Throwing his arms about him he said to any who would listen, 'I spent a night with this fellow once, caught under our own fire. The last time I saw him we were both in a shell hole, up to our knees in mud. And if I'm alive today, by God, it's because he talked me out of dying.'

He beamed with memory. 'And what didn't we talk about, all night long, eh? What subjects didn't you think of?'

Hamond was a cheerful middle-aged man, prosperous. He'd gone back to London after the war, was in overseas trading, buying and selling, he was vague on details, had come to Bodmin on a work-related prospect, only by chance had slipped in for a drink before toddling back to the coast. 'Done well enough,' he said now, with a broad wink, 'well enough to bring the family down to Cornwall and take a holiday villa.

'Several of us meet,' he confided, arm still companionably about Richard's shoulder, 'in the Club of an evening. Plenty of us old warriors about you know, keep together, talk over the past. And by golly we're having a gathering next week. You'd be more than welcome.'

If he noticed Dick's shabby appearance, if he noticed the limp, he was too tactful to mention them. But as they ate and drank, he insisting on Dick's sharing a meal with him, gradually he drew out Richard's story and commiserated. 'Rotten luck,' he said, 'not fair, life, is it. Come to the Club and meet the other chaps and talk about it with them.'

He gave another wink. 'Kill two birds with one stone,' he said, 'if you'll pardon the expression.'

So it was on the night of Iris's 'Panel Discussion', the parties mainly interested in Polmena Cove converged, unbeknown to the others, in the most unlikely of settings, to take part in the most unlikely of discussions, organized by the most unlikely of people.

CHAPTER 10

he evening of the meeting was wet, a first blow. Many of the Club ladies would never venture out through rain. Then, although Michael had arrived early as promised, he seated himself at one side of the room, burying his head in a newspaper, ignoring the other speakers (middle-aged females, slightly eccentric), in such sulky silence it didn't take imagination to guess he wasn't about to give the touch of class or liveliness the discussion desperately needed.

The meeting was held in one of the Club's new rooms, another potential source of trouble. The walls still smelt of fresh wood and paint and the chairs were upholstered in black leather reeking like a butcher's shop. Iris had appropriated it from its strictly male possession without real permission and in the hall outside a few men loitered, a group of what Iris's set called the 'Home Guard'. The arriving audience had to run the gamut of their uneasy patrolling, the war veterans morosely discontented at being displaced from an area they considered theirs.

As things turned out, despite the weather, despite that unwelcoming honour guard, attendance was more than adequate, mostly Iris's set, escorted by men who had nothing better to do, leavened by a sprinkling of older matrons who liked the prospect of an evening out within the safe confines of their little conclave. When Lily arrived there was still room for her to slip into a back corner, almost unnoticed. But Iris noticed her. How dowdy she is, Iris thought, as she waved gaily, like a fisherwoman in her old-fashioned hat. She patted the frill of her own short skirt complacently, knowing it was the height of fashion even if not yet paid for. I should have known Lily was there for some purpose, afterwards Iris admitted with something of a shudder, I should have known she boded no good.

Lily could not have seen Michael behind his newspaper, and Michael himself apparently did not see Lily. Only at the last moment, having folded his paper away, did Michael join Iris and the other speakers, positioning himself at the far end of the table and keeping his gaze fixed glumly on his boots. Nor did Iris point out Michael's sister to him, serve him right if there's trouble, she thought. She meant trouble in the future, in the privacy of their farmstead, the last thing she envisaged was a public family squabble – again in retrospect she shuddered.

The opening hour had come. The newly installed gas-lights were dimmed. The audience grew silent, prepared to be amused. As Iris began her introductions, there was a commotion, a swelling noise beyond the doors which a Club servant was endeavouring to close. They burst open. Lights came on again, heads swivelled. Members of the 'Home Guard' were seen pushing their way in, tiptoeing exaggeratedly with a great scraping of chairs and loud apologies as they found themselves seats and displaced original occupants. Squashed against a wall, Lily watched them; like a herd of bullocks, she thought, loud and boisterous, intent on showing who were masters – and proving that all intrusion should be properly challenged, as they now meant to do to their own satisfaction.

Among them apparently was some stranger – his back was turned, Lily couldn't see who. Introduction still seemed in progress, hands were shaken, names exchanged, the stranger apparently the man they must have followed into the room. Not someone from the Club however, the audience now whispered among themselves, an outsider, surely one of Iris's locals she had been so anxious to ensnare. And a working man, perhaps not exactly 'suitable', as his old army coat, rough shirt and hobnailed boots clearly indicated. Eyebrows were raised.

The men filled a row, a solid phalanx of them, and their settling in effectively drowned Iris's opening remarks, not the best of starts for a would-be public speaker. But even in this emergency Iris's sharp eyes spotted Lily's quick look at the stranger – and Lily's little smile, quickly erased. 'They know each other,' Iris thought, and later, much later when it was too late, 'She must have persuaded him. I knew it was her fault.'

During the first part of the meeting this thought nagged Iris, although soon there were other worries more pressing. The speakers were dull, much duller than she'd feared, and Michael Polleven, for all her prodding, remained dumb. The audience, politely attentive in the beginning, became restless as Miss Starkey chirruped once more about her 'Sweet little birdies,' and Mrs Lester cried, 'Tally-Ho, a-hunting we will go,' not even funny the first time. When someone muttered, 'This is hopeless,' Iris agreed. Suddenly one of the men stood up.

Even in the dim light his shoddy clothes marked him as the 'local' who should have come to be impressed, who should have had the courtesy to remain meekly silent – as now the lady speakers showed, nodding their heads and whispering. Only Michael leaned forward, his shoulders squared.

Iris tried to take control. 'Questions from the floor will be accepted later,' she said severely, in her best chairwoman's voice. 'Don't have a question,' came the soft Cornish reply, 'I've a statement. And my companions here have asked me to say it.

'I've been listening to you talking,' the man continued, 'begging your pardon, you're way off mark. How many of you have killed things living? How many of you have killed a man?'

There was a gasp. 'Look at us,' he said, ignoring it, 'those of us who were in the war. Killed off in our millions. We've had enough of killing.'

There was another gasp. An older Clubber protested, 'I say, that's hard.'

'Count the numbers then,' the other retorted. 'Add up the names on the war memorials.' As the murmurs died away, 'If men are capable of slaughtering each other, why should animals and birds matter? We can kill even more of them.'

Iris gritted her teeth and tried to smile. Grin and bear it, she thought, he won't let go. Only slowly did it dawn on her that the audience was now captivated; even Michael seemed to pay attention. She and her speakers quite ignored, she gave up calling for order, turned expectantly to the local, the misfit, the peasant, who was telling them what they wanted to hear – or didn't want but pretended to because it had become the fashion, because it was the 'in' thing to do.

He was grasping the chair rail in front of him, shaking it gently as he spoke, to the consternation of the rotund lady who occupied the seat. 'Millions of us died,' he repeated, 'keeping this land safe for children. Nothing wrong in that. But who'd want children in a world of steel and mortar, where no living creatures move?

'Isn't only hunters,' he went on, his thin face suddenly enthused with energy, 'hunters are the tip of things. What about your builders, your destroyers of fields and ditches, your ruiners of the Cornish countryside? The place here used to be a beauty spot, just look at it.'

Now he's lost them, Iris thought, now they'll take offence. And in truth once more heads swivelled, faces frowned, whispers spread. Uncertain what to do next, she hovered, torn this way and that. Only the 'Home Guard' muttered 'Hear, hear,' and clapped loudly, drumming with their feet.

With a screeching of wood on metal, Michael Polleven shoved the table forward and started up as if to charge the audience. 'Blackguard!' he bellowed. 'He's no business here. What does he know about property and buildings, he's a squatter on my land. And he's no soldier. Look at him, he's much too young.'

He must also have spotted Lily, for his next broadside was aimed at her. 'I suppose you're proud you brought him!' he shouted. 'Fool that you are, you deserve each other.'

His final insult caught Iris where she was most vulnerable. 'Show-off,' he told her, 'you and your stupid little meeting. If you hadn't been in such a frenzy, he'd not even have heard of it.'

Iris gaped. Never in her life had she had such a talking-to. The two main speakers retreated to a corner, there to be comforted by friends. The audience began to break up in disorder, flustered ladies fumbling for bags while their escorts searched for coats. 'So who let him in?' Michael was saying, his voice heavy with sarcasm. 'I thought this place was private.' Only the veterans didn't budge.

'Private for us, old boy,' Hamond shouted. 'Our room, our guest.' He was ready to be angry, his fists clenched. 'If you don't like it, remove yourself,' he went on, 'we don't need you here. As for Dick Chote, he's a war hero, come to Polmena for peace and quiet. He doesn't need a little squireling stealing it away from him.'

A buzz of fresh gossip erupted, swelled. Polmena, Polmena Cove, was repeated so often there'd be no forgetting the name, nor the implied injury done to its owner. The tide of opinion swung again. 'Poor boy,' Iris heard one lady say, 'it's scandalous. Our soldiers deserve better than that.' Faint-voiced, Iris adjourned the meeting, the vote of hasty thanks lost in the hubbub and, the last to leave, the 'Home Guard' withdrew in battle order, taking Richard Chote with them. And that was how the evening ended, a scuffle barely averted, Michael Polleven goaded into speech of the wrong kind, the rest of the audience united, for who among them was so cruel as to contradict one of 'our dear boys'?

By the time the hall was cleared Michael Polleven had stormed away and Lily Polleven had vanished. Richard Chote and his friends had also disappeared, presumably into those masculine recesses where even Iris didn't dare venture. Iris was left with the humiliation of Michael's words and the wreckage of failure.

Michael had indeed stormed off, striding furiously away into the wet darkness, sure he had been deliberately made a fool of. But Lily waited in the bushes at the end of the drive where Michael used to leave his bike. She had not expected either Michael or Richard; despite the effect upon her brother, she was delighted Richard had come. Having heard him speak, she felt she knew him better than ever. She wanted to tell him all her thoughts, and coax him into confiding back. She saw this moment as a heaven-sent opportunity, a chance to meet on neutral ground. He couldn't accuse her of interference, she couldn't be suspected of ulterior motives, they would meet once more as friends. I want nothing more than that, she told herself firmly, friendship is all I want. She knew she lied. What she wanted, hoped for, longed for, was that Richard would reveal his feelings.

Richard took his time. When she saw him coming down the drive, she wondered why he had lingered, especially if he knew she was there. But she resolved not to question, simply slipped out of the bushes and caught up with him on the road.

'The devil,' he said, surprised. 'You're out late. I thought you'd gone with your brother.'

'You did see me?' Lily tried not to sound hurt. She'd never have stayed if he were waiting. 'No,' she said, 'Michael and I are still at odds.' She smiled through the rain. 'But we scored a point tonight,' she added, falling companionably in step beside him. 'We had an effect.'

'As if we're playing Ludo.' Richard sounded tired. 'As if we're playing games. What I spoke of wasn't a game, for scoring points off anyone.' But it will count, Lily thought stubbornly. Again uncharacteristically she held her peace.

'Took your advice, you see,' Richard was continuing, his tone at its most sardonic. 'Didn't mean to mind you, it just happened. Went out, met an old pal, accepted his invitation. Just to talk over old times, he said. And damn me, at first when I came into his Club I thought I'd really become a hermit.'

He gave a laugh. 'Couldn't get words together, felt a proper chump. Then when I did begin to talk, look where it landed us.'

'But what you said tonight made sense.' Lily was determined to be positive. 'People paid attention, just as I hoped. They'll take up your cause.'

'I prefer to fight my own battles,' Richard said shortly. 'And damn what I said tonight. Shouldn't have opened my mouth.'

He walked on in silence. 'Never meant to mention Polmena Cove,' he said. 'Just wanted to say what I thought about the war. Don't know why. Don't even know why I came at all, except meeting Hamond brought back a lot of memories. It's tempting to remember, feel you still count, show you haven't lost the knack.'

'What knack?' Lily couldn't help asking.

He didn't answer. She thought, leadership perhaps he means; she remembered how he'd led the way and the others had followed him.

He said, 'It's something I learned in the war, and thought I'd find in peace. But I haven't. I resented that. So there's a confession I'm not proud of.'

He stopped still again. 'But I never imagined you or your brother would be here tonight. He'll think it was done deliberate. Damned foolish to have stirred him up.'

Lily looked at him, puzzled. She hadn't seen it that way at all. To her thinking, it was Michael who had made the stir. She started to say, 'What does it matter?' when he interrupted her.

'We can't live down what's been said,' he was saying. 'All in public for the world to hear. We don't need scandal. Or I don't and you shouldn't. So we'd better part. Don't you be seen walking with me, or talking with me, don't come down to Cove again, nothing. Go home and forget.'

Forget me, is what he really means, she thought.

'I can't do that,' she said.

'Why not?'

He sounded fiercer than she'd ever heard him, almost ready to strike out at anyone within reach. Suddenly afraid of what she might say and what he might say back, she began to babble: the importance of keeping Cove intact, her interest in it, their joint efforts . . . 'Rot,' he interrupted, sounding very young, almost as her brother used to, 'that's nothing to do with it.

'It's you,' he said. 'What you build it up into. What you want; what you're afraid of; what's good or right for you. I can't cope with your wants. For myself I really don't care. But don't you condescend to me. I'm tired of your condescension,' he said, equally fiercely. 'Years of it. I'm tired of there being one side with it all, and the other with nothing, as if we're serfs divided by the Middle Ages. So you can tell your fine friends and your grandfather, your brother, yourself for that matter, that what I do or say to keep Polmena Cove is my own affair, for my own pleasure, not yours.'

It was the longest speech he had ever made to her. It burst out from him, overwhelming Lily. But the worst of it, the irony was that it wasn't what she wanted at all. She'd wanted him to confide, but not confidences like these, in as rude and abrupt a way as possible, as if determined to show her all his faults and weaknesses at one time, as if determined to show how little he thought of her, how small his regard.

Furtive tears came to her eyes; she ignored them. 'Go on by yourself then,' she thought of saying in return, 'go on without me. See if I mind.' She did mind, more than mind, she couldn't comprehend. It seemed to her that, whereas a moment before she could almost smell and taste happiness, now she teetered over a precipice she hadn't even suspected beneath her feet.

'There,' he was saying, awkwardly, calming down, 'don't take it so hard. 'Tisn't the end of the world. Run home and make up with your brother.'

131

'I can't,' she said, 'I've told you that. But don't pretend I'm like him. It isn't where a person's from, it's who he is when you're in love with him.'

Afterwards she heard each word she'd said stand out like granite stone. They made a great cairn. And there was no unsaying them.

'Love, is it?' he was saying, softer still, 'love, is it, Miss Polleven? How can you speak of it? Between you and a lame man, without house or fortune, only a strip of beach and derelict mine – if they'll let me keep either, that is. Your parents would be outraged if they even suspected it and your grandfather would call out his hounds to tear me to bits, so much for anti-hunting laws.'

He was trying to make her laugh, but she couldn't. 'And you're dreaming,' he was saying. 'Daydreams that girls like you have time for. Put them out of mind as well. I've no room for love with anyone.'

She heard him stalk away, his heels tapping fast along the road, as if to emphasize his lameness. She thought rebelliously, but it won't be the end, I shan't let it be. He'll come round. She was remembering what else Em had told her: 'You can't change a man by wishing. You can't make him love if he doesn't want to.'

Em was taking advantage of her cousins' absence to visit Will Pendray and had spent most of the evening listening to his mother's string of woes, longer than a trawling net. The two ladies, young and old, sat primly on either side of the fire while the rain spat and sizzled down the chimney and the wind soughed through the slates, a good 'sou'westerly', the old woman called it.

Em herself was content to let Will's mother do the talking. Behind her, at the table, Will himself sat hunched at his work and paid no attention. Bits of machinery were spread in neat piles across the newspaper covering; the floor was littered with tools he had been using; bolts and nuts he had unscrewed were arranged in jam jars his mother had collected. 'Look at it,' his mother said, her mouth working a little in pride, 'never seen the likes. How he knows where it all goes is beyond the likes of me.'

Will didn't hear her, lost in his own tinkering. And that's better than cowering like a frightened animal, Em thought. She contrasted Will as he was now with how he had been only a few weeks ago, two months at most, when she had first seen him, newly out of hospital. Even in profile his face had filled out, had lost its haunted expression, had lost its bone whiteness. She knew he kept himself busy in the garden, had set up some sort of open shed, where he sat building models of pumps and machinery, clever little models that really worked. For use in Wheal Marty, his mother had recently boasted. She didn't boast of that today.

'No sign of letting up.' Mrs Pendray was not speaking of her son's condition, was meaning the weather. 'Look at the coal we'm using, should have lasted to the first part of next winter, not burnt up afore August. Bad luck for the Festival, that's for sure.'

Somehow she made it sound as if the shortage of coal and the worsening of the weather and the approach of the Music Festival were all part of the same story, and all Em's fault. Em pretended not to understand, merely nodded and let Widow Pendray continue her spiral of gloom – the rent now, there were rumours it was to be raised, how was she to pay it, a poor widowed woman with no support.

Here she cast one of her sharp looks at her son, but as he was still bent over his work only Em saw it. 'The Polleven steward were here the other day,' Mrs Pendray went on. 'From the estate. "Hear your son's back home," he says, "hear he's been working with that fellow Chote up at the mine."'

'I'd have kept quiet but Will pipes up, explains he works at home, won't go underground, and all the while the steward's writing of it down in his little book. Been to see your father too, I 'spect, but 'twill be all right for him. No Polleven steward's after making trouble with the Trevarisks, not if they knows what's good for them.'

'Course 'twas Sir Robert Polleven's man,' she explained, emphasizing the name. 'Many of the cottages belongs to Sir Robert, ours among 'em, worse luck. Sir Robert won't take it kindly that we'm allied with Richard Chote. Not when Sir Robert's so set on ousting him.'

She let that thought sink in. 'Don't understand it myself,' she went on, 'don't see the sense of it, what's so special about a strip of beach? But there won't be many others that stupid to support Chote if they wants to keep on Sir Robert's good side.'

When again neither of her listeners made any comment she added, 'Course if your cousin's in with him, Lily Polleven I mean, that's different for her too, I suppose. But Will'd never have met Chote if she hadn't lured him there.'

Em felt her cheeks flush. She didn't know how to defend Lily, certainly not in Will's presence. She knew Lily had seen Richard again, perhaps often, although Lily never said and she didn't like to ask. I know it isn't the way to behave, she wanted to tell Will's mother. Lily shouldn't persist; she shouldn't go pestering Richard Chote. But it's no more than that, a childlike interference. There's nothing between them.

She suddenly thought, I hope there's not. Bad enough Michael misunderstands Lily, Richard mustn't. Not only for Lily's sake but for Richard's own. I like Richard, Em thought, as Mrs Pendray's voice droned on. He's been kind to Will. He deserves happiness after all his troubles. Lily can't make him happy. She won't know how.

At the same time Em couldn't help feeling sorry for Lily. And sorry for Michael. They both looked so unlike themselves, forlorn, she'd have called it, turning the house into a morgue. Lily wouldn't explain her troubles but Michael had confided his. Iris was everything to him, he'd said. She remembered how he'd said that once about his other loves, about his horse, his hounds, the farm itself, but she hadn't the heart to point that out.

I've enough problems of my own, Em thought now,

as Widow Pendray's voice crossed and recrossed her consciousness, then drifted away like some sea current. But that would never enter Michael's mind. Nor Lily's either. They'd never imagine how it is for me, torn between them and worried by their flouting of common sense. Poor young things, she thought, I feel responsible for them, and I don't want to be responsible.

Before Mrs Pendray could dig deeper or question more closely, Em stood up hastily and reached for her coat which was draped on the back of a chair. 'I'd best be off now,' she told her hostess, not giving chance for further prying. To her surprise and delight, Will put his tools aside.

'I'll walk with you a spell,' he said, almost as he used to do in the days before he had first left the village. ''Tis a dirty night to be abroad.'

He nodded to his mother. 'Leave the coal bucket by the door, I'll fill it on my way in.'

As they went down the street together Em had the strangest feeling that time had reversed itself, as if all the days of painful wondering and hoping and despairing had come together in a rush. She tried to beat down the feeling, for fear it should end in disappointment, crossing her fingers as children do when they want to ward misfortune off. This actual offer to walk with her was the first sign since his return that Will had the slightest interest in her, or even really acknowledged who she was. In the arid desert of emotions where she had been existing, even so small a thing as concern for the weather or a coal bucket revealed great possibilities.

It's been so long, years, Em thought, since we even walked like this; the last time was the night before he left, when we promised to write and he asked me to wait for him. Half ashamed, she wondered if he remembered it. Why don't you ask him, Lily had urged her. Lily might but Em never would.

When Will spoke, she thought perhaps he did remember after all, for he said in a wondering sort of way, ''Tis mortal strange to me, Em, that these streets, these stones underfoot, these cottages and the people in them haven't altered at all since I've been gone, seem to stand waiting for something, I don't know what.'

He stopped and looked down at her, his shadow in the lone street lamp tall against hers. 'And you're not different,' he said. ''Tis only me that's changed.'

She wanted to say, 'But you haven't, Will. Underneath you're the same.' She wanted to protest eagerly, 'But it doesn't matter. I can change with you.' Wisely she said nothing, recognizing in some way that it was better to have him speak than interrupt his train of thought. And recognizing too that what he was fumbling to put into words was perhaps the most important thing he'd ever said.

'I feel as if I've been gone on a long journey,' he was saying, the words faltering as if he still had to search for them. 'There, don't know if you can understand that for a man who'd only been up to Devon for the wrestling, going across to France was a trip to the moon. And being there was moonlike, having nothing to do with earth. Earth was left behind, like now, like I used to dream of it.'

He said, 'And now I'm back 'tis as if my feet can't walk on it, they sinks through to ash. And I'm like a shadow, like that shadow there on the road, with nothing of me in it – don't they say there's no weight on the moon? And for all of mother's yattering, for all this work I'm doing for Richard Chote, I'm not back in myself. My hands seem to be doing things of their own accord, as if I can't control 'em. Can't explain it except to say 'tis as if I'm sitting outside watching my head breathe.'

He took a great gulp of air then, said simply, 'But that doesn't help you much, does it? And I'm that selfish, talking of myself all the time.'

He said, 'Just don't leave me, Em. For in all that darkness there were only one light, like at the end of a tunnel, that I would come home and be with you again. And if, or when, I go on from being a shadow back to a man, and I don't know if I can, I don't know how to make myself begin, if it isn't too selfish, if you aren't against it like, I'd appreciate it having you waiting at the other end.'

It wasn't much, it wasn't the world spinning in circles, yet Em felt as once Lily must have done when Lily had shouted, 'Isn't it great to be alive!' Em wanted to reach up to Will, promise him anything, promise to keep him safe. She didn't do any of these things, it wasn't in her nature. But she took his hand that was hanging at his side as if all the energy had drained out of it, and holding it tightly promised that he need have no fears of her, she'd wait.

And so she left him, striking out up the hill, turning at the corner to make sure that he had gone back to his mother's cottage. She took the inland road towards the farm. The rain might drip, and on the upper reaches, the wind might lift and sting her face, but she never felt a thing.

Iris was angry. Iris was humiliated. She'd make Michael pay. Whatever she did, Michael would be seen to be at fault. Avoiding her companions who were waiting to gloat – and reiterate Michael's insults under pretence of commiseration – avoiding any social gathering in the Club's bar, Iris hurried home to ask Hugo's advice.

Iris tackled Hugo directly. No need to hide. His mother had been one of the ladies present and would soon return full of the story. She found her cousin at his favourite occupation, smoking on the cane-backed sofa in the so-called conservatory, an unopened *Punch* on the floor beside him and the lights off. For a while she sat unnaturally quietly, watching the rain stream down the panes and the scrawny aspidistras sway in the draught from the ill-fitting windows. Then she told him what had happened, bracing herself for sarcasm.

'You wanted success.' Typically Hugo took pleasure in being perverse. 'And success you've got. Thanks to you, dear cousin, a nice fat scandal on a plate, a veritable feast. And two facts for the rest of us to chew over, good pickings for a shilling.'

And when she asked him, pretty please, to elucidate,

'Why, Iris, two facts that anyone with common sense and possible interest in Polmena Cove ought to be aware of.'

He wasn't teasing now, was deadly serious. 'One, your betrothed's sister, or should I say former betrothed, seems to be over-familiar with Chote, and that'll cause a nice in-family squabble, daggers drawn all round, war to the hilt. Michael Polleven'll never have his sister involved with someone he thinks beneath her, or rather beneath his own idea of class. And two, now Chote knows what the Pollevens want, won't he fight them just. In business parlance that means trouble. Development won't go forward as easily as we've been led to believe.'

He drummed with his fingers, suddenly interested. 'And then there's Chote himself,' he added thoughtfully. 'He won't leave easily. Chote may be a simple sort of fellow, a former shoemaker, so they say, but there must be something to him. Look how the "Home Guard" rallied to his standard. Suppose he does own the place? Suppose he thinks of developing it himself, to his own advantage, he'll find backers. You say the Clubbers were smitten with him. I tell you, Iris, if I were in the way of betting, Chote's the man for my money. He may have the staying power the Pollevens lack.

'Just the type to attract attention,' he added, reverting to his more sardonic manner, 'especially with the ladies. Dark and mysterious and exciting. Look out, Iris. Little Lily may have found the bargain that you've missed.'

Iris never mentioned her chagrin nor her desire for revenge. Too clever for that, she simply shrugged, saying with a smile, 'Well, that's the way things go,' when during the remainder of this rough evening Mr Farell Senior found fun in teasing and Mrs Farell oozed sympathy. Her brain was busy with ideas of how she could pay Michael off and get even with his simpering sister. So when Sir Robert Polleven approached her, she'd no hesitation in listening to his offer. Not for his ends of course, but for her own.

*   *   *

Sir Robert seldom left the Manor. Only events of great importance lured him out; had he Zack, his old retainer, bring in the horse and polish the brass. Seated in the pony trap, bowling along the Cornish lanes, in his top hat and frock coat he looked what Richard had called him, an anachronism. Since first he'd talked with Michael he'd not been idle, had been occupied with renewing personal contacts, diminished by the war and increasing age; had begun to put out feelers to find financial backing, writing letters, making telephone calls, 'getting in touch', he called it, with old friends. Making a survey of his rents and income he'd begun to count his personal assets. Pleased with his progress on these fronts, now he was intent on two other related projects where personal presence would prove essential.

The first of these was going badly. He was seated in his solicitors' office, beneath those frosted windows which for Richard had symbolized obtuseness. All should have been clarity today, the glass washed so that the partners' names were clearly visible, the chair on which he sat dusted, the table cleared of papers except for one large chart over which Messrs Treful and Lurkin now hovered. But the fools he paid to do his business were obviously stalling.

He raised his stick and poked at the map. 'Look at it,' he said testily. 'There's no mention anywhere of Polmena Cove. Only the old name, the real name, Polleven Bay, written plain as a pikestaff.'

Again a jab with his stick. 'To my mind proof positive. Forget the beach, I'm not stupid. I know tidal property belongs to no one. And I don't suppose Chote lives in a hut half under water. I'm talking of land. Of the entire cove, the valley above it, all the Polleven land in fact, along that stretch of cliff.'

The map he was referring to was old, tattered about the edges and yellowing along the seams. It too had been dusted off, its edges flattened by books, laid out for Sir Robert's inspection. In great detail it showed the one-time boundaries of Polleven property, including farms and fields and coverts, now sadly out of date. Large parts of the map had been crossed out and boundary lines erased. Words like 'Leased' or 'Transferred' or 'Sold' had been scrawled in various handwriting, some entries long before the present century when most of the actual sales occurred.

Treful, the senior partner, shifted his spectacles and gazed at Lurkin. What a jumble, the look said. The interpretation of the map – the redrawing of it to mirror present facts, the locating of primary buyers and subsequent ones, the searching through deeds and records of land conveyance – would be the work of months, not weeks. And so Sir Robert understood the look. He rested his chin on the silver handle of his cane and glared.

'Alas, old nomenclature counts for little,' Lurkin took up the burden of explanation, spoke soothingly. 'A change of name might actually strengthen an opposing claim. Take Wheal Marty for example. Because of its name are we to presume the Martins own it?' He laughed at his little joke.

Sir Robert was showing impatience. 'And what of the mine?' he asked belligerently. 'It's within my boundaries, it's on my cliffs. I assume I own it since no one else does.'

Again Treful looked and Lurkin spoke. 'Again, alas, being on your cliffs (supposing of course that you still own the cliffs) does not automatically make it yours. If the mine is still in use, then a court of law would probably give possession to the man at present working it. Or mineral rights may have been granted separately. And if you look carefully at the map, Sir Robert, as indeed we have been doing,' (here a faint reproach came into his voice) 'you will see that the boundary line along the cliffs above the mine is marked in such a way as to suggest erasure.'

'Fiddlesticks.' Sir Robert's snort of derision was final. 'In my lifetime there's been no sale at Polleven Bay.' (He stressed the name defiantly, hanged if he'd give it the new one.) 'And, unless a complete idiot, no one's likely to give it away.'

He began the slow business of getting up. 'If that's your

final word,' he said, 'I don't pay through the nose for nothing. I'll take my business elsewhere.'

A third time the partners exchanged glances. Neither wanted to offend the old man. On the other hand the matter was a complex one, at the end of which dangled money. Of two tactics, prevarication or speaking out, the first offered better pickings.

'Perhaps.' Suggesting all kinds of possibilities, Lurkin allowed his voice to trail off, letting his senior, Treful, take over. 'No need for pessimism,' Treful now said. 'With your permission, Sir Robert, we'll make a search. There may be villagers who, for a fee, will swear to Wheal Marty's closure; some may even remember the former owners; we'll have depositions made. But to our mind, more work is needed to sort out estate land, still owned, from land sold, given or deeded away. Nothing can be proved or disproved until that's done. And so we told the other claimant.'

Sir Robert didn't like the expression 'other claimant'. Nor the cunning way old Treful slipped it in. If Treful was thinking of pitting Sir Robert against Chote, then the devil take it, Treful had already been given instructions. He'd been told to show Chote the door, he'd been told to shut him out. Best make sure, Sir Robert thought, best underline that as far as I'm concerned Treful and his toady work for me.

At the entrance to the inner sanctum he paused for one last thrust. 'I expect results. I want the deeds of Polleven Bay prepared. As for the mine, if St Marvell villagers balk at helping, remind them I can always raise their rents. My steward's already been round once; I can send him round again. Times are hard,' he said, his own voice hard, 'cottages are not easy to find. Nor is property like this.'

For the final time he tapped with his cane upon the walls. 'You'll never find an easier roost on such easy terms.'

That should make them trot, he thought, as he came out into the daylight. That should make them jump. Damned if they'll get the better of me, for all their legal twaddle. My grandson won't be robbed if I can help it. As he climbed into the pony trap and Zack took up the reins, he thought again of that grandson and what he planned for Michael's future. And Iris Duvane wasn't part of it. And so he meant to tell her, in this second of his encounters to which he now gave his full attention. Iris Duvane was nothing but a fly-by-night, a woman on the make, a conniver and a harlot whom he'd have no trouble in buying off and saving his grandson from a serious mistake.

If he remembered how he'd once tried to buy off another woman, if he thought of Jenny Trevarisk, that was so long ago his failure had faded with memory, and wouldn't have mattered anyhow.

Iris had chosen the setting. Might as well get a free meal into the bargain, she thought. She'd made sure to arrive early, sat in the bar of the Majestic and thought how nice it was. Nicer than the Club for sure, as nice as the London hotels she frequented, very posh. She gazed round with satisfaction. She liked the banks of mirrored lights, she liked the chrome and glass. She sipped her drink reflectively, her back turned to the windows. Below them the grey expanse of sea heaved and swelled but she wasn't aware of it.

Her first thought on seeing Sir Robert was how like Michael he was. Give Michael white hair and a white moustache, straighten his back and narrow his eyes, there was the Polleven image intact. She had a moment's fancy of a line of Pollevens stretching back to 1066 and almost giggled.

She even liked Sir Robert's clothes. And the way the waiter hurried to take his hat, like being at an opera. Funny old duck, she thought, as he joined her. But he didn't take her hand, or kiss it, with old-fashioned gallantry, as she expected and as he ought to have done. Instead, the studied formality of his greeting didn't deceive her, nor hide his contempt. She strengthened her resolve.

Sir Robert was as direct as Lily. When he spoke he didn't mince words, earning her grudging respect. But he wasn't as clever as he thought he was, as Iris soon found out.

'I'm Sir Robert Polleven,' he said, heavily correct, 'Michael Robert's grandfather. You'll understand I've Michael Robert's well-being at heart, he's as dear to me as my own son.'

That's a lie, Iris thought, he hates Michael's father. She tapped her fingers on the table top and began to enjoy herself. But when Sir Robert added, 'In his father's absence I feel responsible for him, he's young of course,' as if being older she'd understand, as if in fact he had already estimated her age, she wasn't so pleased. Damn his impudence, she thought.

'You're said to be fond of the country,' Sir Robert went on. He didn't offer her a drink, although her glass was empty, sat up very stiffly, arms not touching the table, like some ghastly Victorian prude, as if, she thought, he's afraid of contaminating himself, as if I might do the contaminating. 'But we expect you prefer the town. No doubt, for all concerned, it would be better if you returned there. And as we're sure you'd expect something to cover the expenses, we're prepared to offer that.'

He thinks of me as a whore, she thought, one of those worn old London bags that hang about the back streets. And what's this 'we' he's so fond of using, as if he belongs to royalty. For a moment she was tempted to tell him to go to hell. Then she saw the funny side.

'Depends how much, doesn't it, dear,' she said, lighting a cigarette and blowing the smoke carefully through her pursed lips ('Just like a doxy, a real hoot,' she told Hugo afterwards, in a carefully edited version, in which Sir Robert was made a fool and her reactions were displayed to best advantage).

When he felt in his breast pocket and produced a cheque, the amount took her aback; it was more, a great deal more, than she might have expected. She hadn't thought he was prepared to go that far, in fact she hadn't thought he was well-heeled enough to pay such a high price to keep the Polleven blood line clean.

Before she could decide or even put out a tentative hand,

he coolly pulled the cheque back out of reach. 'We don't give something that large for nothing,' he said, 'we expect something in return.'

That surprised her. She stared at him. 'Aren't I giving up your blessed grandson,' she almost said, 'aren't you getting him back intact? Or almost intact.'

'By all accounts Richard Chote's a country bumpkin,' Sir Robert was continuing, suave as silk. He didn't explain who Chote was, he expected her to know. 'He'd be easy pickings.' He didn't say, 'For someone of your experience,' but he suggested it, actually patting her hand where it lay on the table. 'We'd like to find out what he's up to.'

Iris took a deep breath. 'Let me get this clear,' she said, matching coolness for coolness. 'You'll pay me to give up your grandson if I spy on Richard Chote. But suppose I don't like spying? And suppose your grandson owes me something? There's breach of promise, you know. He did promise me marriage.'

Sir Robert began to tremble. He ran his hand beneath his collar as if it were too stiff, and his scraggy neck seemed to swell, like a turkey cock's. 'Don't bandy words with me,' he said, his voice shaking. 'Do you know who I am? And don't even think of blackmail or you'll regret the day you came into this county. We know what your morals are.'

He looked more than ever like his grandson, thrusting his chin forward petulantly, his face heavy with anger. So that's who Michael copies when he doesn't get his own way, Iris thought, that's why everyone's afraid of him. But his grandfather has no hold on me like the poor creatures he lords it over. 'And don't you bully me,' she told Sir Robert. 'I don't like bullies.'

She lit another cigarette, fitting it into her holder, at her most confident. While he spluttered she began to think. She knew she was not good with money, was always in debt, would have to scrape in the bottom of her beaded purse to find enough to pay for the drink Sir Robert obviously wasn't going to buy for her. It occurred to her now, not for the first time, how nice it would be to have access to money and enjoy all its benefits.

The idea of spying on Richard Chote, for whatever reason, was certainly distasteful, but she'd no personal interest in Chote or his quarrel with the Pollevens. And she didn't like being taken for a whore, albeit a well-paid one. She'd better luck with men than that, she didn't have to stoop to having them buy her favours. But if she wasn't squeamish she could take the money and afterwards do or not do with it what she wanted. It was then that Hugo's comments came back to haunt her. 'Lily Polleven's found a bargain.'

Suppose, just suppose, she thought, Richard Chote's capable of doing all that Michael boasted of, he certainly looked 'interesting' and 'fierce' enough when he disrupted my meeting. If he does own Polmena Cove and does become rich, Lily doesn't deserve to have it all.

Tracing her thoughts out in lines on the polished table, she began to paint a new picture which would keep her busy and give her a new interest. If she did what the old faggot was asking, gave up Michael and turned her charm on Chote, when Chote left Lily – Iris smoothed her skirt complacently, a country bumpkin'd be no match for her – wouldn't that be a nice revenge! She began to smile. It suddenly struck her that she'd been offered payment to do what she actually wanted, make Michael suffer and get Lily jilted.

'I'm not up for buying,' she said to Sir Robert, calling his bluff. 'Nor spying. Hold tight,' she added when he again began to bluster. 'That's not to say I won't work for you, I don't mind finding out what someone's like. But if you want me to give up your grandson, after all we've been to each other, pay me what you offered, without further questioning, and there's an end to it. You can put a stop on the cheque if you like,' she added contemptuously, for she thought such bargaining beneath her, 'so I can't cash it until you're satisfied I've done what you asked.'

('I almost told him to forget morals,' she added to Hugo, with another giggle, of course not mentioning the money or

145

her acceptance of it. 'I'd have liked to see his expression when I said I don't have any. As for giving up Michael, he could have offered me the crown jewels to keep him, I wouldn't have cared.')

It was only when the old man had fumed hatless out of the hotel in his agitation, leaving his cheque on the table, and she was congratulating herself on her cleverness, that the last final way of showing up the whole lot of them also occurred to her, although she tried to put the thought aside as quixotic and foolish. It's not for me to make the Polmena Cove venture succeed or fail, she told herself sternly, only to ensure the Pollevens don't benefit. The new thought wouldn't go away, lingered the more she tried to push it under. And it would truly make the whole adventure exciting, would truly make it 'fun'.

CHAPTER 11

Unlike his grandfather, Michael Polleven wasn't thinking of the future. It was the present that filled his waking moments. Although the marks left by the fight had disappeared, the effects of them still lingered. As did the way Iris seemed to have dropped him like an empty glove. He didn't yet know of his grandfather's efforts on his behalf, they would have driven him mad, but he did feel Iris's rejection like a personal affront.

Unwilling to return to the Club after that disastrous meeting, fearful of ridicule and openly hostile to his sister, Michael had buried himself once more in farmwork, nominally seeing to the repair of ditches in Barrow Meadow. It didn't help.

The field was long and narrow. It rose from the stream to a stand of ash trees crowning an oval mound of earth, the barrow which gave it its name. There he had taken himself at midday, supposedly to eat his sandwiches. Below him on the western side of the field, the old ditcher, Arlie Rowet, was still working steadily, methodically moving along the boundary with his spade. He'd not stop to eat until he was finished, only taking a gulp of cold tea from time to time.

When Michael had been a child his father had told him that the barrow was a grave where some ancient Celtic chieftain had been buried. It had always been one of his favourite places at Nanscawn where he used to dig for buried treasure, but today he thought nothing of that. After the rains of the previous week, the fine weather had come back, but it wouldn't last. From this high position he had a view across fields towards the strip of sea, already lost in mist. Clouds were beginning to mass on the horizon and his head ached. There was a heaviness in the air like the mutter of thunder and the flies were biting, always signs of change. And the way the ash leaves trembled he knew the wind was backing to the west again, another indication of trouble. Tied by the gate, his pony flicked its tail and stamped.

The rain wouldn't come yet, Rowet said, 'twould be fine 'til St Marvell's Festival. They was always lucky with the weather then, Rowet said, never knew it otherwise. Damn the Festival, Michael thought, damn the weather. In his thoughts all was dark and storm.

He turned and lay on his side, pillowing his head on his hands. When he was a boy, centuries ago, he had always looked forward to the Festival. He'd loved the carnival atmosphere, culminating in the music at the week's end; for years his father had been a sponsor; until his old battle charger died, always used to ride it at the head of the opening parade; this year Michael had planned to take his father's place. Had planned also to escort Iris, another opportunity to impress her with Polleven influence. But something had gone seriously wrong.

These days Iris was never at home. When, greatly daring, he telephoned the Farells' bungalow, Farell replied. Iris did not answer any of his letters, or at best sent a single postcard saying she was 'off visiting'. Visiting who? Where? There were no answers. It was as if Iris had cut him off, root and stem. He groaned.

Even before he had had his first falling out with Iris he had sensed her steely disapproval, once held in check, now turned on him. But what had he done to merit it? If he'd lashed out at her, surely she'd known he was jealous, jealous because he loved her. Suddenly all the suspicions he'd had of Iris flared.

What most tormented him was the memory of her sexual freedom. He'd never imagined it in a woman. Thoughts of her naked body over his, lithe and agile, brown with north-coast sun, made him sweat in anticipation, as if he could never have enough of it. He could feel the smoothness of it, he could taste its warmth. Yet conversely its coolness excited him even more, like a pool, deep and mysterious. She had seduced him, he couldn't deny that, but what did it matter; seduction added to the excitement. He groaned again.

'You'll never find a Cornish girl to give you this,' she'd laughed at him. He knew it for truth. She had spoiled him for any other woman, and seemed to get pleasure from the knowledge. Yet he knew in all his years, even if he lost Iris now, even if he recovered from that loss, she would haunt him. But he wouldn't lose Iris, he couldn't.

But, his thoughts wouldn't keep quiet, what if Iris never came back? He would drag through life, like a man sucked dry, like a . . . like a . . . he fought for the image, a dry husk, another William Pendray, doomed to waste away. And all because of Richard Chote's interference; all because of Richard Chote's good impression at Iris's meeting, where he himself had failed. Anger rose in him thick as bile.

And then there was his father. He knew how displeased his father would be. Julian Polleven might not say much but he would look volumes. 'I trusted you,' his look would say. This flurry of activity today wouldn't hide neglect. The sheep hadn't been dipped, there were fences down, his promise to repaint the stables hadn't been kept. Again he burrowed his face in his arms. He'd been so proud of being left in charge, he'd had such plans.

His reverie was broken by Rowet's shout. The old man was standing peering down into the ditch, leaning on his long-handled Cornish spade. As Michael started up, Rowet turned to wave his cap to attract attention. Damn your impudence, Michael thought, leave me alone.

Reluctantly he came out from under the shelter of the trees into the open heat where the glare of the sun made his head ache even more. All about him was a haze as if the sun had sucked the moisture up; he felt sweat break out as if he were in a Turkish bath, and his boots slipped on the baked earth. He plunged down the hill, the yellowing grass coming loose in tufts.

Rowet was staring down into the ditch which here ran beside the hedge, choked by parsley and meadowsweet. Where he had cleared the ditch, the soil still showed signs of damp; ahead of him long grasses still covered it. 'Look here,' the old man said. Carefully he held back the grass, poking with the triangle of his spade so that Michael could see an opening burrowed into the side of the hedge above the ditch, a neat opening with used bedding spread out at one side. In the damp earth leading to the hole claw marks showed.

'That be the sow's work.' Rowet bent down and touched them. 'Here and here.' He pointed at a flurry of scratches. 'Don't know where she's gone, but the little 'uns'll be inside. Creatures of habit, use the same hole or sett for centuries; follow the same pathway at dusk, along this yere ditch to the stream.'

He eyed Michael as he spoke, an old country hedger, at heart a kindly man, knowing nothing of fancy arguments for or against animal hunting, knowing nothing of sophisticated reasons for animal preservation, accepting by instinct that nature takes care of its own. If stories of Michael's new girlfriend, or Michael's disgrace, had filtered down he'd never mention them. What would he care about such new-fangled ideas? But he'd remember Michael as a boy and what such a discovery would have meant to him.

'Let's have them out.'

Michael watched as the old man deftly cut through the overhang of the sett with his spade, the triangular blade and the extra-long handle designed to keep stooping to a minimum, slicing through work that those claws had taken years to build. Back the dry soil peeled, like an apple pared, until the whole thing was opened and the cubs lay curled in their primeval heap at the bottom of a tunnel.

Despite the aching in his head, Michael looked at them curiously. He'd always wanted to see a badger's sett; it had been one of his boyhood wishes, old Rowet would remember that. The cubs mewed, squirmed, helpless in the sun. He should tell Rowet to cover them up again.

Suddenly he heard Chote say, 'What do you know about killing?' He heard himself say, 'He's no soldier', and Hamond's retort, 'Dick Chote's a hero.' The words seemed to arch overhead. They concentrated the aching in his forehead to where the cut that Richard Chote had given him had almost disappeared. As if the sun were blinding him, he saw a crimson glare like the glare outside Chote's hut; his head swelled as it did when he'd had too much to drink.

'Bloody things,' he heard himself say in a voice he didn't recognize. 'Get rid of 'em.'

And as Rowet hesitated, 'Go on, kill 'em, or I'll do it myself.'

And, snatching the spade from the old man, he laid about him with its sharp edge until there was nothing left alive.

Down in Wheal Marty Richard was also hard at work. Or trying to work, trying also to forget everything else, putting Lily Polleven out of his thoughts as he had put another girl in another village, years ago it seemed.

It was not the knowing of the girl that mattered, there was nothing to it, a young man's dream. But when he had come home she had taken one look and turned away. 'Can't marry you,' was all she'd told him, but he'd known why. Well, she couldn't help it, but it had helped drive him from his village to live in exile. And her disgust was what made him leery of other women, what at bottom made him suspect Lily.

Richard had told Michael Polleven mining fascinated him, and it did. He had not added that the more he struggled with it, the more it taxed his ingenuity, the more he proved that a lame miner was not handicapped, was not disgusting. He swung with his pick again. 'Stupid,' he told himself. 'Lily's not like that. She told me so.'

He knew he'd been reticent with Lily. It wasn't her fault. If he'd driven her away, he had only himself to blame. But it wasn't only his lameness that held him back, there were his emotions. He didn't want them to show again. He picked up his pick, tore the rubble loose, swung a second time. One thing he could be sure of, he thought, Lily would never understand how secure he felt working underground. Certainly Will Pendray wouldn't, although perhaps before the war Will Pendray might have shared the same feeling.

For Richard it was like being in the trenches just out of gunfire range, burrowed down snugly, a rabbit in its warren. The weight of rock overhead, now so terrifying to William, he thought, wrapped you round like a blanket, gave a sense of protection that only war could enhance, as if no harm could come to you, as if nothing could find you, as if you were safe.

In the intervening weeks since he had told Lily he would see her no more he had regretted his words, cursed himself for a fool. As he cleared out the entrance tunnel to the mine, inching his way towards the entrance of the first shaft, some twenty feet beyond, he felt that every swing of his pick hacked at his own stupidity. Passing through the rusted tangle of tracks and winches he'd told himself that was what he was, a tangle of indecision.

He shook his head, forcing himself to the task in hand. The shaft he had come down was as perfect as the day it had been cut. As was the gallery, or adit, to which it led, where he now was working. This gallery slanted gently uphill away from the cliff face, its floor carefully paved, its walls shaped like a beehive, domed and fluted. Lily would have liked looking at it, he thought, would have run her fingers along its edges, would no doubt have given him a lecture about ancient Greece and the tombs of Mycenae, in her own fashion confirming his impression how old it was.

The mine was deeper and more complex than he had first thought, another proof of how old it was. When he paused and let the slide and shift of the stones settle, sooner or later he would catch the sound of water slushing, a rush of sand and pebble as the tide receded somewhere deep in the workings. And the quality of air was too good for there to be only one entrance, although there was no sign of another entrance on this side of Cove. If the other opening were on the far side of the headland, then the mine must be very much larger indeed. One day soon, he must make the effort to look at it from the outside; if he could get an oar he'd take Will's boat out, and row around, close enough to scan the cliff.

He tapped the ceiling tentatively. As he worked his way along, he'd found the original stone roof had given place to rougher workings, shored up by wooden supports which had rotted in places. He'd have to think of a way to haul replacement timbers up from the beach, perhaps using the neat little pulley which William Pendray had designed in miniature – and which Will had promised one day to come and show him how to build. 'But how will you get rid of the rubble,' he could hear Lily's question, 'where will you put the rubbish when you've finished?'

For the present the rubble, such as it was, was stacked out of sight, behind great boulders seemingly placed there for that purpose. On the outside, the only trace of his labours was the brownish-red colour of the stream which now trickled among the bracken down the cliff, to lose itself in the rocks at the foot. He had managed to unstop a large pool which had become dammed up inside the entrance, but whether the stream originated from that pool or drained from some other source he wasn't sure. He'd come to suspect there was another gallery, higher than the one he was working on, perhaps between it and the entrance level; the water may have come from it, but he hadn't found it yet.

He knew drainage was one of the greatest dangers in a mine; wherever you went, water accumulated. He couldn't rely for ever on self-drainage, and he couldn't be sure that it worked efficiently, especially in wet weather. He needed Will to design him a pump. And he needed the money to build it with.

The sound of a pump's thumping and groaning was the first thing to prove a mine was in operation. One of his books had mentioned a pump whose noise was so strong it reached from Trethurgy all the way down to St Austell. He'd ask Will about it. If Will could come up with a model of a neat windlass pump, even a 'rag-and-chain' sort would do, perhaps he could afford to buy it. Or even better, perhaps somehow Will could piece a pump together from the old pieces of machinery that were left over, then the sound of the Wheal Marty pump would tell the Pollevens he was in control.

Ahead of him the gleam of the lamp caught a thin tracing of reddish rock. When he put his hand to it he could even feel its warmth, like fire underground. He had told Michael it was only a question of following the veins of tin and copper for which this mine had been worked for so many years, of letting them go on until they revealed their secrets in all their plenitude. But that was idle talk. If there were a sort of Midas touch for tin or copper he wasn't sure he had it, wasn't even sure he'd recognize the ore when he saw it or be able to distinguish it from other related rocks like quartz. He'd had no formal training and the books he consulted were more confusing than helpful. The letter from the assayer in Bodmin he'd visited had been encouraging but vague, for who could tell, even if there were a vein, how long it would go on for or if it were worth the digging out . . . but it wasn't that letter which now burnt a hole in his pocket, which made seeing Lily Polleven more of a necessity than he wanted to admit.

With a gesture of disgust he threw down his pick again so that it stuck in the ground. All his fine gestures, his farewell speeches, what use were they when they only hid his own sensitivity about his limp. But what his mother had to say made it imperative he have dealings with the family he wanted to despise because he was so sure they would despise him.

With typical female logic Beth Chote, born Beth Martin, had by-passed the essential questions he had asked her. Instead she went back to the beginnings, her own and her brother's, and before them to their mother who had first lived in Polmena Cove. Only by slow degrees did she come to what he wanted to hear. 'Our hut was a rough place in those early days, I believe,' Beth wrote. 'My mother chose it, poor soul, to hide her shame. At least to hide shame as the outside world would deem it, the outside world which condemned and abandoned her.'

Beth's writing was carefully formed, the 'a's and 'o's wide and rounded, just like her speech; the uprights by contrast stiff, crossed neatly or looped. It was clear she had taken as many pains with the actual wording of the letter as the forming of the letters; he heard her voice in the lettering, not the words. In speaking she would have said, 'My Mam called us love children, 'tis a pleasanter name than what they used to shout after us.'

He knew about that of course, it was no secret. But what else she'd written he'd never heard before. 'My Mam didn't marry,' Beth Martin continued. 'Couldn't. The man was already married himself, with a Devon wife, important folk, her family matching his. They say she was delicate, spoiled, always wanting to be the centre of attention; always off to her childhood home, leaving her husband alone. She didn't want, and therefore didn't have, children. It was a barren marriage, a loveless marriage, a sham.

'The man was a gentleman farmer, cousin to the Pollevens, without much money or land of his own but having the same name. He must have called on the Polleven relationship, had to, else he couldn't have done what he did.

'I think he was a good man,' Beth Martin wrote. 'He wanted to do right. I've never seen a picture of him but I have of my mother. She must have been beautiful when she was young. When she came calling at the back door with milk he noticed her. He began to take pains to be in the kitchen or barnyard when she was expected, began to watch for her coming, waited for her in the woods.

'It wasn't her fault,' Beth wrote firmly. 'Nor for that matter his. My mother told me once he doted on her, would even

155

have left his wife if my mother'd let him. What land he had was part of the main Polleven estate, he couldn't give it away. But he could ask the head of the family, Sir Robert's father, and bargain with him. "Give me something for her," he must have said, "or else the world will know." And so she got Polmena Cove.

'There was no need of bits of paper,' she added, 'no deeds between him and my mother. I don't suppose she even thought of it, and probably he wasn't able to. But he wrote her often, not love letters as you'd think of them. They were ordinary letters, like those a man might write his wife, about the hay and cattle, and the losing of a dog, about what her children did, and how they got on, things like that. When I was born he gave her the hut; when Jeb followed, he gave her cliffs and access as birthing gift, well, people didn't think of the value of those things in those days. When, after that, he died, no one took them back again, nor even tried. I was born in 1858,' Beth wrote, 'when Sir Robert Polleven would have been over thirty – old enough, you'll say, to remember who I was and who my father was – more than old enough to have stopped what happened at the time – had he been at home. But he wasn't. He was overseas with his regiment, was a soldier like his own son, Julian; was stationed in India. When he came back it was over with. It was Sir Robert's father,' she wrote, 'who must have closed his eyes to what was going on.'

She had sent the other letters in a separate package but he hadn't had the heart to look at them yet, other than a casual glance, all those closely packed pages a half-century old. He thought, so it wasn't my old miner who fathered my mother after all. And didn't know whether to be sad or sorry. For the man who had been his grandfather had been a Polleven, although dead also these forty years, and whatever gossip or scandal dead with him. And he was Sir Robert's second cousin, whether Richard liked it or not. And again whether Richard liked it or not, Polmena Cove had once belonged to the Pollevens, just as they claimed.

It wasn't to his liking to have to reveal this fact. He didn't want to be beholden to the family he was set against. The problem is, he thought, the thing that eats at me now, is not whether I own or not, but whether I have the right to own. 'As for me,' his mother had written, 'I leave it up to you. You are the only one who has gone back there, I trust you to act for us. But one thing I will say, although I've bit my tongue for years. To my way of thinking, Jenny Trevarisk, she who now is Mrs Julian Polleven, destroyed my brother Jeb, took him and threw him away like a piece of wood. If Jeb was the rental price the Pollevens exacted, then they've had more than enough. So if it happens that you meet with Jenny's daughter, Lily, well, I named the girl when she was born, and nursed her like my own child. But I don't want her to destroy you neither, nor make you part of their rental price. Not set you up and drop you down because you aren't good enough.'

She isn't fair about Lily, Richard told himself rebelliously, for once in his life at odds with his mother. Contrarily he ignored the fact that the warning was exactly what he had himself been afraid of. As far as he was concerned, things were much more simple – he hadn't wanted to like Lily, had sent her away. Now he had changed his mind and wanted her back. But he wasn't going running after her, no good would come of that.

So he worried, like a dog with a bone, if he should see Lily again – and how to arrange it so it didn't seem arranged. He could write – she might throw his letters away or her brother might intercept them. Suddenly he'd had enough of letters to last a lifetime. He could go to her home – she would slam the door or her brother would, and he wouldn't blame them. And how to get there, how to get anywhere with one leg shorter than the other and nothing but his old army clothes . . . had he but known it, had he but realized it, like Michael, like Lily, even like Iris Duvane, he was fretting over something of minor importance. In a microscopic Cornish world avoidance rather than rendezvous is surely the difficulty.

CHAPTER 12

ike her brother, Lily had buried herself in her old life; practising for the St Marvell Festival gave her something to do. She had been singing in the Festival since she could remember, as a child, as a schoolgirl, and now, after the lapse of the war years, as a young woman, the leading soprano in St Marvell's Women's Choir. She had little formal training, took part like many of her fellow Cornish from sheer joy. But somehow for her, this year, the joy had gone. She had to force herself not to think of Cove, not to wonder what was happening there, not to question her brother about the progress of their grandfather's schemes. Pride wouldn't let her see Richard again, not since he had warned her off – like Michael, like Richard himself, she found no pleasure in pride.

The contest songs were ones she knew; she should have liked singing them. Now she had shut herself up in her bedroom, sheets of music propped against the pillows. As when she was a child, the black symbols seemed to lie trapped between black bars, waiting to be freed into sound, but she couldn't concentrate on freeing them.

Her bedroom was square and old-fashioned, like all else at Nanscawn, opening on to the sheltered side of the house. Abandoning all pretence of practising, Lily leaned on the window ledge, looking into the garden she had shown Iris, created from a barley field by her mother, in the first years of marriage. The beech trees along the hedge were old; their tops swayed to and fro, their leaves rustling. The lawn they shaded was cut to velvet shapes. I've known this view for twenty years, Lily thought; I've known this room, and never really wondered what they meant. Could I live without them? Are they so important?

On clear days, if she went to the other side of the house, she could see the headlands on either side of Cove and the strip of sea caught in between. Somewhere down there lives Richard Chote, she thought, without clutter, pared down to essentials, like an otter, neat and clean.

For the first time she realized what discipline, what restraints, were needed to exist in that austere fashion. And what strengths. My mother must have known them too, she thought, she didn't start with comfort. It was only as she grew older that she spread into this luxury. She wasn't like me, beginning with luxury, moving to restriction. Half daringly she let herself wonder what living in the hut would be like. She had seen the inside in summer; what of winter? What of days like this when winds blew? Presumably Beth Martin had managed, so had Lily's mother, could Lily? Uncompromisingly honest with herself, she admitted that she wasn't sure.

But Richard would be there as companion, Richard would have to offer her the choice. He might never make it. She blocked the thought. As days had passed without his presence, she had tried to feel indifferent, had learned not to speak of him, not to mention past events, not complain. In a house which once had bubbled with her enthusiasm, her reticence seemed unnatural. Like her brother, like her cousin, Lily was learning new balance, alternatively borne up or plunged down as hope or despair fought for dominance.

Part of her still hoped for reconciliation with her brother – she had not known hate before. I've been too sheltered, too inward-looking, she accused herself, too prejudiced. If my mother is part of those 'lower classes' Michael despises, well, so are we, her children. It doesn't make me feel inferior. Why should he?

Wearied by introspection, another novelty, Lily drew back from the window. Catching a glimpse of her reflection in the old oak mirror, she saw no difference from the Lily who had first spied smoke at Polmena Cove. Yet she knew she was different. If my cheeks aren't white, she mocked herself, pinching them to give them colour, if they aren't lined and drawn, if physically I haven't pined and wasted, well, I don't suppose girls die of love. And if conversely now it's Em who seems younger, if by contrast I have grown quiet, it's not that I've aged exactly, only become wiser. But what's the use of wisdom, she thought rebelliously, it's not wisdom that satisfies me.

Down in the dining room Em was polishing the table. She liked the feel of the old wood; she liked dabbing the polish on and then rubbing until the surface shone. She was thinking about the Pendray cottage and like Lily making comparisons. Not so much about the furnishings or her possible adjustment to its more humble surroundings, that didn't bother her a scrap. She'd no pretensions about her own background. But she did think about Will and his mother, supposing that Will would ever ask her to be mistress of the house, and his mother would still be alive. She wondered how Mrs Pendray would take to another woman in the little cottage where she had always been in charge. And how she herself would feel in the company of another woman who so far had shown such little liking.

But that's perhaps her way, Em told herself. Lots of village women are like that, their bark worse than their bite. It's only Aunt Jenny who never has a sharp word, who never bites back. But when Aunt Jenny was young, when life was hard on her, perhaps she was forced to be harder, when Uncle Julian was a prisoner so far away.

And that's what Will is, she thought suddenly, a prisoner. Locked in his mind. If I could find the key to open his prison, he'd be himself again.

The week of the Festival dawned fair as usual. The early events proceeded as scheduled: the opening ceremonies on the Monday, when the Vicar and Methodist minister climbed through the village to the war memorial; the races on Tuesday, which Jack Trelethy, the butcher's grandson, won. On Wednesday the young men of the village climbed a greasy pole suspended over The Cut, fell in and were fished out with elaborate regularity. Thursday's tea and carnival, with its decorated milk floats and flurry of children in costume, came and went without incident. By Friday, the first evening of music, rain was already falling. The wind had freshened, flattening the grain. Out to sea white horses galloped, bringing the surf in with the tide.

Faced with unprecedented disaster, the organizers of the Music Festival had to work fast. One of the reasons for St Marvell's popularity was its open-air theatre, an overgrand name for the hollow shell cut in one side of High End Field. Now the area was hastily draped with canvas in an attempt to shield competitors and audience, the canvasing borrowed from the local army camp.

The theatre was very old, perhaps of medieval origin, used originally for Miracle plays and mimes. More recently it had served as a pulpit for preachers, of whom Wesley had been the first. Its seats were of rough stone, covered with turf; the stage, constructed afresh each year, was of wood, braced with wooden scaffolding; from a distance the whole formed a vague half-circle, like a pagan amphitheatre.

Its acoustics were also famous, another grand name. There were those who claimed the quality of sound was as good as any in London. Whether the slope of the hill produced this clarity, or, as was also claimed, the effect came from grass on granite, the many basses and baritones, the sopranos and contraltos who came to St Marvell to sing in competition never forgot the village saint's affinity with music and swore it was the special blessing of his martyrdom – endured to the playing of a reed pipe on this very tract of land.

Friday evening was devoted to the women singers, Saturday to the men. As Lily and Em now hurried towards High End Field, the wind whipped at their hair and skirts,

161

and the rain blew in their eyes. Rain or not, in normal circumstances, Lily would have been dancing on air, would have been tugging at Em's arm to look here, look there. Now she hurried on towards the makeshift tent, lost in reverie. How different it would be, she was thinking, if I'd never met Richard, if I was as I used to be. Or if I knew he would be here to listen. It seems wrong somehow to be doing something that has been so important in my life and not having him to share it with. She scarcely looked up when Em said, 'It looks dreadful, like a barracks. Even the hydrangeas have wilted. Where will everyone sit?'

She was referring to the canvas now spread in a large khaki circle, and to the participants, who since late afternoon, as soon as they could get away from work or home, had been arriving, on foot, by bike, in horse-drawn carts and in charabancs. Some of these ladies had travelled a great distance. Now they huddled in mackintoshes under umbrellas, practising. In spite of much unnecessary clearing of throats, their voices rang out in harmony, while, as if in counterpoint, their male supporters also joined in, the male voice choirs for which Cornwall is most famous. From various wet corners, discordant sounds rose as cornets and trumpets vied with tubas and trombones against the constant drips.

'Well, at least you'll be dry inside.' Em kept up a running commentary, although she was talking to herself. Lily wasn't listening, and as they climbed over the stile from Nanscawn fields into High End, she could see her other cousin, hanging back so as to seem not part of them. Poor Michael, Em thought with a sudden pang. He's in a bad state, as bad as Lily. But if I try to get either to talk, they won't say anything, for fear I'll tell them it's their fault. I wish I could convince them to share their troubles. I wish both could know neither's a threat.

She and Lily had expected to come alone. At the last moment only, Michael had emerged from the library. 'Suppose I ought to,' he'd said, without show of enthusiasm, 'but don't hang round my neck.' And, pretending to be busy mending a riding crop, he'd let them go ahead. The two girls had exchanged knowing glances, sure he had been drinking again. And now he had almost caught up with them, Em was as sure he would refuse to sit with them, would skulk off on his own, the picture of misery. 'Wait a moment, Lily,' she said, 'we can at least arrive together.' But although they slowed, Michael never joined them, loitered ten feet behind.

Inside, the tent was already crowded. Various choirs edged together in friendly pre-competition rivalry, and musical directors and conductors, even some London critics, jostled elbows and knees with village worthies and proud relatives. Equally as many came to listen, some, like the singers, from miles away. Conspicuous in the audience were the Clubbers, Iris Duvane among them.

The Clubbers were out in strength. Following Iris's lead they had taken to the idea of patronizing the natives and support of village customs had become popular. All week, their summer finery hidden beneath large waterproofs, 'in case', they had strolled along the St Marvell streets, admiring the flower arrangements and commenting loudly on the strings of paper garlands which hung over the cottage doors. En masse they had clapped loudly when the decorated floats passed, and cooed at the children. 'What dears,' they said. Equally patronizingly they had purchased the most expensive seats for the music contest, prepared to go 'slumming', as they called it, smiling with supercilious experience. As always they stayed to listen and be silenced.

Iris was seated in a front row beside the older Farells. The stone seats were hard even with the air cushions they'd brought especially; the grass underfoot was trampled into mud and like the tent itself smelt of wet hay and wool as various participants now pushed their way inside through different side openings, shaking themselves collectively out of their soaked coats – like dogs, Iris thought, half amused. But she was only partly interested. She had other thoughts in mind, namely, what Sir Robert had offered, and how much she might use his suggestion without compromise.

Iris had had no trouble in avoiding Michael. She did so because she wanted to, not because Sir Robert had offered her payment. She just was waiting for the right moment to administer the final *coup de grâce*. However she had been thwarted in how to reach Richard. A recluse, wasn't he, living in a hovel, spending his days down some godforsaken mine, she didn't fancy trying to find him, ruining her shoes and getting soaked into the bargain. Iris had had enough of country living to remember about mud and rain.

Now, after giving up any attempt at sensible conversation, she had idly turned round to see what was happening behind her, was more than gratified to recognize the intense stranger who had created such an effect at her meeting and who was now staring about him with the same disconcerting intensity. Like Lily before her, she thought the opportunity perfect. Except, as Richard paused, presumably to study the programme before finding a place to sit, she felt a touch of doubt. Bumpkin or not, he didn't look like a man who could be made to do anything against his will, certainly not coaxed into revelation of the sort Sir Robert was looking for.

She suppressed her misgivings. Even doubt added 'interest', would make pursuit less boring, would add to the fun of the risk. If she muffed this unlooked-for chance she wouldn't deserve a second.

The reason for Richard's presence was so naïve, Iris would have been scandalized. He'd heard Lily sing, he'd heard her speak of the Festival, he knew she would be there. If he told himself he owed it to his father's memory to make an appearance, he was only partly telling the truth. When, muttering an excuse, Iris slid from her seat and made her way towards him – not easy with all the incoming throng – he was as startled as she meant him to be.

'We meet again,' she said, standing on tiptoe to whisper in his ear, her enthusiasm false even to him who was not expecting falseness.

Iris must have sensed it. She shook her head in that gamine

gesture men were supposed to admire, then forced herself to slow down and start again.

'Quite a walk from your cove to here,' she said in what was supposed to be a sympathetic tone, stressing the words 'your cove'. No point in offending him. 'And doesn't the sea look grand today with all those waves.' She made a vague gesture to indicate the outdoors. 'Good enough to drink.'

'Not unless you like salt.' Richard Chote's voice was ironic. He was looking at Iris without smiling, summing her up, Iris thought, so she tried to smile herself and ran her hands through her hair again. Wondering if perhaps he didn't recognize her, 'I took the chair, you know,' she volunteered as if that explained everything, and as he still looked blank, 'I chaired the meeting you came to.'

She spoke loudly, as if he were deaf. 'And what you said, I thought you handled very well.'

When he shrugged as if nonplussed, 'And the other men, how did you come to know them?' she asked, even more cunningly, for she already knew that, had wormed it out of them. ('Dick Chote, MC,' they'd told her, 'everyone who was out there remembers him.') But he was not to be drawn easily.

'I've been thinking of coming to see where you lived,' she went on, pressing hard. 'To thank you for your comments. My goodness, it must have taken courage for a real hermit. And a hero too. We were honoured.'

'Don't know about hermit.' Richard sounded irritated. 'Don't know about hero neither. I just prefer quiet.'

Iris considered and tried another tack. Although she was sure his so-called hut was a filthy hole, full of horrors, once she was inside it, had her foot in the door as it were, then she could really begin the work of softening him. 'So when am I to see this beautiful retreat of yours?' she asked, smiling at him openly now, putting her hand up, ever so gently, to touch his sleeve. 'I've heard so much about it. And about the cliffs and beach. When the tide's out sometime, won't you show me them?'

And when again he made no reply, greatly daring, 'Is the

cliff path difficult? Or, like Sir Walter Raleigh, will you have to carry me?' And once more she put her hand on his sleeve.

He never answered. Over her head he had seen Lily. And behind Lily came Michael.

Lily saw Richard at the same time as he saw her. She and Em had entered together, but Em had immediately crossed to where her parents were installed, was bent over talking to them. If Lily had remembered Michael was so close to her, she might have hesitated, but she wouldn't, couldn't have acted differently. For she not only saw Richard, she saw Iris Duvane, saw Iris's bright fingernails spread clawlike on his arm.

Lily felt her face grow red, felt the blood drain from it so quickly that she feared she might fall. And heard Richard exclaim her name, and plunge forward in a kind of double leap on one leg. Then he was holding her round the shoulders, saying in a voice that was harsh with concern, 'Are you all right? Can I do, get you anything?' It was music to her. And Em was also hurrying up and saying, 'What's the matter?' And she was shaking her head, replying, 'Nothing, it's all right, don't fuss,' just as she had at Cove when the boat had almost overturned. But this time she was the one who never took her gaze from someone's face. And Richard never took his from her. And in that steadfast look all the lights and bursts of music that she had ever imagined poured out their richest song.

None of the three saw Iris's dissatisfied pout, nor her final flick of hair. Nor at first took in what Michael said to her, or she said to him.

Michael did not see Richard. That is to say he did not see him immediately as a real person. Rather Richard appeared as what he had always been, a figment of imagination, to be bent and twisted as Michael's own imagination bent and twisted him. It was Iris on whom Michael was focused, an unrepentant, even jubilant Iris whose momentary disappointment at losing her hold on Richard was being rapidly overtaken by sheer delight in the effect she was having on

Michael. If she had planned it deliberately, it couldn't have been better timed.

Like Lily, Michael concentrated on Iris, her proximity to Richard, her confiding smile. Like Lily, Michael noticed Iris's hand, that little hand he had loved to take between his two great paws and hold ever so gently, and which had often, in other circumstances, been laid on Michael's own sleeve in trusting birdlike fashion – when Michael cried out Iris's name, his voice revealed an anguish that contained all the revenge Iris could ever have wanted.

'Iris,' Michael said, 'Iris,' as if repetition would make her turn to him as she used to. 'Iris, what are you doing here?' He didn't say, 'With him?' He didn't have to, Iris knew he was thinking it.

Iris's hand smoothed down her hair in its customary gesture. She smiled, her wide-mouthed, scarlet-lipped smile that showed neither mirth nor pleasure. 'Why, Michael Polleven,' she said in her bright artificial voice, 'I think you're jealous. Fie on you.

'Not that I'd blame you,' she went on, eyeing him, assessing him, seeking the best way to make him squirm. 'Richard's positively a dear, dying to show me round. And so brave. Even his limp makes one feel protective. Don't you think he's attractive, the most attractive man for miles?

'Not like you,' her look said, 'with your round country face and round bloodshot eyes. And your petty little difficulties and clumsy little pleasures, like a stale old man.'

And when he didn't move, impatiently, 'Oh do get on, you're staring like a dummy.' Again her little shrug. '*Mon Dieu*,' she spoke over her shoulder, hissing in French to hide the final killer's dart, '*comme je suis bête*. What a fool I've been. Whatever did I see in you. But it's all right, darling,' she was mocking him, 'you're safe. Granddaddy's offered me, oh, so much lovely money to stay away from you.'

She brushed past, her perfume enveloping him. He stood staring after her, his own fresh complexion and thick fair hair inappropriate for mourning. Then, as if he had been poleaxed, he slumped, his shoulders drooping, as if all the listening world had heard what she said. Dummy, oaf, hayseed, the names they used to mock him with, burned in his head, he couldn't stop them. And his grandfather an accomplice. If he could have seen his grandfather, he would have killed him. Turning clumsily, he blundered past his sister and cousin. Only when he was outside, like a man whose hurt begins when the adrenaline stops, did Iris's words stab. 'Whatever did I see in you? What a fool I've been.' And as if to make the murder complete, 'How attractive Chote is.'

Behind him, in the tent, Lily and Em and Richard stood looking at each other in dismay while Iris minced back down the aisle. 'That'll show them,' her walk said. As she went, she reached in her purse and pulled out an envelope. They couldn't have known it was Sir Robert's cheque, but they did watch her as she tore it slowly and deliberately into little bits and ground them with her heel into the mud.

Richard moved first. Perhaps he would have gone after Michael had Lily not stopped him. 'Let him be,' she said. 'He'll want to be alone. We can't do anything.'

She hid her own concern, smiled at Richard. 'Are you here for the concert?' Her question was mundanely obvious, but her smile asked, 'Are you here for me?' And responding to it, Richard let himself smile in return, nodded, said abruptly, 'I'll wait for you when you're through, outside.'

It was all that they had time for, latecomers were pushing their way in, the thrust of people parted them. But Lily knew if Richard had promised to wait, he would. As for Michael, she suspected her brother'd go off somewhere to lick his wounds, all the life knocked out of him. Yet, although the hurt would be deep, the cause of it would be finished with. There'd be no more dragging pain. She and Em and he would come together again; they would tell him at last what they had always thought of Iris, persuade him that he was well rid of her.

'Go and sit down,' Lily said to Em, who was anxiously staring after Michael as if she wanted to follow him. She suddenly laughed again, as she hadn't done in ages, 'Don't frown so, Em. Things will finally be all right.'

CHAPTER 13

The final event of the evening had come. Already individual ladies had sung, been judged and been found wanting or rewarded according to the judges' decision. One by one the Women's Institute Choirs, the Chapel Choirs, the Church Singers, had risen as their names were called, left their chairs, trooped out to the platform. Last, out of courtesy as hosts, came the turn of St Marvell's Women's Choir.

Dressed in long black gowns and strange flat hats, they lined up in a row, waiting for the signal to start, their conductor teetering nervously on a little dais in front of them, while Mrs Treful, the solicitor's wife and official accompanist, spread her skirts. When she was ready, like some gigantic crow she nodded her head, her plump hands poised over the keys to emphasize the opening chords, her bracelets jingling.

By now they'll be tired of the same thing, Lily thought, watching the baton hover, waiting for it to point. She meant the judges, a group of them seated in a special box with flaps at both ends – to stop the crowd from influencing them, she thought. Once she would have liked to win, would have given anything to have read their notes. And winning still would be nice if Richard were pleased. I sound like a wife, she thought, almost laughed, almost missed the first beat, came in triumphantly.

'The morning's at seven,' Lily sang. She watched the conductor's baton swoop and dip, like a swallow, she thought. They had already sung the 'Hal-an-Tow' and 'Merlin the Diviner', and this, the third, was her favourite. 'At seven, at seven,' the contralto answered her, and 'The lark's on the wing,' the full choir replied. Competing with a thrum of wind as the canvas lifted, the notes soared, burst like bubbles, disappeared. Lily clasped her hands. Not in nervousness, she'd never felt so confident, but to keep from clapping as the voices swelled.

The baton pointed at her. 'Lark,' she sang, 'lark on the wing.' She saw the larks on the cliff break from the grass, lifting until they were specks too small for the naked eye. The mass that was the audience blurred, blended, split into individual faces; Em's there, a glimpse of her; beside her, Em's father, mouthing words, using a rolled-up programme to beat time; beside him again, Charity, nudging him to be quiet. Somewhere, Richard would be listening, waiting to the concert's end. For the time that sufficed, no need for anything else. 'God's in His heaven, His heaven,' she sang. 'All's right with the world.'

And so it is, she thought, as she sang the line again and again.

The singing was over. Now came a pause, while singers and audience discussed the performances, praised and commiserated, goodnaturedly making light of their rivals' mistakes and laughing at their own. Suddenly everyone grew still. The judges' heads came together; they whispered, dipped their pens, wrote. Their spokesman, a dapper little fellow with a tight-collared shirt, climbed onto the dais with the results in his hand. One by one he called the names, read the verdicts, recording faults and excellences with impartial gravity (although as a St Marvell man, dressed up for the occasion and barely recognizable, everyone knew where his true interests lay). 'St Marvell,' he read, his lips twitching. 'Second prize. And a special word of praise for the young soprano, most promising.' He beamed openly as a great round

171

of applause followed, led by Ben Trevarisk, the conductor saying, 'Well done, all of you, never do for hosts to be first,' and Mrs Treful gave over complaining that they'd gone too fast, too slow, and the tent smelt like a midden.

After the prize-giving, Lily lingered, pretending to help, picking up the debris, gathering dropped sheets of music, and finding Mrs Treful's glasses. Iris's scattered paper had disappeared and so had Iris. Good riddance, Lily thought. 'You go on,' she told Em, 'I'll be back later.' She didn't say why she would be late, let Em guess. This was no time for explanations.

It was well after nine o'clock when she stepped out into the twilight. The wind was still rising and she felt the cold – inside, the tent was warm, hot even, like a greenhouse without plants. She paused for a moment, looked round. The rain, fined to a drizzle, had almost ended but the grass was soaked and puddles stood along the hedges. It was still early enough for there to be some light, but the long summer sunset was obscured by clouds. They emphasized the grey twilight, were folded down, thick as blankets. The field was deserted. After the crush and frenzy of the afternoon, the quiet was unnerving. The gloom, the greyness, the sudden swift swoop of bats from the church tower heightened melancholy; she had the eerie feeling that someone was watching her, was creeping up unseen. The thought made her glance nervously from side to side. When she heard a footfall behind her, she jumped. And for the first time remembered Michael.

'Feeling guilty?' Richard's voice was reassuring, even although, underneath, it still held a cautious note as if he were warning himself to hold back. 'You should. If you hadn't missed that rehearsal you might've won.'

With a sense of relief out of proportion to the moment, Lily let her nervousness slip away. Michael would have gone home long ago and Em would take care of him. As for Iris Duvane, she'd never mattered, Michael would be himself again. And here was Richard as he'd said, and he was merely teasing. Whatever misunderstandings between them were about to be cleared away, old unwanted rubbish. All's right with the world, her thoughts sang.

'There's something I should tell, show you,' Richard was saying. He sounded over-polite, well, he'd be bound to be embarrassed, she thought, contradicting himself after he'd been so fierce. He'd have to get over that, she decided, embarrassment's just a form of shyness. When he fumbled in the pocket of his army coat – which he has the right to wear, she thought, suddenly proud of him, more than any other soldier I've met, except perhaps my father – for a second she supposed the letter he brought out was one he'd written himself. She was about to tease him back, ask if he found it easier to write than speak, when he began to explain what the letter contained. To her surprise she was disappointed. At that moment, ownership of Cove was the last thing on her mind. 'What of us?' she wanted to ask. 'Shouldn't that be discussed first?'

She banked her disappointment down, took up the letter and started to read by the light of a torch he must have brought especially. He had halted against the field hedge by the open gate which led to the road, out of the wind where he could hold the torch steady as she turned the pages. There were so many she was afraid she'd drop them; one already had a piece torn off, presumably part he'd censored. The writing was large, laborious, as if someone had taken pains with it, but where the torch's little circle of light made round golden patches on the page, the words danced; she could scarcely make sense of them. What am I supposed to think, she wondered, it was all so long ago.

He was waiting expectantly. 'I'll leave it up to you,' Beth Martin had written, and presumably in turn he was leaving it up to her. She tried to reread the letter as carefully as it deserved. What she was thinking was: he's just handed me proof that Polmena Cove was once ours after all, just as I said. But now, ironically, I don't care. She almost blurted out, 'I've changed my mind. I want you to have it. You deserve it more than the rest of us.'

173

She picked out the one thing that to her seemed the oddest in the whole odd business. 'We're related,' she said and wanted to laugh at his expression. 'But it's so confused I can't work out how. If your mother's father was my great-grandfather's cousin, what does that make us?'

When he didn't reply, she thought, I believe it's not even occurred to him, and I don't think he likes it. The old Lily would have laughed. The new Lily, suddenly aware of a fresh complication, thought, dear God, don't say it'll cause more difficulties between us. 'It's only a minor relationship,' she hastened to assure him, 'some sort of second or third cousin once or twice removed. Hardly worth mentioning.'

She looked at him under her lashes, daring him. 'So, Cousin Richard, how does it feel to be one of us?'

She had never called him by his given name, it gave her a strange feeling. She watched how his face contracted, shuttered down, as if he thought she was mocking him.

'No doubt your grandfather could tell you,' he said. 'It'd not be welcome news. Unless perhaps he already knows and that's why he's so anxious to get rid of me. Forget the relationship; I'm only an illegitimate Polleven. It's the moral issue that's got me foxed.'

Lily folded the pages, spread her hands as if to make a tray, handed the letter back to him with a formal bow. 'Take it,' she said. 'That's what I think of it; Cove's yours, by gift. And as far as I'm concerned, there's the end of it. As for being illegitimate,' she stammered at the word, 'what's new in that? I am too. Or was until father married mother. Surely your mother told you that.'

'No,' he said, 'no, she didn't.'

Something about the tone of his voice made her take a deep breath. This is important, she wanted to warn him, but her voice came out casual, non-caring. 'And would knowing or not knowing make a difference to how you think of me?'

When he said, almost impatiently, 'Of course not,' she felt her shoulders relax as if she were breathing again. She looked at him. Standing there in the dim greyness, his shabby greatcoat darkened in patches where the rain had soaked, he looked more than ever like a soldier about to go into action. She felt him bracing himself for a blow as a soldier might. 'And it doesn't to me either,' she cried. 'I told you so before. It's what a person is, not where he comes from; it's what he's like inside. And if you want to know what I think, well, I'm glad we both are only partly Polleven. It makes us more alike, different from the others. Certainly different from my brother and grandfather. As far as I'm concerned, that's a good thing.'

She blushed afterwards, bit her lip. He'll think me forward, she thought, vexed with herself. She came up close to him so the golden circle of torchlight lit up her face. 'We're still in this together, aren't we? We're still friends?' She might have added, 'Be honest now, because this is even more important.'

The wind blew, the hedge dripped. Darkness was coming fast, almost a winter night in August. He put out his hand and touched her cheek, tentatively at first, then with firmer touch. 'Friends?' he asked her. 'Or more than friends? And if so, are you sure? Can you swear to it?'

'Yes,' she told him; her eyes sparkled. To every one of his 'nos' she had a 'yes'; to every one of his hesitations she had a firm response. And then there was no more time for questions or any kind of answer, all was positive.

After a while he drew back, laughed himself. She remembered how once she'd thought she'd hardly ever heard him laugh and she liked the sound of it, deep, a hearty man's laugh. 'We'll never get on if I don't stop kissing you,' he said. 'What a greedy little thing you are. Hasn't anyone kissed you before?'

'Only you,' she said. 'I'll stop if you will.' But it was a long while before he did, as if only by touching and holding her he could shuffle off those lonely days of doubt; as if only by clinging to him, letting herself be touched, Lily could convince herself he was real and the moment real, that in truth they could be more than friends. It was not the best of evenings for lovemaking, nor at that moment would Richard take advantage of Lily's inexperience. But what Lily lacked in experience she made up for in ardour; all the passion of her nature came pouring out; and Richard, responding like to like, matched and surpassed her with eager hunger. When at last they left the field and went into the road, it was as if they had been so locked together that they had almost forgotten how to walk, their legs trembled so.

Without really planning to, they followed the inland road, where overhanging hedges would shelter them from the wind. The bushes were drooping now and great drops of moisture splattered as they brushed past. Above their heads the tops of the trees which lined the road dipped and swayed with cracking sounds like ship sails, and bushes rustled as if animals were scurrying to hide. The inland road ran roughly parallel to the cliff path which Lily and Em had originally followed – on a day that now seemed like a prelude to this – and as Em had done that day, so Lily and Richard now used the interlude to reveal to each other what they really had hoped and feared since their first encounter.

It was still early enough that they were free to talk, to stop, to embrace and then walk on again, without worrying about being late. Nor did they have to worry about being seen together. The bad weather had driven everyone indoors, even the trombonists would have put their instruments to rest, and although singers still lingered in the village pubs, quenching their thirsts or lubricating their throats (depending on whether they'd sung or not), they were not likely to come out until closing time.

Richard's arms were about Lily, hers about him; it seemed to Lily that suddenly they had no more secrets. Out everything came, to be shared, wondered at or dismissed as no longer having importance. Yet her own feelings about Cove as the place where she'd been born; her longing to go there, live there even; her desire to reconcile her past with her present life, seemed of so much less consequence, compared to his aftermath of war. The consequence of physical deformity and the fear of rejection because of it overcame her, made her remorseful at her previous lack of sympathy. Yet, she knew she mustn't show it. Pity would really make her lose him, better to be brusque.

So, 'Rubbish,' she told him stoutly, although she longed to show him how mistaken he was. 'Rubbish. To have been wounded is a dreadful thing, but it's never something to be ashamed of. If it doesn't matter to you, it certainly doesn't matter to anyone else. Besides I'm used to it. I've told you about my own father. And if any girl's so stupid as to dislike you for it, well, I'm glad. It leaves you free for me.'

And when she had convinced him of this, shown him with all the intensity of which she was capable, 'Rubbish,' she said with even more certainty this time, when he spoke of his lack of money, lack of a proper job – and lack of status in her parents' eyes – 'They think as I do. My father was a soldier, you'll see.'

It was useless for Richard to point out all the reasons why the advantages were on her side, the disadvantages on his. 'All silliness,' Lily told him. 'As soon say your mother won't like me because I'm who I am. And don't say you know better,' she added when he began to argue, then stopped, as if thinking it wiser not to – leaving her with the impression that she had touched some truth – 'I've worked something else out. I must be older than you by several months. Imagine.' She stopped and looked at him. 'Your father would have known me when I was a baby, before you were born. So he must have liked me. He'd have thought I was good enough for you.'

An observation that also had to be reworded the other way round, had to be attacked, defended, mulled over so once more he could refute it to her full satisfaction. 'It seems to me,' Lily said finally, at her most contrary Miss Polleven self, 'if I say I'm not good enough for you and you say you're not good enough for me, that makes us even. So there's no point in speaking of it again. And if we haven't decided for ourselves by the time mother and father are back, then we'll ask their opinion. But I don't think we'll have to,' she said. 'I know what's right for me.'

She may be thoughtless, Em had said, she may be wild, but when she's made up her mind there's no changing her.

They had been walking on like this, engaged in this most absorbing of arguments, and then walking on again without real sense of direction or purpose except the vague one of making their way towards Nanscawn Farm, when suddenly Lily stopped. 'Look,' she said. 'Whatever's that?'

They had come to the parting of the ways, down towards Polmena Cove, up towards the farm. The gate in front of them gave a view over the fields towards the sea, like the gate Em had once leaned on. To their left the lights of St Marvell twinkled vaguely in the distance through the mist. To their right the headland forming part of the cove loomed before them with the valley entrance on its far side. The wind was stronger here again; as they came closer to the sea, they had to shout to make themselves heard. But Lily was not referring to any of these things.

The sky above the headland was clearer as if the clouds had parted. As they watched, it became tinged with red like a sun trying to shine through. Lily, beginning to say, 'That's strange,' stopped and frowned, as if realizing that at this hour the sun couldn't possibly be shining on the east side of the headland, even if there were sun. A sudden golden streak, followed by another, made her cry in equal surprise, 'Fireworks,' followed by the equally quick realization that neither could they be on that side of the bay and in any case they weren't supposed to be set off until tomorrow.

Richard had stopped too. He dropped his hold on Lily's arm and stared, then started forward at a great rate so she had to run after him. 'What is it?' she cried. 'What's wrong?' But she knew before he told her. No fireworks this glowing colour, no sun, but fire itself, rampant and spreading. Fire in Polmena Cove. But how, after all this rain?

Even as the realization sank in, the first of the explosions went off, shaking the earth where they stood as if a giant had

178

tipped it sideways. They both stopped again. Neither spoke. They felt a gust of air stronger even than the wind, a long-drawn-out sigh. 'By God,' Richard said at last, 'someone's trying to blow it up.'

He spoke quietly. But Lily could feel the anger taut in him like string. Suddenly all her own anger broke out for him. But with anger came guilt. For as sure as if she'd seen Michael herself, she knew her brother was responsible, and for what final reason.

'Go home,' Richard said at last. 'There's nothing you can do. Go home and wait.'

He started forward again. 'And where are you going?' Lily wanted to cry, wanted to catch hold of him. 'You can't stop him by yourself. You can't fight him again.'

She might have been talking to the wind, as soon tell the wind to cease its blowing.

'All right,' she cried, 'do what you must. But I'm going back. All of St Marvell will have heard the noise; they'll be out in full force, they'll help.'

She cried louder, screaming it above the sound of the wind, 'It's Michael, don't you understand? It's Michael. But it's not his fault.'

'I know,' Richard said. 'Don't think I don't know that.' She watched him limp away into the darkness, and vanish. Then she turned herself and began to run along that road which but moments earlier had seemed to be leading to a safe haven. As she ran, images formed and re-formed: Michael with a flaming torch, like an archangel, full of vengeful anger; Michael at the mineshaft entrance, peering down into it as he lit some fuse. These in turn were supplanted by the one of Richard and Michael fighting – she thought, if Richard got the better of Michael that first time, it must have been by some lucky fluke. But a lame man can't fight like that and always expect luck to be with him. She saw Michael waiting to push Richard off balance; she saw the waiting rocks and sea. She heard herself shouting a warning. The thought made her run the faster but the uneven pavement tripped her and she slid on the wet road surface until she felt she hadn't moved a yard.

When she burst into the first of the pubs, the Cormorant, perched at the beginning of the narrow village streets which twisted down from High End Field, her breath was coming in great wheezes, and she had such a stitch she couldn't speak. She leaned against the door jamb, fighting to recover, her heart thumping like a mine engine, while overhead the great oak rafters, festooned with strings of onions, seemed to bend and sway. She'd never been inside the Cormorant, but even before she'd reached it she could hear the singing, the landlord, one of the basses in the choir, having just finished a noisy rendering of 'Going Up Camborne Hill Coming Down'. He and his daughter were now standing by the bar counter, wet towels in their hands. Through a haze of cigarette smoke she saw men swivelling on their stools, mugs of beer in their hands. She heard someone exclaim, 'Why I never, 'tis Miss Polleven.' She continued to hear people talking, see them coming towards her, saw them bending over her, but didn't have the strength to reply. And sometimes she felt she might have remained like that for ever, opening and shutting her mouth without sound, like a hooked fish, had not the second distant explosion suddenly ripped through the building.

Either it was louder than the other or, now that the door was open and the singing stopped, they could hear it. They began to shout; some ran into the road outside; others, still crowding round, heard her piecemeal explanations with curious silence, as if they had been shocked back into sobriety. The words 'Cove', 'Chote', 'Wheal Marty', even 'Michael Polleven', echoed round her, each taking shape independently, as if they had hardened to glass. She found she was being fussed over by the landlord's daughter, a mug of whisky was thrust into her hand, as men who knew how to deal with emergencies at sea now hastened to deal with one on land.

Quicker than she would have thought possible, they had organized a rescue party. From house to house the message ran. 'Trouble at Polmena Cove, boy, Richard Chote's in trouble. Miss Polleven's here a-giving of the word. Some tale about her brother against Richard Chote, can't make head or tail of it, but we'm needed. So get a move on.'

Lanterns were lit, men roused out of bed began to struggle into their clothes. Some set off at once with ropes and picks; others staying for blankets and hot drinks made plans for a longer emergency, such as they were accustomed to if a ship went on the rocks. Only in one or two houses did the windows remain obstinately closed and the rooms dark.

One of these was the Trevarisk cottage. The other was the Pendrays'. The Pendrays they left alone, but they hammered at Ben Trevarisk's door. ''Tis Chote,' they shouted underneath Ben's window, 'Jeb Martin's nephew,' calling it through the letter box and rattling the unlocked door until it opened with a violent pull and Ben stood there in his long underwear. 'Won't give me my trousers,' he cried, shaking his fist at the upper window, which was shut. 'By gum, won't she just. But I'm a-coming, boys. Just let me get my boots on.'

He heaved and pulled. 'Come into my mind,' he said, grunting, 'that in this weather, if 'tis the mine that's gone, they may do with some rescue work on the other side of the headland. So I'll just go down to The Cut and get the boat ready. As for you, you old crow,' he shouted up at that shut window, 'shame on 'ee for an ingrate.'

The window opened a crack. Charity's head poked out. 'And shame on 'ee, pious old faggot,' she cried, 'don't interfere. 'Tis between them Pollevens and Richard Chote and the Pollevens hold the money bags. As well as the keys to our house.

'And yours and yours,' she added, pushing up the sash and leaning out to point at the men underneath. 'Gert great silly fools. You'll end up as houseless as Chote is.'

A strange silence followed her remarks as if the truth of them had suddenly gone home. The men looked at each other; one or two of them shifted uneasily. They would all have known about the visits made by Sir Robert's steward and the probable reasons; some had already been approached by Treful and Lurkin and warned of the consequences of non co-operation. Aware of the danger to themselves and their families they hesitated. But only for a second.

'Bugger that,' one said stoutly. ''Tis a man's life, missus, that's what may be at stake. And if you sits there smug like, thinking you be safe, then, by God, I'm sorry for 'ee. When your man was in danger on a worse night than this, Richard Chote's uncle didn't hesitate.'

They left her still shouting, surged up the street, making for the cliff path as being shorter than the road. The lights from their lanterns twinkled in a steady line. They were followed by some of the younger women, the fisher girls, who ran with them, their striped skirts and headscarves bound up tightly because of the wind. In the village, the older women, the mothers and wives, watched from their doorways, hands folded on their chests, their lips drawn tight. By their sides their children, most in nightclothes, stared or jumped up and down begging to go too. 'Stop still,' the women told them, jerking them back, 'bain't safe.' Whether they meant danger on the cliffs or danger here in the village, man-made danger possibly threatening their own homes, they didn't make the distinction, but their expressions showed they felt there was one. Yet they too made no complaint, after a while turned and went inside to do what they had to do to prepare for the present emergency, making up beds, sorting out clothes, warming up food and brewing great jugs of tea to carry over the cliffs at first light.

As if recovering from a nightmare, not sure which was nightmare, which real, Lily was witness to all this without being able to say a word in defence. She was bitterly ashamed; ashamed for her family, and for her grandfather's vindictiveness; ashamed that she had once almost been part of it. At the same time she felt relief that stout Cornish goodness had once more prevailed. She too followed behind the men, trying to keep up with them. And as she ran, became conscious of one last person hurrying beside her.

It was Will Pendray, his big body scrambling awkwardly from lack of practice. He had obviously dressed in haste, his coat unbuttoned and his miner's helmet slung on his back over a rucksack from which his pickaxe hung. 'If 'tis the mine,' he panted, 'need a miner, see. Know what's what. So I told mother when she tried to stop me. Need a miner, I told her. If someone's trapped.' And added one more image to frighten Lily and keep her company on the way back.

CHAPTER 14

ither the wind had quieted at last, or, caught up with so many people, Lily scarcely noticed it. She scarcely noted anything except the need to conserve energy so she could keep walking as fast as she could. It was not until she reached the entrance to the valley that she saw the signs of fire, although the actual fire itself was out. Proof of arson was clear here, the odour of kerosene, strong and pungent, overwhelming the charred smell.

In the place where Richard had built his original barricade, the timber had been set alight and the gorse and bracken were scorched in a great patch all around it. 'Without this rain, 'twould all have gone up like a tinder box,' the men called to each other, treading gingerly through black streaks of vegetation which still smouldered. But when they reached the beach, the stack of driftwood beside the stream was still blazing. Fanned by the wind which whipped in round the point, it blocked the way across the bridge, the crackle of wood vying with the duller roar of the waves. But although the wind blew spray in sheets, even that was not enough to put the fire out, only made it hiss and spark.

The tide was in and the flickering flames lit up the edge of the sea. From time to time breakers mounted from the darkness beyond, surging high up the shingle, even occasionally reaching the base of the cliff before recoiling in a smother of foam, making access along the beach dangerous.

The flames also lit up the cliffs, revealing the ledge where the Martins' hut stood. Had stood – there was little left of it, the roof caved in, the walls split outward, the wooden frame still smouldering, the interior already burnt to ash.

Lily and the other girls waited by the stream as the men began now to pick their way cautiously across the beach towards the ledge. Judging the size of the incoming waves by the suck of the undertow, they tried to make a dash between each set, were swept back, pushed forward again, clinging to each other to prevent being washed away. One by one they gained the ledge, clambered up, stood in a group talking softly among themselves.

For a while the girls watched, not saying anything, having nothing to say. Then slowly, under their breaths, they also began to comment, not looking at Lily but showing they knew who she was. 'Gone up like tinder too,' they said, speaking of the hut. 'Old wood. Pour a bit of kerosene and light a match, nothing'd stop it. But look how the walls are blown apart. Who ever done that? Whatever for? 'Tis turrible sad.' They eyed her, instinctively too kind to say what they thought. Michael Polleven against Richard Chote, they sensed tragedy in the making.

As the men on the ledge began gingerly to poke among the stones, striding up and down with long sticks, talking among themselves in undertones, 'Where's Richard Chote gone to then?' the girls now asked. Again they eyed Lily. 'Didn't he live here all alone? Why couldn't he stop it?' When someone, greatly daring, asked, 'But suppose he tried and failed,' someone else volunteered. 'Wasn't he at the concert, didn't he wait afterwards?' They all looked at Lily for confirmation. Lily didn't hear them. Where is Richard, she was thinking, where's Michael, 'Where are they?' she shouted to the men. The wind took her words and blew them away like spume, and no one answered.

Lily could endure the waiting no longer. She too jumped down on to the beach and began to run. The first of the waves surged round her feet but she scarcely felt it. The second came

185

harder, out of the darkness beyond the fire, like a wall, the froth of its breaking spreading like a carpet, waist-deep. It made her stagger, her skirts swirled like seaweed. Then the backwash caught her, dragged her down. For a moment she lay spread-eagled like a heap of washing, her eyes blinded with salt, her mouth and hair filled with the grit and shingle that rolled over her. Got to get up, she remembered thinking, scrabbling with her fingers for purchase before the next wave broke.

She was lucky. Either there was a lull, or the shouts of the girls now alerted the men on the ledge. As some of them started to run back, several of the girls themselves came floundering after her, clinging to each other as the water eddied about them. They reached her and dragged her up just as she scrambled to her knees. When the next wave came towering towards them, its crest breaking white, they had formed a chain, arms locked about each other as the first of the men plunged towards them from the other side, arms also locked in similar fashion. All the same the wave knocked them apart as if they were rotten apples, set them bobbing about like corks. Had the men not got to their feet first, not been there to fish the girls out with their stronger hold and greater reach, they would have been swept out into the darkness, where there would have been no finding them.

Lily lay on the ledge where someone had dropped her. She was completely spent. Bruised all over, soaked from head to foot, she didn't feel the cold or wet. She didn't even hear the men's angry shouts at the other girls to clear off and stop being fools. What the blazes did they think they were a-doing of? That the men were angry because they had been frightened was obvious, but they became even more angry when some of the girls, too exhausted to argue, began to cry. Other girls however, hardened to knocks perhaps and used to working alongside the men, sat up and gave back as good as they'd got. 'Didn't see 'ee hurrying to reach us in time,' one said, while another, a large fresh-faced girl, shook out her skirts and cried, 'Ruined, but the water were just right fer swimming,' which made them all laugh. Blankets were now shared round, the flasks of tea unstoppered. Lily tried to ask again, 'Where's Richard gone?' but her throat had dried and no words came out.

'If it's Richard Chote you're asking for,' one of the men said, as if guessing, and in his good-natured way trying to set her mind at rest, 'he bain't here, for sure. But he may be at the mine.'

He jerked with his thumb towards the east cliff, along which Lily saw lights twinkling. Carrying lanterns, men were climbing up the track. They went slowly, for here they were on unknown territory and the grass would be slippery, the soil underneath turned to treacherous slime. But Lily cared nothing for that. She too wrung her skirts out and threw aside the blanket. As soon as she could stand, she began to hurry up the mine path, although at times she could feel herself staggering. Again she was conscious of someone just behind her, and although she did not turn round, she guessed that it was William Pendray.

In daylight, in good weather, the path wasn't easy, winding a few inches wide through the bracken, although in places it had been enlarged, as if Richard had been trying to restore it to the way it once was. Now the rain had brought water gushing down it which made the rough footing even more uneven, and if Lily stopped for breath, which she had to do more often than she liked, she could hear the crash of the waves against the sheer cliff face. Keeping her eyes fixed on the string of lanterns, using them for markers, she forced herself on, felt with each foot carefully, tried not to think of what lay on the seaward side.

She had no idea how long this took. All her efforts were concentrated on reaching the entrance of the mine. And if behind her she felt the presence of her silent companion, she could only guess at the effort it cost him to keep up with her.

The path itself had fortunately not been blocked by the explosion, probably because as it neared the entrance it wound away to one side and levelled out and so no longer ran directly uphill. But even before Lily came to Wheal Marty's entrance, she could see evidence of the explosion that must have loosened stone and shale and sent large boulders crashing down the cliff. When she reached the actual opening, she saw how the great rocks at either side had been blackened and split by the force of it, while the little stream that had run from the tunnel had completely disappeared. Meanwhile, inside the entrance itself, men were already probing among the debris, where shattered spars of engines leaned at unnatural angles, as if someone had tossed them like toys, twisting them out of shape. And beyond this tangle of old machinery, just after the first shaft opening, a wall of fresh fallen stone was piled.

A man came out, leaning against the wall as he picked his way forward. He was carrying a crumpled rucksack which he threw down. 'Here's the bag,' he said, 'my own stuff.' It was only when he limped forward into the light that Lily recognized him. Once more her throat contracted.

'Must have found it before he burnt the hut,' Richard was saying, with a trace of bitterness. 'Knew enough to save it. Must have tossed one stick in to finish what the flames started, didn't leave enough to finish off the mine entrance as I suppose he planned. Saw him up here when I first got to the hut. He was using my Davy lamp and must have come outside for shelter, because there was a second explosion, the one you heard. Almost blew me over. Then afterwards, when he saw or heard me coming up the old mine path, he ran inside again, for he wasn't here when I reached the entrance and there's nowhere else he could have gone.'

Richard must have seen Lily now, for suddenly his voice changed. 'The second rockfall's my fault,' he said slowly. 'I went in after him. Shouted, heard him moving ahead of me, saw the lamplight. Then, what with the rubble, I lost my footing, grasped for a timber strut. It gave way and the roof started to go, but I managed to scrabble back.'

His gaze was fixed on Lily; he spoke in a monotone.

'Fortunately for me the fall went inward but trapped him on the far side. When the dust settled, I thought I could still hear him moving about, saw the gleam of light through chinks in the stones. I shouted again, kept on shouting, but he didn't answer, must have continued further on. There was no way I could get through to him, didn't even have a torch myself . . .'

His voice trailed off.

'Then he'll be all right too,' Lily said. She watched Richard as closely. 'He'll be safe.'

Richard didn't answer, neither did the other men. They all stood there scuffling with their feet among the shifting shale and rubble, not looking at each other, not asking in her presence who the 'he' was, but, like her, knowing. It was Will Pendray who spoke for them.

'Depends.' Will also stood at the entrance, peering in, his shoulders hunched. He took a tentative step, then retreated as the other men moved to make way for him. 'Depends,' Will repeated, 'how the first charge was laid for one thing. If not set properly, it could've caused damage beneath. Even the rest of the entrance could collapse, so you'd better all clear away from it.'

And as the men came hurrying out, 'The drainage channel's stopped, see, so that means water's blocked. There's bound to be flooding eventually in the galleries it drained. And that may cause more falls. The shoring's old, rotten; it'll snap under weight. But by gum, it's the machines that's gone to waste, more's the pity.'

Oblivious to the rest of them, he crouched down beside one especially misshapen piece of metal which had been thrown clear outside, as if he personally meant to straighten it with his own hands. And for a moment he seemed to forget where he was, or who he was, as he fiercely concentrated.

While he was talking, Richard took the opportunity to come and stand by Lily. He was as bedraggled as she was, his clothes drenched, his sleeves torn and his boots larded with red mud. 'I'm sorry,' he was saying, 'I hoped you'd not have to know. But if we're to find him, there's no hiding it. And we shall find him,' he added. 'It only means clearing out that fall and going after him.'

He said, 'For God's sake, Lily, don't look at me like that. I had no idea he'd go inside, no idea the roof would collapse. Why did you come back, I told you not to.'

He stopped, for she had burst out, 'Sorry, you're telling me you're sorry, when I should be on my knees to you, when my brother has burnt down your valley and destroyed your home and mine. Shame on you, Richard Chote, you've no sense.'

And he was saying then, 'And you've come down the valley with all that fire.' He had his arms about her, oblivious of the curious stares. 'Looks as if you've been swimming,' he said wonderingly, then, 'My God, you've never fallen in the sea, you've never crossed the beach.'

A shout made him turn. The men who had been handing out picks and shovels at the entrance had stopped and crowded round Will Pendray. And Will himself had straightened up and squared his shoulders. Under the summer sunburn his face was white but his voice came out steady. 'You'd be fools to move them stones,' he said. 'Dig at them, you'll bring down more, unless you can shore the roof up as you go. Trap him for sure then, maybe trap yourself. The whole thing'll cave in.'

Everyone was quiet.

'But we've got to,' Richard said, 'it's the only way to find him.'

'No one else a miner here,' Pendray said, his voice still steady. 'Not as far as I know, that is. And with due respect,' he went on, turning to Richard, 'what you know I've forgotten before I was grown. So what I says is this. Before you move them stones, you'll need timber for props. And you can't go in the dark anyway if he's got your lamp. And when you get through the stones, if you do, you'll need to have some idea where you're going to, not thrash about.'

He suddenly seized a stick, drew in the mud. 'Look here,'

he said, standing back. 'Don't know this mine in particular, but in general they was built like this.'

He'd drawn what looked like a maze of lines, with other lines coming off at different levels, a confused tangle, some lines joining, some not, some running at right angles to others, some circling to join at another place.

'There's the entrance,' Will said, jabbing, 'and here's the first shaft. We know she leads to a gallery where Richard's been working, but we don't know how far or in what direction that gallery runs. And we know now that there must be another gallery coming in off the entrance, if Michael Polleven's gone along it, but we don't know where it goes either. It may go up or down, 'tis a jigsaw in there.'

He paused a moment to shrug off his knapsack and loosen his own bundle. 'And I'll tell you something else,' he said simply. 'This isn't a small mine, not a one-man-and-his-son caper as you thought. I can smell it, and 'tis big, a whopper.'

'Think of it this way,' he said when they all looked at each other in dismay. 'This cliff face is what, three hundred feet high, top to bottom, and God knows how much more under the sea. And what's the distance round the headland, a half-mile or more.

'So we best wait 'til sun up,' he added, 'give us time to plan. And pool resources. He won't go far by then.'

When Michael saw and heard the rocks falling he had had time to jump back out of the way, and after he heard Richard's voice calling, he had run on to avoid him. Now he inched along, had scarcely moved more than a few feet beyond a second shaft which he hadn't seen in his haste. Almost falling down it had terrified him back to reality.

Although the lamp he had taken threw off some light, it seemed to be growing dimmer and the rocky surface underfoot was constantly worsening. Now he felt as if he were clinging to a precipice, although in fact sometimes the walls of the gallery appeared to be narrowing while the roof lost height. He already had to stoop, might soon have to crawl. He had the feeling if he didn't brain himself first he would be wedged in tight. From time to time he heard vague rumblings; they could have been echoes of the first explosion or they could have been caused by subsequent falls of stone; he couldn't be sure which direction they came from, in front, behind, underneath.

Michael shuddered and buried his head in his hands. The sense of excitement that had filled him had long gone, had disappeared in that awful moment when the roof had come crumbling down. Originally it had seemed so easy, almost a joke, when the idea had first come to him that now was the best opportunity to destroy Richard's world – a punishment to fit the crime, as Gilbert and Sullivan would have put it and as Lily was always singing. That would show her, show Iris Duvane and her precious Farell, even show Grandfather Polleven that Michael Robert was a chip off the old block, a force to be reckoned with.

And it had been easy, nothing to it, to drag out the big can of kerosene from Nanscawn barn, and carry it all the way to the valley; he'd plenty of time. Once at the valley he'd paused only to douse the first timber pile. The blaze of wood on the beach, even the explosion when he'd tossed the stick of dynamite into the hut, paled with the thrill of lighting that first match and seeing the first flames snake up.

And the second explosion at Wheal Marty had seemed as easy, nothing to it either. He'd looked in the entrance, seen the engines – he knew enough that without machinery Chote's mine would never work again. He'd put the remaining dynamite beside it, near what looked like an old winch, lit the fuses, raced outside. He had expected the whole entrance to be blocked, not for it to blow outwards with a mighty roar, cracking the rocks under which he had sheltered like rotten wood.

Nor had he expected Chote to arrive back so soon. When, dazed and deafened, he had staggered up, he'd seen Chote down by the hut and knew he'd been caught. Then, as he realized Chote was climbing the cliff, in a panic he'd ducked back inside. And thus been trapped.

Familiar waves of giddiness made his head spin as the effect of the whisky too wore off. He vomited. Afterwards he lay exhausted, wiping his mouth on his hand, the sour taste almost making him vomit again. It seemed an injustice that in a moment, just like that, all the excitement should have vanished, leaving the knowledge that although Richard Chote's hut had gone up in flames, Richard Chote hadn't gone up with it, that although the entrance of the mine had been blown up, it was he himself who was caught.

With a rush of apprehension, Michael now heard a sudden sigh, like a shift of stones far below him, and started with fear. Surely that's the sea, he thought. The circle of the lamp in his hand swung as he turned. Its light picked out the rocky surface overhead, certainly closer, just inches away now. It picked out too the end of the passage, the closed wall with its reddish streak of mineral running vertically – and the rusted iron of a ladder leading up and down a new shaft, the third he'd counted so far. He leaned against the wall and again wiped his mouth.

No way forward then. And no way back. He couldn't bear to go back, not see Richard and have to face him, not to be dug out, like a badger when the dogs are on him. Suddenly he thought of himself in the ditch with Rowet, the spade lifted. Trapped, Michael thought, until they come to get me, if they ever do.

That was a new terror he hadn't contemplated before. It drove him forward. He edged towards the opening of the shaft, tried to estimate what to do. The light caught at the rusty rungs of the ladder which stretched both up and down into dim and dreadful darkness. He felt for a stone, dropped it, heard the sound of its falling, rattling against the sides. Upwards would be safer. But when he tried the ladder overhead, it crumbled away in his hands.

Downwards then. He tugged at the lower ladder, strained at it as best he could. It held. Lying on the ground, he shook the bars to see if they were firm. They groaned and creaked but didn't budge. Still he hesitated. He sensed this shaft was deep, like a well, hopefully without water. And old mines sometimes wound about for miles.

As he lay he heard the sigh again, and then, for the first time, the thread of cold air, fresh air, with its taint of salt. It revived him. That's it, he thought, another exit. But he wouldn't take chances. Sitting up, he fumbled for the rope he'd also taken from Richard's bag and looped it about his shoulders. He'd fasten his lamp to it, lower the lantern first; then, when he'd seen what lay ahead, he'd bring up the lantern, keep one end of the rope tied to himself and the other to something firm, turning the rope into a safety strap for him to hold on to. When he had got down so far, he'd unhook himself, retie the rope, lower the lamp, and so begin the process again. Slowly he edged himself backwards, feeling for the rungs with his feet. The lamp swung beneath him in arcs, lighting up his feet and boots but showing little of the shaft beneath.

After the third stopping and retying of the rope, the slowness of his progress irritated him. Blast it, he thought, must be almost at the bottom. He tried to pry another rock loose to check the remaining depth, failed, hung the lamp from his belt and went on without bothering to use the rope.

The walls of the shaft were wetter here, he could feel the moisture dripping, seeping through the rocks. And it was growing hotter again, although from time to time he still felt the gusts of cooler air. At the twelfth rung he felt his foot slip as the iron gave way.

For a moment he dangled by his hands, flailing for hold, before they too gave way. And he was falling slowly, slowly, towards a ground that came rushing up at him.

By midnight the news of the fires at Polmena Cove and the disaster at Wheal Marty had spread through the neighbourhood. Everyone knew that Michael Polleven was still in the mine, presumably still alive but cut off. As Will had predicted after the explosion and the subsequent rockfall, there had been other falls, stressing the importance of his advice. Men put their ears to the ground, listened to the subterranean rumblings, heard the shift of stone far under the ground, and agreed that 'twould be madness to try and force a way through without proper precautions. For the most part they retreated homewards, promising to return with additional help and equipment as soon as it was light.

Only Richard and Will remained beside the mine entrance. They sat on the ground with their backs resting against some rocks, saying little, staring out into the darkness. Further off on the open stretch Lily had settled down with Em. Em had lost no time in joining Lily, although the returning men had tried to persuade her to go back. 'Turrible dangerous,' they warned her, 'a big tide running and the mine path wicked underfoot.' But Em had persisted, the tide had turned and the big waves had retreated. When she got to the bottom of the mine path, Richard and Will heard her and went down to help.

None of the four slept. The two cousins waited, arms round each other, not speaking either. From time to time during the long wait, one or the other stirred to offer tea or food. It was close to three o'clock before Richard came himself and asked to speak to Lily alone. And although she felt Em's disapproval, Lily went with him.

He took her down the path a way, then, knowing it well, moved off it obliquely, the lantern left by the St Marvell men swinging in one hand while he guided Lily with the other. A few steps on he motioned to her to sit down and, as she did, the lantern lit up a small stack of timber which he must have already brought up from the beach. It was built into an overhang of rock and was dry, with space enough to squeeze in side by side, their feet sticking out.

'Listen,' Richard said, as if he thought Lily wouldn't. 'I can't bide waiting like this. I'll take Pendray's lamp and see if there's any chance of getting past that rockfall on my own. I can move the stones by myself, one by one if need be. I shan't disturb much. And I don't need much space to crawl.'

He said, trying a smile, 'I'm good at crawling.

'Now don't you fret,' he added as Lily began to argue. 'It's better so. Then, when there's light, the others will be back. With Will to supervise 'em, they'll soon get the rest cleared.'

He drew her deeper into the shadows, until they were backed against the planks. 'Listen, love,' he said, again as if he thought she wouldn't. 'I'd thought to bring you home tonight. There, I've admitted it. But since I have no home left, we'll have to be patient . . .'

'No, we don't,' Lily was fierce on his behalf, suddenly wanting to make amends, wanting him to be happy. 'Here's good enough for me,' she said.

She clung to him, all her passion revealing itself. He held her against him; she could hear his heart thudding in time with hers. Suddenly the sound of that thudding drowned every other noise, as if they were one person.

Richard stroked her hair, desire hot on him despite the moment. He wanted to touch her breasts, her body, he wanted to say, 'Hold me,' as if to convince her and himself he was still alive, as if in her he could find refuge from the danger that waited. He wanted to make love to her so they would both remember, so that when he was gone she would have that at least for a memory.

For a while they stayed together, immune, safe. Then Richard breathed out slowly, let his clasp loosen, pushed her away. 'Not yet,' he said, 'wait. When I come back we'll find a better place.' He rose to his feet, she'd never know the effort it took. 'And I'll bring your brother with me,' he said.

He left her then, spoke quickly to Will Pendray, took up Will's lamp. The three others watched as he went to the entrance, paused a moment to coil a rope over his shoulder, listening. Then he went inside, feeling for each step with extra care. They heard the clink of stones, one by careful one, as he set about the task of removing them.

196

Will watched him, too. His mouth worked. He let out a violent oath, startling in its obscenity. 'I'm the miner hereabouts,' he shouted, throwing back his head as if he were baying it to the sky. 'If anyone knows about mines, I do.'

He turned to the girls, spoke quickly to Em, almost unintelligibly, as if the words were stuck around his tongue. 'Tell them not to touch a stone until they've shored the roof up,' he said. 'We're going down the shaft.'

And to Richard, who was working his way forward stone by stone, he called, 'You'll never do it that way, boy. We must go down.'

He stood for a moment in the entrance. They sensed his muscles tensing, even in the darkness they could feel the fear on him. When Em came to stand beside him and put out a tentative hand, the sweat on his palms was like water and water was dripping off his face.

He gripped her so painfully she cried out, then, stepping on the balls of his feet, lightfooted, as if he was remembering how once he used to walk, he went through the entrance to the first shaft. 'Get out of that, boy,' he said to Richard. 'We'll go down the shaft, then work our way inwards along the gallery you were on. If we're lucky we'll find a way up somewhere. So give me the lamp. I'll lead. Stay way behind me in case of trouble.'

And to the girls he repeated, 'Don't let them do anything, mind, until they've done the shoring.' With that he lowered himself down the shaft with unexpected ease, was gone. And as quickly Richard followed.

The light of the lamp had made a welcome spot of colour inside the mine. Without it there was darkness. And silence, only the sea's angry lash.

'I'm that sorry Will's involved,' Lily said to Emma at last. She said nothing about Richard, of course, nothing about what she and Richard had just been doing, spoke calmly, as if she were speaking of ordinary day things, about things that had to be done or not done in everyday life.

And as calmly Em replied. 'Don't be,' said Em. 'It's what's needed. It'll make a difference for him.'

Her forehead knotted. 'It's a hard lesson,' she said, 'and not one he should have to learn. But this way he's nothing on his conscience. And that's what he needs, nothing to blame himself for, nothing to bring on shame.'

She turned to Lily. 'And I wish Richard good luck,' she said. 'If anyone merits luck, he does. It's a pity we can't say the same for Michael. But we can't change that. And there's the three of them gone,' she continued, as if she had just waved them goodbye on a railway station, 'but they'll come back. If they meet up with each other, that is. I believe they will. God'll have them in His keeping, for they deserve no less.'

And slowly, painfully, she began to cry while Lily comforted her.

CHAPTER 15

s dawn was breaking, a calmer drier dawn, the first of the St Marvell villagers reappeared. Among them was Ben Trevarisk, who as an older man naturally assumed the lead. When he heard that Richard and Will hadn't waited, had already gone inside the mine, he expressed what all must have thought.

'By Christ,' he cried in wonder, 'a Martin, or so we thinks of him, another Martin to be rescuing of a Polleven, why 'tis incredible.'

He slapped his thigh with a sound like thunder. 'Damme, if it don't take the biscuit,' he said. 'And damme if he bain't a fool, risking his life for someone that did him wrong.'

And to his daughter he added, almost defiantly, 'There, won't deny I would have preferred to be the one that done the rescuing, that'd even things a bit. But I don't take it hard. There'll be place yet for Ben Trevarisk. Will Pendray may know his job, or used to, but we'm still needed. We bain't wasting time, not with the work he left fer us.'

He spoke dramatically, but the other men were quiet. When they did speak it was in mutters, the unexpectedness of Will Pendray's action overshadowed by the irony of Richard's. If it made an extra complication, if it added to the bad news they brought, they didn't admit so at first.

The bad news was serious. And to be fair Ben didn't relish the telling of it. He explained that to save time they had wanted to bring timber and supplies round by sea; this had been Ben's idea from the start, Ben himself had been preparing his own boat for that very purpose. But the wind had backed. Although it had certainly decreased, it had set up a swell which in turn had built into surf. Getting out of The Cut would be bad enough but coming into Polmena Cove was well-nigh impossible.

'A wind like this can blow for days,' Ben grumbled, as if the wind also had conspired against him. 'And when it's in this quarter no boat afloat can manage along this coast. So I had to come on foot.'

To counter this bad news however he also brought good. During the night, leaving nothing to chance, the villagers, who hadn't slept either, had tried to round up extra help. Friendly neighbours had been pressed into service, had immediately offered farm horses and carts. Seeing Em's dubious expression, Ben explained it was for transport. 'If we can get the timber to the cliffs,' he said, 'we'm set to roll it over. Or lower it from the headland direct to the mine mouth. Listen, you can hear 'em already hard at work.'

And sure enough, through the early morning quiet, they could hear a rumble, as if plough teams were moving on the fields above. 'Meanwhile we'm here to collect the wood that's left,' Ben went on, 'it can't all be burnt, there's surely some to hand.'

With flamboyant enthusiasm, he heaved up a plank washed ashore by the storm the night before, and set off up the cliff with it on his back. Following his example his companions, tackling the stack Lily now showed them, began dragging it out, while others, armed with bars, contemplated the pile of stones that blocked the entrance passage. This measuring and assessing went on until shouts from the cliff top told them that the first of the wagons was approaching. But all this generous activity ground to a halt when Sir Robert's cohorts arrived.

It was also Ben who told the girls about Sir Robert. And who warned them when the first of Sir Robert's troops appeared. Afterwards Ben said he believed Sir Robert had been on the watch all night; there'd been reports of someone on the cliffs above Wheal Marty, although in the darkness no one had recognized who it was, and had assumed it was just another spectator, drawn to the spot by the noise. But this morning, when they came up to the valley entrance, Sir Robert Polleven certainly had been waiting, mounted on his old hunter, put out to grass so long it was almost as decrepit as its master.

As they'd passed, Sir Robert shouted to them in a hoarse voice, asking where his grandson was and what was being done to save him. If he remembered another day when his son had helped in a rescue attempt, he didn't mention it, but the villagers remembered. He heard the story of fire and explosion without sign of emotion but the details of the so-called rescue made him burst out in fury.

'A handful of farmers and a piece of string,' he shouted, 'a cripple and an idiot, to bring me back my grandson! I'll see about that.'

'We tried explaining,' Ben said, 'tried to tell 'un ours was the only way, that Pendray knew mining like we know fishing. He wouldn't listen. "Don't talk to me of fishing," he shouted, "drowning more like." Without another word he whipped his horse into a gallop, making us jump off the path. Slashed with his whip he did, rode at the hedges like a steeplechaser.'

He shook his head. 'Mad,' he said. 'Mad with fear, I 'spose. On reaching the first farmhouse he shouted for help, cursed and swore at the farmer for not having, what do they call it, a telephone. Were they still relying on word of mouth, like some primitive African tribe? They was to send off double quick, to summon proper assistance, damn the expense, who did they think they were? "Don't you know who's in danger," he shouted, "don't you know who I am?"'

'Although beats me where he thought he'd get new help from,' Ben added, 'what with the local police and most of St Marvell already here. And all the expense, all the effort, for a sneak of a chap, who thought he could play fast and loose, and get away with it. If it weren't for his father, although he be my nephew, I'd say leave him be; let him find his own way out and be damned to him.'

The assistance Sir Robert summoned lost no time in arriving. When the villagers saw who it was, they stared in disbelief as a platoon of soldiers, from his former regiment, came trampling down the valley and up the mine path. They were all young, eager to take over, their officer a young engineer rather like Michael Polleven. When Ben, stationing himself in front of the mine, told them to halt, 'March on,' the officer said, 'you and your amateurs, playing with stones.' And when again Ben tried to stop him, 'Out of the way. Old fool,' he added, brimming with callow arrogance, 'what do you know of engineering? Stick to crabs.'

Refusing to listen to advice, next he dismissed the farmers. 'No need of them,' he said. They took their dismissal to heart, unhooked their horses and stumped off, leaving the timber piled on the carts. Finally, giving the rockfall as cursory a glance as the one bestowed upon Ben and his 'amateurs', he pronounced it a nothing, easily got rid of by trained professionals. Before anyone could stop him, over every protest, he gave his men the order to blast the blockage.

'You'm crazy, boy!' Ben Trevarisk bellowed. 'Blow that rubble, the whole thing'll blow. There're men beneath it, another behind. 'Tis signing of their death warrants, I tell 'ee, to put a charge to them rocks. Might as well shoot 'em and be done with it, it's that useful.'

The soldiers listened to this exchange, turned away to smirk, not daring openly to laugh. But the officer saw their expressions, and their suppressed laughter put him on his mettle.

'Clear the path,' he ordered. 'Keep those women back. Set the charge.' Forcing the villagers to retreat, he had his soldiers unload their equipment, a supercilious smile upon his face. Even when Lily, thrusting herself forward, cried out that she was Sir Robert's granddaughter; her grandfather should know they were mistaken, it was her brother, Sir Robert's grandson, whose life they endangered . . . 'And

I'm the Queen of Sheba,' he retorted. 'Endanger! Stuff and nonsense. We'll have him out in minutes, just you watch.'

His men knew how to set a charge all right, better than Michael Polleven did, enough to finish what he had begun. With a great rumbling the explosion blasted through the rockfall into the tunnel. A massive internal eruption followed; the whole cliff face fell outward in a slide of liquid mud. Like a waterfall it sheeted over the entrance, sealing it as thoroughly as ever Michael had intended. And, in burying the entrance to Wheal Marty, blocked any future access in or out.

On the beach, the watchers witnessed this with horrid fascination, realizing the consequences sooner than the young officer. While he reeled backwards, his face turned white, feeling for support, all smugness gone, the word spread in a whisper, 'Buried, by gum, buried 'em alive – if any survived the blast, that is.' And like him, like the old Polleven stationed on the cliffs, Lily and Em turned to each other in horror, all hope gone.

Down in Wheal Marty itself, Will Pendray's sixth sense must have alerted him. He had time to shout a warning before the hot blast came surging in a thunderous roll. Behind him, Richard, caught off balance and exposed, crouched awkwardly until Will pushed him to the ground, shielding their heads from bits of stone which crashed around them in miniature cascades.

The explosion seemed to reverberate for ever. Like the waves on the beach, it surged against the rocks ahead and then surged off, a mighty backwash of sound. With all the force of water, it kept Richard pinned, spread-eagled, showered with shale and grit, smothered with dust. It might have been moments, or years, until he saw Will Pendray's feeble clawing movements – and heard his own retching as he dragged himself upright.

In the beginning they'd made good progress, had got easily down the first shaft and then turned inwards, along the gallery where Richard had previously been working, and into the passage beyond, as yet unexplored. Pendray naturally went faster than Richard, the light from the Davy lamp showing what lay ahead. He moved light on his feet, like a dancer, Richard thought, and the way from time to time he put his hand to the side of the walls, or reached up to touch the roof, suggested a manner of communication, as if the rocks themselves could speak and he could interpret. But this early progress had not lasted long, began to slow almost immediately after passing through this first area. The reason wasn't only the rough ground, nor even the rotten state of the timber struts, although all that didn't help; it was the number of small rockfalls that blocked the passage. These were all old falls, Pendray said, and even Richard recognized them, of indeterminate duration, nothing new or worrying, not surprising, given the age of the mine, but each needed to be cleared away before they could proceed.

This work Pendray took upon himself. A few neat blows, a careful aim or two with his pick, and space was made. Then they were pressing onward to the next blockade. It was as if he can't stop, Richard thought, labouring after, as if he's got to go on, as if once stopped, he'll realize where he is and never move again. Richard had heard of mountaineers becoming immobilized with fear; what'll I do if fear overtakes him, he thought, I'd never get him out. But he refused to let that thought stay with him.

They hadn't seen or heard signs of Polleven. 'Not yet,' Will had said, stopping again to put his ear to the wall, like a doctor listening for a heartbeat. 'He started above us. We have to find a way to go up to his level; or with luck meet him somewhere coming down to us.'

But when they came to the first branch in the gallery, the uphill passage dwindled to blank walls. They were forced to retrace their steps and continue along the original gallery. It was already morning, and work was beginning on Wheal Marty on the outside, when Will stopped again as if to listen, breathing deeply – looking for the current of air, Richard thought, understanding that at least, feeling for the wind I told him about. He himself was trying to remember when he had last felt and smelt it – this time instead of that cold, welcoming draught had come a boom and a hot, killing, blast.

'Dear God,' Richard spoke first. His voice seemed to come from someone else; he wiped the dirt from his mouth and nose, felt for his head as if it had come disconnected. 'What the devil was that?'

But he knew. There was no disguising that sound or force. As when he had been under heavy bombardment, when the guns had pounded for hours without cease, he felt anger rather than relief at their stopping. 'Damned idiots,' he panted, spitting out the dirt, 'damned fools, what're they playing at?'

Will Pendray didn't say anything, sat slumped as if the force had knocked him speechless. Even in the lamplight it was hard to distinguish his expression. Under the dirt which engrimed his face Richard had the impression of great pallor, as if blood was draining away as it does sometimes with shock.

'It's all right, old man.' He was talking in the same intuitive soothing way he'd used on the beach, the way he spoke to men cowering in terror, when human brains couldn't contain the firing a second longer, when human sight and hearing would burst apart under the relentlessness of it. 'It's over with. On your feet, that's the ticket.'

Will seemed not to hear, had collapsed within himself like a pricked balloon. 'Done for,' Richard thought, 'my God, he's done for.'

He'd seen it happen many times, the noise, the pounding, until it eroded away control, eroded sense. You could hector, threaten, you'd not get a man back from that world he'd escaped to. Even kindness was not enough to bring him back. Yet somehow you had to try.

After a while, when he himself had recovered enough to pull himself upright, he managed to get Will on his feet. This seemed very important; once down, like a sick horse, a man might never get up again. Richard used all his strength to pull and push, at the same time alternately coaxing and bullying. Possibly he may have struck Will, he couldn't remember. The effort left him drained. Yet he knew, again intuitively, that they must keep on, either forward or back, it didn't matter as long as they kept moving.

One glance backwards told him that they'd never return the way they'd come, not with Will like this. Dust and debris still hung in choking clouds but he could see the fresh rockfalls. From time to time the continuing rumble of stone came from the direction of the entrance, the eddying of the eruption. Even he knew an explosion of this magnitude must have caused enormous damage to a mine so fragile and old. 'You've killed us!' he wanted to shout.

No way except continue forward then, but he knew himself hopelessly lost, in the mine he had wanted to call his. He felt like taking Will by the shoulders and shaking information out of him. 'You're the expert,' he wanted to shout.

He took up the lamp, shone it ahead. The passage veered round almost at right angles, but just after the corner another rock wall blocked it, an old blockage, layered with scatterings of fresh fallen stones. He could recognize the newness now by their colour, lighter, cleaner. The rocks underneath had a different look, he sensed the difference, deeper, thicker than the others they'd come through, more solid. Where the light caught there was a reflection of darkness shining with a russet gleam. 'You'd know how to assess that heap of stone,' he said accusingly to Will, 'you'd see the flaw. You'd hit the weakest point, force a way past as easily as knifing butter.' To himself he said, 'This wall may have no weak point.'

He picked up Will's pickaxe, balanced it, balanced himself, swung. The sound came back heavy, dead. 'A dead end,' he told Will angrily, swinging again and again. 'Blocked.'

All the while he kept on talking to Will. He found talking easier than working in silence. The impenetrable silence, the impenetrable weight suddenly seemed a burden he couldn't carry; like Atlas he was bowed by it.

206

Furious, he resisted the knowledge of defeat, swung and dug. The years of debris swirled, choked, settled, thick and clotted. Sweat started from him, he could smell his own fear. It steadied him. He made himself relax and move in rhythm along the line of blockage, starting at one end and progressing to the other. Each time he swung he felt the jar of an unyielding mass, swore, and swung again. Impassively leaning against the wall where he'd been propped, like a lifesize doll, what remained of William stared over his head.

Richard was exhausted. 'One more,' he panted, and then, 'one more.' He could scarcely find the energy to raise the pick handle, let alone swing it, when he felt the point catch, dig in – and the mass shift.

Now he swung and dug in a frenzy, a terrier scrabbling. When the pick no longer served, he used both hands, shovelling away at what appeared to be fine dust. It caked him head to toe, again he was choked. He had just reached the point of drawing back or being smothered, when he felt his hand go through to space.

After that it didn't take long to widen the hole and clear out a passage; he worked like a man possessed. When the opening was wide enough, he put the lamp in and found a place to steady it, then forced Will's head down as he would have to stoop. He had to make Will go first, he'd never be able to drag Will after him.

'Come on, come on,' he muttered, persuading, cajoling Will, and forgetting his own lameness that made him such a dolt. And when, as if he had capitulated, Will obediently bent and slid through the gap, wriggling through with professional instinct, Richard followed with such awkward haste he pitched forward on his face.

He fell awkwardly, but without hurt. Dragging himself up, swinging the lamp, he stared about him. The place they'd come to appeared enormous, as if the original gallery had trebled in size, had widened into what, after close confinement, seemed more like a cave. This never was the work of one man, he thought, suddenly awed, here's the proof.

Taking Will by the arm, he ventured out into the cave. It gave him the strangest feeling to see their footsteps in the dust on a floor where no one had come perhaps in a hundred years. 'Or more,' he said, 'perhaps much more. How old is this?'

Will never replied.

At least five passages branched off from the cave. He went from one to the other, trying to listen for what Will would have listened for, trying to smell that cold open smell. Once more the thought came to him that today of all days he hadn't smelt or heard anything, and if Will had, surely he'd have mentioned it. Could the earlier explosion have caused a blockage lower down; suppose the second exit, if there were one, was already blocked? Again panic clawed his gut.

It was then that as if in answer he heard a sound, not the one he'd been listening for, rather, a moan, a quaver of a moan like an animal. It came from the middle passage and made his hair stand up. 'What's that?' he cried.

After what seemed a long wait the cry was repeated. He knew now where he'd heard sounds like that before, in No Man's Land in the aftermath of some raid. 'We'll try this way,' he told Will. Picking up the lamp, he took Will by the hand. 'Forward march,' he said. 'No hanging back, one two, one two.'

At the start of this new venture he had to drag Will forward as if even in his state of shock Will was reluctant. 'If it stops or narrows,' Richard promised him, 'we'll turn round.' But it maintained its original size, and after a while took a deep plunge downward, then levelled off again.

That made walking easier. 'It must be very old,' Richard answered his own question, still talking to himself. 'And in much better state than my original gallery. The roof must still be in place. No rockfalls here.' And presently as if to give emphasis to this observation, as if instinctively assured by the firmness of the ground, Will himself no longer held back but followed Richard's lead, if not of his own volition at least without resistance.

The lamp picked out the walls ahead, smooth-hewn rocks; they seemed to glitter. There was a quality about them Richard had never seen before. Small side passages branched off the one they were on, like side chapels off a church nave. He sensed a kind of purpose to them, not a random hewing. Sometimes the dark original colour was stained with red and gold, a shining. He was awed by it also. Despite his fear an excitement grew. 'What do you make of it, then?' he wanted to ask Will, wanted Will to reply. 'What do you think it means?' Like a zombie Will kept pace with him, a child held by the hand.

They passed one shaft, but, 'No one's been here in the longest time,' Richard told Will, 'even the ladder overhead's crumbled.' They moved on. Suddenly the cry was closer now, a whimpering. It seemed to echo and re-echo in thin imitation. Ahead the lamp picked up the rock, fastened on something on the ground, a thing that moved and strained as the light caught it, and cried out again, a shout.

'Well,' Richard said, 'here's a fine thing. How to get the walking wounded out.' He spoke more cheerfully than he felt, came up to Michael, said, 'What've you done to yourself?' And as Michael tried to rise, more sharply, 'Lie still, you idiot, let's look.'

He propped Will against the wall, bent down, felt for broken bones. He sensed Michael's gaze fixed on him, felt the clutch of his hands. 'I thought no one'd ever come.' Michael was whispering as if after all that shouting he had no voice left. 'There was one great explosion. I thought I was dead.'

He said nothing about the reason why he was there, or why Richard had had to come after him, said nothing about what he'd done. Suddenly Richard was reminded of a young German soldier he'd once found in a shell hole, where he himself had stumbled in the dark. They had looked at each other, almost face to face, two enemies, sworn to kill. The German had been young, his age; had seemed absurdly young

209

and vulnerable. They had both spoken at the same time. He didn't know what the German said, but, 'Get out of here, and good luck, you poor sod,' Richard had told him, sickened by the senselessness of hate. He'd deliberately turned his back, for a moment had felt the other's indecision. When he looked round the German had gone, and after a while, when a lull came in the shooting, he himself had gone on as well.

Michael must have had a blow to the head, must have lain unconscious, the lamp he had stolen from Richard's bag smashed. When Richard shone Will's lamp up he saw the dangling ends of rope in the shaft above. But apart from a twisted ankle, Michael appeared to be of a piece, no broken bones. It's fear that made him cry out, Richard thought, fear that stopped him from going on.

The ankle was so swollen he couldn't take the boot off but he thought he could tie it up so that it would bear weight. Got to get him moving too, he thought, the halt, the blind and the deaf, got to get us all moving on. He almost laughed.

As he worked quickly, using part of his own shirt and a piece of snapped-off wood, he was thinking, planning, rejecting. He could see the broken rungs overhead, no way up this shaft, although he'd never have got William up it anyhow, and by now probably the gallery above, the one Michael had been on, was blocked as well.

'What's wrong with him?' Michael had regained the use of his voice, was staring at William.

'Nothing that time won't mend.' Richard was curt. 'Now up, in a row, one behind the other. Take Will's arm, let Will lean on you, you lean on me.'

He had got them shuffling forward in a line, himself in front, like convicts chained together, but that was better than he'd hoped. 'That's it,' he encouraged them.

'Where are we going?' Michael had made a quick recovery now he knew he wasn't going to die. He sounded truculent. 'Why this way?' he repeated.

Richard beat down the answer, 'Because there's no other.'

Instead, deceptively mild, he asked, 'Where would you prefer then?'

When Michael told him, he almost yelled with relief. 'You've felt it too,' he wanted to shout, perhaps he did, 'you're sure, today, while you've been inside. Then we aren't cut off from it, I've not been imagining things.'

They were still moving one behind the other, slowly, Richard hobbling with the lamp, his knee by now so stiff he could scarce contain the pain; next to him Michael, equally lame, unable to put weight on one foot at all, perhaps it was broken. And next to Michael, Will, bringing up the rear, intact in body, only his mind gone, leaving it a shell. Yet he almost succeeded, Richard thought, by God he almost did. If those fools, whoever they were, hadn't done what he told them not to, he'd have gone on to the end. Damn them, he thought again. If only Will would talk. He stopped, said carefully, loudly, 'Will, you can hear me. I need your help. I need you, Will, you're the only one I've got. If there's an exit, how can we find it?'

He found he'd taken Will by the lapels of his jacket, was shaking him. 'I haven't felt the current of air at all but Michael says he did earlier. We can't feel it now, where's it gone?'

There was a long silence. He won't answer, Richard was thinking; he felt despondency shut down. Can't or won't.

'They're waiting for us outside,' he said in what afterwards he realized was divine inspiration. He shook Will again. 'Em's waiting for us outside. Help us get to her.'

To his amazement Will spoke out, a thin thread of sound. So sometimes, even when unconscious, men will drag speech up from the deepest recesses of their minds. 'The wind,' Will said thickly, 'changes in the wind. But it's still there all right.' He might have been laughing at their ignorance. 'Got to be,' he said, 'no other reason. Smell.'

And suddenly it seemed to Richard, to Michael, that they could taste the freshness in the air, the coldness they had been looking for, the raw smell of sea and salt. And perhaps even Will felt it too because he began now to herd the other two along. And after the passage made one large final sweep, again almost a right-hand turn, they could see it, the small speck of greyness against the dark, the speck, cut into rock, that grew larger until it became an oblong of light through which fresh air poured and the sound of salt waves beat.

But when they came out of it, the second exit they had all been so sure of, they found they were perched on a spit of rock like a ledge. It had an overhang above it like a porch roof, and below, some forty feet or so of sheer slate plunged down into a raging sea that seemed to reach tentacles up to suck them off. And overhead again, twice as high of slated rock and scree stretched in a stillness to the cliff top.

CHAPTER 16

Before the sound of the explosion had ebbed, the villagers had begun to calculate the effect. They weren't miners, weren't 'professionals', but that didn't prevent them assessing the damage in human terms. 'No way back in there,' Ben said, shocked into simplicity. 'No way out neither. But don't you grieve.'

He put his large arm round the girls, for once his natural kindness asserting itself, that kindness which somewhere in his past hardship must have stifled. 'Just have to wait,' he said.

Waiting came hard to Lily. 'No!' she screamed. She started to run up the mine path, knelt, thrust her hands into the mud, scooped it out. 'Dig,' she cried, 'dig.'

The mud settled, her hands were glued with it. Her arms were coated with the red wet earth. ''Tis no use, my lover,' Ben said. He pulled her away. 'Digging won't bring 'em back.'

Before the charge was set Em had scarcely breathed, had sat as if even the batting of an eye would disturb the balance. Patience was part of her nature, Lily used to say, Em's inheritance from a line of fisher folk, forged by harsh environment. Now Em stood up, and like her cousin, screamed. 'Waste,' is what she cried, 'vanity, greed.' The words were lost as if she'd never uttered them.

Waiting was nothing new for the villagers. Their patience was unending. They had often had to wait – for weather to change, or storm to die down, or boats return – wait for the sea to give up its dead. They didn't speak yet of death but they prepared for it. Practical and efficient, they also knew how to prepare. 'Oh, Em,' Lily said as the day wore on, 'there's Mr Jarvis, the carpenter. Whatever's he come for?'

Em didn't tell her. In another role Mr Jarvis was the undertaker. He made coffins, of the best oak. He knew the Pollevens for monied people. They'd need his work.

Sir Robert Polleven didn't relish waiting either, had expected his gamble to pay off, had willed it to do so. It had failed and he had to live with the consequences of failure, having no recourse except to rely on that 'cripple and idiot', as once he'd had to rely on the cripple's uncle. But he wouldn't think of that. Like a block of stone he sat close to the cliff, on a chair he'd had brought from the Manor, shawled and blanketed, chin resting on his silver-topped cane. The waiting didn't make him change his mind, they'd find no weakness in him. When Michael was safe, he'd still get rid of the other two; if Michael was safe the destruction of the mine would save him destroying it himself, he'd be glad of it. The thought that Michael might not return at all, that all three might be lost, never entered his mind. He wouldn't let it.

Such unwavering confidence in his grandson's invincibility might have given Lily comfort, might have comforted Emma. He acknowledged neither girl, made no concession, ignored their presence, ignored their fears. Had he been asked, he might have replied, and believed what he was saying, 'People of that class aren't capable of feelings.'

The north-coast Clubbers also gathered – the word 'waiting' didn't fit, there was nothing of patience in their curiosity. Since Iris's meeting most of them knew who Michael Polleven and Richard Chote were, and the cause of the quarrel between them. Strangely enough their sympathies were more for Richard than Michael. Echoes of the ill-fated confrontation at the Club and the veterans' championship of a war hero lingered. And although they liked to ape country squires they were secretly pleased that a real one should get his

214

comeuppance. Already there was talk of 'doing something' for the missing men. They meant making a money collection in their memory, for the benefit of their families – if they had families, that is, and of course excluding Polleven.

On the other hand, if somehow Iris Duvane's name was now mentioned, if 'one of their own' was coupled with this tragedy, they also felt duty bound to keep Iris's reputation unsullied. Even Hugo Farell, from some ill-defined family feeling, although he would have denied the charge, eventually hauled himself out of bed and struggled down the valley path until he reached the beach.

Polmena Cove didn't look as he had imagined it, he thought, gazing about him with distaste. Nothing inviting today, the eastern cliff plastered by a giant red mudflow, the narrow strip of beach blackened with refuse caught among the seaweed and crowded with spectators. Already reporters had come crowding down, scenting a story, putting Polmena Cove really in the news. He almost felt like tackling Sir Robert Polleven direct. 'All this publicity hinders business,' he would have said, 'makes a bad impression. A beach resort linked to a mine disaster, what a contradiction!'

He couldn't help thinking how interesting it was that in times like this simple people acted with the same instincts as their more sophisticated brethren, closing ranks and presenting a united front. No one'd get much information out of the inhabitants of St Marvell if they set their minds against it. And he listened with a half-smile of appreciation as he heard villagers swear that the mine belonged to the Martins, didn't Richard Chote work it and wasn't he a Martin, when a scant week or so previously they'd been swearing the opposite to Sir Robert's solicitors.

Only one person made no pretence of waiting at all, had already shaken Cornish dust (or sand) from her feet, with the firm avowal never to tread thereon again. Returning from the concert, Iris had wasted little time, had packed her bags and left, taking the night train. She had penned her hosts a charming little apology (in case their hospitality might come in useful next year) but to Hugo she was somewhat more explicit.

'See you in London,' she'd written, 'or so I suppose, if you can ever drag yourself away. As for me,' (he imagined her little shrug) 'I always said the Celts are complicated creatures. These Cornish machinations are too involved for my taste, so I leave them in your hands, dear cousin. Who better suited to sort them out. I'll enjoy my victory. But I will admit,' she'd added in a last postscript, 'victory could have been sweeter if there was someone to share it with.'

A group of people waiting, a village waiting, loved ones, friends, relatives, the collective wishing of all of these surely recoiled upon itself like a gigantic spring, releasing some hidden energy. And it is perhaps possible that on the other side of the headland, trapped on that isolated ledge of rock, the three marooned men felt its presence like a lifeline.

Richard recovered first, at least he recovered sufficiently to assess the position. They lay in an exhausted heap, safe enough for the moment, but facing horrendous difficulties. Although they'd found a second exit from the mine, and although Richard was sure along the way they'd also found signs of ore, veins of tin or copper that must have been forgotten years, centuries before, none of this served if they couldn't get off the ledge. And how were they to do that, two lame men and an 'idiot'?

Richard had had a moment's hope when Will had spoken. Perhaps reaching the open would revive him, at least restore him sufficiently so that he would be of use. But he knew he couldn't count on that. And Michael had already said, 'Don't expect help from me. I've no head for heights,' weighing his own chances, afraid to take risks. Pointing to the lower rocks, Michael had added, 'You'd need climbers' gear, ropes, crampons, a whole damn mountaineering expedition. Besides, what hope is there if you did get down, look at the bloody surf. No one with even both legs working could swim through those breakers or survive those currents. And where would you swim to? For God's sake, I've not survived a mine collapse to make food for fishes.'

But if going down the cliff, and up it, was beyond them, then a rescue party must be summoned to make it possible. And to summon a rescue party someone must do the summoning. And if indeed the sea blocked the way down, then perforce the way up was the only solution.

'My God, you're mad to think of it.' Michael paled at the prospect. He hobbled to the side of the ledge and strained to peer round that overhang of slate which concealed the entrance so effectively that neither from the cliff nor from the sea would anyone ever spot it unless they knew what they were looking for. Above this first barrier, what Richard thought of as a roof over a porch, slate crumbled into landslips where additional outcrops of harder rock thrust like beetling brows; above them again, scrub covered the face of the cliff like a grey-green fuzz. 'You can't get up there,' he told Richard, 'not crippled like you are. You bloody cripple,' he suddenly shouted. Fear made his voice ragged. 'You'll get no thanks from me. This is a bloody impasse you've brought us to.'

I don't want your gratitude; you've forgotten it anyway, Richard thought wearily. And I don't need your insults. But they suddenly didn't seem to matter. He said in his deceptively quiet voice, with its hint of anger, 'First we'll eat a bit and think a bit and see what we come up with. So sit down and shut up if you aren't capable of thinking.'

Manoeuvring Will with care, he got him in a safe position, backed inside the entrance where there was no danger of his stepping off by mistake or reeling over the edge; he'd known of men, coming out of shell shock, flinging themselves over the trench parapet in an apparent suicide bid. He unbuckled the bag Will had brought, set the pick and rope aside, found bread and a flask of tea.

The tea was almost cold but he shared it out in equal parts, each drinking in turn, as he divided the bread. Michael wolfed his share down hungrily; Will sat with his on his knees, his throat working spasmodically as if he wanted to eat but didn't remember how. Richard himself ate and drank neatly and quickly. While he ate, he assessed their chances. He knew they were slim. They couldn't stay here indefinitely with no hope of rescue and little expectation of ever being seen, not with this sea running: as bad as being trapped inside. Something must be done before their condition deteriorated and they lost heart.

It went without saying that he was disappointed. Naturally he'd assumed that a passage of the size and importance of this one wouldn't just peter out in a piece of ledge perched on nowhere. Most likely, he thought, lying back for a moment, there must once have been a way out. Probably to the sea. At the foot of the cliffs, jagged spires of free-standing rock had broken off from the main part. Although their only purpose now seemed to be to add to the sea's turbulence, and to block effectively any random sighting of the ledge, at some time in the past they might have formed a flight of cleverly hewn stone steps. Idly he imagined how men might have run up and down those steps, with wicker baskets, he supposed, in those days, full of ore, to lower them into coracles that were later rowed out to deeper water where Mediterranean adventurers stared down from their anchored galleys.

Or perhaps there had been a trail going up the cliff like the one he'd discovered at Polmena Cove – he'd come across that by accident. Not until he'd actually started up had he stumbled upon it, with its cleverly positioned paving stones underneath the heather and bracken, and its cleverly plotted twists and turns.

At first he had thought it was just some animal track, like those little lines crisscrossing the scrub here on their left, an animal track leading to nowhere. He shook himself. If he could get up to those tracks, work his way to them over the scree, if he could rely on roots and plants, gorse bushes, to give him leverage, if he could find hand- and foothold, if his foot would hold . . .

He swore to himself. It wasn't the height that bothered

him, nor the sheerness of the cliff, nor even the possibility of falling, it was whether his crippled leg would hold.

He made himself think the route out carefully, forced himself to imagine it, like a sequence of photographic stills, in black and white. He didn't want to fall of course, he didn't want to feel his leg give way, his hands give way, the void open out – but it could happen, it was a chance he had to take.

But he wouldn't fall, not now he had all the world suddenly ahead of him to live for. Not now when he didn't have to keep proving to himself, proving to the real world, proving to Lily, that being crippled didn't hinder him. Not now when he had Lily to believe in him.

Thinking of Lily brought her there, in a flash so vivid he wondered the others didn't see her. 'Forgive me,' he heard himself saying, although he spoke no word aloud, 'I know I've not had much time today for thinking of anyone. And I know I promised to come back, it's coloured all my actions, it'll dominate what I do next. But you know as well as I do what has to be done and who's left to do it.

'It's like in the war,' he told her, 'a team effort. Each one does his bit, then someone else takes over. There's no reason for it being that way, no fuss about heroism, it's just because you're there, that's all. So, although I'm no expert at this climbing stuff, there's no point in putting it off; got to get on with it.'

Leaving all the gear behind, what use were pick and rope where he was going, he rose stiffly, his knee rigid like a piece of wood, like one of those burning sticks that were all that was left of his house. 'You watch out for Will,' he told Michael, his voice full of sudden menace, 'you keep an eye on him. If he wakes, you make sure he knows where he is, don't let him blunder off. And if I'm not back or help doesn't arrive, then wait until the sea drops and try to get down.'

He didn't add what he knew as well as Ben, 'When the wind's in this quarter the surf can stay for days.'

Getting on top of the first outcrop, the porch roof, was the hardest. No, the first step was hardest, the first letting go and edging out away from the safety of the ledge itself, body flattened against the cliff, injured leg dangling, not looking down, one foot inching delicately, fingers feeling for a hold not yet visible. His shoulders and hands were strong enough to take his weight, he told himself that over and over, but that didn't make allowances for the fact that there might not be anything firm to hold on to.

He had decided to go to the right of the ledge first, then work his way back left, merely because on the right, a few inches up from the ledge, he had noted an indentation, less than that, a flaw in the rock wide enough for a foot. It was all he had. But if he could find another similar indentation above it, at the moment out of sight, if he could find a handhold – all he'd need then was a bit of luck, a firm stone, a firm root to cling to and he could swing his other leg round and be standing on the roof. Then he could really decide the best route to follow.

And that is what he did, although if asked he could never have said how. Nor explain how he could have got back to the ledge again if he hadn't found those three essentials – a first handhold, a second foot- and a second handhold, as if carved for him specially. But once up he could sit astride the roof (which from above even more closely resembled his name for it, having a distinct peak in the middle), let the sweat dry, and plan. He noticed for the first time that the sky was grey, that the waves came in against the cliff with surprising regularity in great grey-green curls, tinged with white, and that there was a smell of thrift here close to, a clump of pink thrift growing out of season.

He leaned over the roof and shouted down, 'There're black-thorn bushes and gorse here, I'll hang on to them and move off to the left now, over the scree.' And hope I'm still lucky, he thought, as he fought with the prickles and burrs of this unexpected growth of stunted trees and gorse from which the roof emerged.

The gorse probably wouldn't have held if he'd had to

put weight on it, it was shallow-rooted, embedded only in shale, and the blackthorns were so stunted they looked like plants rather than bushes. But the feel of them gave him fresh confidence. He crept out from their cover on to the scree, edging upward where he could, moving sideways if he couldn't.

The scree was made up of small slates that ground themselves into his hands, the whole stretched like a skin over the cliff underneath so that when he moved upon it he felt the whole skin move. Once, when his foot slipped for a moment he felt himself going. The stones slid beneath him in a small flurry of dust, the very smell of the dust was cold, as if nothing had disturbed it since it had been first formed.

If he hadn't been used to balancing, if he hadn't become good at what he'd jokingly called crawling, he would have gone through that outer skin, ripped it off, and slipped away with it. But he didn't. He stretched across it, he gave himself to it, he caressed it, all the way towards that spread of scrub which suddenly looked as safe and sheltering as an entire forest.

It was amazing what minutiae of detail one saw, he remembered thinking as he now edged his way through the thin scattering of plants and grass, blurred by distance until one got right up close to them. The shape of a single heather patch for example, its feathered flowers already bursting into pink and purple; the withered clumps of grass that grew in places, burnt colourless and treacherous, coming away in his hand; even the butterflies that fluttered as he moved flatly across shallow ground which here smelt like summer, a mixture of hot blackberries and sun. Perhaps it was better to concentrate on these small things than on those that lay beneath, revealed now in all their hideous, vacant beauty, the green-grey water, the waves, smooth as oil until they broke, the great gouts of foam.

If he had been an artist he could have sketched from memory every inch of that sparse passage. He didn't look down, didn't look up, just kept going. And when he suddenly realized by the change of texture, by the feel of thicker soil, by the actual physical lessening of the tension round him as if even the air was more solid, that he must have almost reached the top, he resisted the temptation to rest for just a moment before he made the final effort. He knew too well what that 'rest for a moment' meant, too many men died because of it.

He crawled on as slowly as before, not letting himself imagine the end, a stretch, a heave, another stretch, relying on his shoulders, his good leg almost as useless as the bad. His hands reached in front of him, he scarcely recognized their bloodstained shape as they clawed over one more outcrop of rock, a small one this, fastened on its upper side, and heaved. And suddenly he was up where all was level, a level field, where at a distance cows munched ruminatingly and never lifted their heads.

The ground no longer sloped under him in a vast empty sheet; the sea, reduced once more to its proper perspective, lay confined in its blue-grey bowl; he lay on the grass by the cliff verge, not thinking anything, only that he was very thirsty. And after a while, when he could move again and straighten his back, when with shaking hands he could heave himself upright like a man, not like a creeping crawling insect, he edged away from the cliff edge, found the trace of the path that led down the field towards the valley entrance.

It was Ben again who brought the word, came almost running down the path if so large a man could be said to run. 'Dick Chote,' he shouted, 'by God, he'm back!' And in an excess of affection he caught Em up and twirled her off her feet as if she were ten years old. 'They'm all trapped on a ledge on t'other side of the point.'

'Climbed up the bloody cliff,' others were exclaiming now to any who would listen, voices rough with admiration, 'up the bloody cliff, mind you. But how to get them others off?'' They shouted to each other, 'Surf's not so bad now, 'tis gone down some with the tide. But the wind's holding, still can't get out from The Cut. If only there was another boat.'

They couldn't say more, others were hurrying round, crowding round, the whole world was echoing the words. They must have reached Sir Robert in his lonely vigil. They finally reached Lily, made sense.

Lily had been concentrating on remembering Richard's face, it had seemed to her the only thing left for her to do; she had been willing him to show himself in her thoughts so that he would be alive in them. Sometimes she felt she'd almost succeeded, he appeared to her clearly; sometimes she felt him slipping away and she'd had to concentrate the harder, afraid if she let him go for a moment, she would never summon him back again.

At some point, she didn't know when, she and Em had given up standing as close to the mine entrance as they could, as if willing that mudslide to draw back like a red velvet curtain in a theatre and reveal the players behind it. Instead they had come down to the stream where the debris across the bridge had been cleared away and the ruins of the hut made blackened outlines. Vaguely she remembered that people had brought food and drink, speaking softly, urging it on her as one might coax an invalid; vaguely she supposed the tide must have come in again and then retreated, because now once more the roar of the waves was held to a distance and soft folds of wet sand spread between the sea and themselves.

The old Lily shouted out. 'Em,' she cried, 'isn't it good to be alive!' The new Lily felt it, deep in her heart's core, like a thrust of blood, like a surge as if she were connected to some current of energy and she and it had fused. She looked up at the sky where the sun was only a brightness under the grey of clouds, it must be well on in the afternoon, where had the day gone? 'There is a boat,' she heard herself saying, as earlier she had said, 'There is some wood,' in so calm a voice she wouldn't have known it was hers. 'Will Pendray's boat, the one he rowed me in.'

And while the men went searching, for Dick Chote would never have left it in the open after the past week of storm, even if he wasn't a born fisherman he would have made certain to have hauled it well up from the beach, and surely Michael Polleven wouldn't have had the malice to burn it too, she went up the valley path to the top of it, not exactly running but moving swiftly as if, she thought, I'm gliding along, as if I'm walking on air.

She passed the place where her grandfather was installed with his shawl and chair and his manservant for company, passed by, then turned and came towards him.

'You've got Michael back,' she told him, bright-eyed, serious. 'That should be enough. You should let Richard have the rest. Nothing in this world is worth all this, not even Polmena Cove.'

He didn't say anything. She went on up, beyond the burnt-out barricade, to the field where she had climbed the hedge and sat counting flower petals, when she had still been a child.

The people there parted when she came towards them, letting her through as if she had the right. They know, she thought, and the idea warmed her like sunlight. Richard was sitting against a hedge, his legs stretched out in front of him. He looked pale under his sunburn; suddenly she was remembering how he had looked when he had risen up under the keel of the boat. But his eyes were smiling at her, not burning with anger as then.

She knelt beside him, not caring what anyone thought, not even knowing that she didn't care. 'I'm here,' she said, she whispered, ''tis finished with.' And she took his hand, and held it and felt under its torn palms the surge of energy running faster like a fever.

How the men of St Marvell got Widow Pendray's boat down to the sand flats, gliding it along as if it were fitted to wooden runners, and how Ben Trevarisk got himself fitted into it with one of his sons to pull at second oar, joined at the last moment by a third crew member, one of the Clubbers, a former rock-climber, and how Ben took the 'Seagull' out through the surf, has passed into legend, is the stuff of courage. And makes up the sum of Ben's real atonement – although for once he didn't have time to make a production of it, had to save that for another day.

The 'Seagull' dipped into the waves like one of the birds for which she was named, her sides barely lifting above the spume of foam. Once beyond the surf, getting round the point was not that difficult, it was coming in to the rocks at the base of the cliff where the figures on the ledge could now be clearly seen that taxed all of Ben's skill.

'Heaved up and down, me handsomes,' he used to say, 'like a bucket in a well. Up in t'air one second, down in the trough another, takes some powerful rowing to keep a boat level in them conditions, if you bain't sea-sick first.'

And he'd laugh, a great bellowing laugh. 'Never saw a man so white,' he said, 'as that there foreigner. "Now Tom, me lad," I says to son Tom, "get your coat off 'cos 'tis two to one he'll be in the drink afore 'ee can say Jack Robinson." But he didn't. Went at it like a proper trooper once he got the hang of it.

'"Jest let me get me bearing," he says, cool as cucumber. And to Michael Polleven, hanging over that ledge in a fret to be off first, "I'll come up and take Pendray down with me, then come back fer you."

'And so he did,' Ben'd add with what was surprising humility, 'up and down like a ruddy squirrel with his ropes, never saw its like, had claws instead of feet. If Dick had had he there afore he made it on his own, he'd have been that grateful I expect. Brought down poor old Will first, never knowed where he was to, poor chap, and were laid out in bed in his mother's cottage afore he did. Then went back for Michael Polleven. Well, he's my nephew, as I said afore, but I told young Michael a few home truths. And damned if the foreigner didn't round on 'un too.

'"Know Dick Chote well," he said, well, words to that effect like. "Going up that cliff weren't a patch on what he did in France. Got a medal fer that, and he'll get a medal fer this too, you see. But if all this caper were to steal a man's home from him, why, bugger it."

225

'That's what he says,' Ben would repeat, 'bugger it, just like we would. And then goes on to add, "I'll not sit idle by and see misjustice done. And if they wants to raise a collection, that's what I'll put my money on."

'Don't know about no money,' Ben'd stop to explain hastily, prompted no doubt by Charity's resentment that he should have done, 'don't know about justice and all, but know Richard Chote deserves a medal like Jeb Martin got. And know that of all the things I've done in me life, nothing pleases me better than to have helped him when he needed it.'

CHAPTER 17

A nd the rest passed into legend too, or rather into the stories legends are made of. Or so Lily used to think. Not that Lily realized it at the time; for Lily it seemed just natural.

'It was like this,' she used to say, 'when the shouting and the tumult died away – I do like those words, the shouting and tumult, they fill the soul, they're words to sing to – when Michael and Will were safely back, and Ben and Tom, when Grandfather Polleven took Michael home with him and Em went to stay with Widow Pendray, why then, Richard and I found a carter to bring us up to Nanscawn door, and that was an end to it.'

She didn't add how at first Richard'd refused, saying it wasn't right, swaying with fatigue while he argued. And she, fierce as a vixen, had argued in return that hadn't he wanted to bring her to his house, hadn't that been his intention? And if now it was a day, two days later, and if he had no house to go to, wasn't it only fair and just that she bring him to hers?

But she did explain how when they got to the farm they found Hetty in such a fluster, alternately weeping and laughing, that if Lily had asked her to make up a bed for a horse, or told her that the end of the world had come, Hetty would have believed her and would have run to do it out of joy and happiness. And that she had said to Richard, emphatic for the last time, 'We cost you your home. Where else should you go but here?'

But the greatest secret of all she never did tell anyone, how in the middle of the night when everyone was sleeping, when a great calm had come across the fields, like the coolness of moonlight, she got up from her bed in that square familiar room, crept softly down the corridor and opened Richard's door.

He'd dropped like a log when they had got him upstairs, if they'd but known it, in that sleep that only soldiers know when a battle is over. Now she sensed somehow he was awake. In fact he was looking out of the window, across the fields to where the cliffs dipped down, where, had it still been in place, he might have seen the lights in his hut.

She came to stand beside him. 'It can be rebuilt,' she told him, knowing too what he was thinking. 'We can rebuild it. And the mineshaft can be cleared in time; you'll make a go of it.'

For he had told her of the galleries they'd seen, the carefully layered passages leading from that underground cavern, and how when Will recovered they'd go back and explore it thoroughly, go into partnership.

He'd sighed then, leaned on the sill beside her, dressed in old clothes borrowed from her father's wardrobe. The wind, almost gone at last, stirred his hair, and ruffled the lace on her dressing gown, so that she drew the window close.

'And we'll be together,' she told him, 'it's better so. We'll put the bitterness and evil out of mind and rebuild on that too.'

He laid his hand upon her cheek, she could feel the calluses, the cuts and blisters. 'Such confidence,' he told her, ''twould move a mountain. But I think, like you, that when an end's reached, there's no going back on it.'

'What does that mean?' she asked him; she felt a silence, like the silence before a judgement, a coldness as if the start of autumn had come before its time. And when he didn't answer, 'You can't let evil win,' she'd cried, 'we've gone through too much together.'

She clung to him as she had done on the beach before he left her. 'Hold me,' she cried, 'never let me go. What do I care about what's proper? Or if you want to sleep, I'll keep watch for you, I'll sing for you, whatever you want, just don't leave me again.'

And she began to sing, 'God's in His heaven', softly, haltingly, under her breath, a thread of broken song like a mermaid's singing, until he took her head in both of his hands and stopped her mouth with his. And then it didn't matter what was proper any more, was as improper as he could have wished for, and yet as right and natural as rain and sun.

Michael never came back to Nanscawn, at least not for many years. He was the real casualty of the struggle for possession of Polmena Cove. Nor did he stay with Sir Robert as the old man begged. He went abroad, to try his luck in various foreign countries, had made an attempt at farming in Kenya, was married with his own children before he returned.

William Pendray gradually improved, but many months were still to pass before he was fit enough to marry Em Trevarisk. If there were those who grieved to see Em's youth wasted, Em wasn't one of those, nor was Lily, nor was Richard. And when Will was ready Wheal Marty had been cleared again and the ore it contained ready for the working. Copper, that was what it was, copper hidden under the tin, and when they had it started, they rebuilt the entrance on the other side of the headland where it had always been. The mudslide over Polmena Cove gradually grew over, disappeared, the cove was left to its own self. The only new thing was the small house built at the bottom of the valley where the spring came out of the undergrowth.

Sir Robert never gave up his fight for it, still insisted on his rights, eventually brought a legal suit against the Martins, more out of stubbornness than hope of winning. His fight for possession of Polmena Cove became his obsession now that he had lost his grandson, but any money he hoped to obtain from it went into his lawyers' pockets. It was only with his death that the immediate threat disappeared. His son, Julian, then formally made the whole of the cove over again to the Martins as a wedding gift, to ensure there would be no further misunderstandings.

But by then Lily's parents themselves had long returned, had been on the way back ever since Lily's first letter, had hastened with redoubled urgency when the news of the mine disaster at Polmena Cove had frightened them.

'Here's Richard,' Lily had said to her father and mother when they all finally met. She held her parents' hands in both of hers as if she wanted to anchor them.

'And here they are at last,' she told Richard. She came over to him, and put her arm through his. 'What do you think?' her gaze asked.

Richard saw a woman about Lily's size with Lily's eyes and smile, a gentle laughing woman with Em's wide forehead. And a tall thin man with a limp who held out his hand and said, 'How can we thank – or repay you?'

'Oh,' said Lily, her eyes shining with fun, having the last word after all, 'he only wants me, that's repayment enough for anyone.'